CHASING
THE
VALLEY

A Random House book
Published by Random House Australia Pty Ltd
Level 3, 100 Pacific Highway, North Sydney NSW 2060
www.randomhouse.com.au

First published by Random House Australia in 2013

Addresses for companies within the Random House Group can be
found at www.randomhouse.com.au/offices.

National Library of Australia
Cataloguing-in-Publication Entry

Author: Melki-Wegner, Skye
Title: Chasing the valley/Skye Melki-Wegner
ISBN: 978 1 74275 954 8 (pbk.)
Series: Melki-Wegner, Skye. Chasing the Valley; 1
Target audience: For secondary school age
Dewey number: A823.4

Cover illustration and design by Sammy Yuen
Photographs © thinkstock
Internal design by Midland Typesetters, Australia
Typeset in 11.25/16.5 pt ITC Galliard by Midland Typesetters, Australia
Printed in Australia by Griffin Press, an accredited ISO AS/NZS
14001:2004 Environmental Management System printer

Random House Australia uses papers that are natural, renewable and
recyclable products and made from wood grown in sustainable forests.
The logging and manufacturing processes are expected to conform to
the environmental regulations of the country of origin.

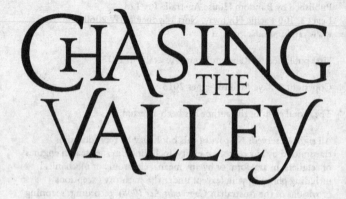

CHASING THE VALLEY

SKYE MELKI-WEGNER

RANDOM HOUSE AUSTRALIA

For Shirley Elizabeth Melki

My grandma, my inspiration, my friend

CHAPTER ONE

THE BOMBS

IT'S A QUIET NIGHT WHEN THE BOMBS FALL.

Just before they start, I'm scrubbing dishes in some grungy bar. The Alehouse, it's called. Stupid way to mark the night your life changes, isn't it? When you think of important occasions – dangers to your life, near-death experiences – you don't think of soap and dishrags. I'm sixteen, too young to be working the bar circuit, but no one cares about laws down here. In the grime of downtown Rourton, I'm hardly the first kid to ramp up my age and make a few coins under the table.

'You ever dream of running, kid?' Walter says.

I freeze, elbow-deep in soap and potato grease. It's just the two of us in the kitchen now. Anyone

1

with a brain has nicked off home to beat curfew. For Walter – a grey-bearded old drunk who takes bar jobs to steal the grog – it's worth the risk to take closing shifts. And for a scruffer like me, this is as close to a home as it gets.

'What do you mean?' I say carefully.

Walter stares out towards the empty bar. Moonlight sneaks in the window, dappling the table with shadows. The markings on Walter's neck reveal his magical proclivity is Darkness, and I bet he could manipulate the shadows into moving if he wanted. But he just stands there with a weary look on his face, swaying a bit, as if his legs are considering a new career as exotic dancers.

'You know what I mean. Sometimes I reckon that staying here's not . . .' He stops to take a swig of whiskey. 'I could join a crew, take the refugee route out of here. One day, kid, one day I'm gonna find that Valley. I'm gonna . . .'

There's a pause, as he tries to find his words.

I nod, letting Walter know it's time to shut up. I know what he means, but it's risky to let him ramble on about it now. He's too woozy to be careful and watch his words, and downtown Rourton is notorious for its rats. Informers. Scum who hide in the shadows and sell people's secrets to the guards. They get three silver coins for dobbing in a traitor. That's enough for a week's worth of meals, if you're smart about haggling and don't mind stale bread.

'I just reckon . . .' says Walter. He stops to belch, then kneads a hand into his forehead. 'I reckon I could do it. I could join a refugee crew, make a run for it. Maybe make it all the way to the Vall–'

'Stop it,' I say. 'This isn't the place.'

'There's gonna be a meeting tonight in the sewers,' Walter slurs. 'For a crew, you know. A few scruffer kids are putting a crew together to get out of here. I wanted to join, but they reckon I'm too old. They only want teenagers, not –'

The bombs hit.

There's half a second's warning: the mechanical rattle of royal biplanes and the shrill hiss of a whistle, like a mis-launched firecracker. Then light and heat and death come for us, tumbling like a star from the sky. It blasts a crater into the cobblestones outside. The window shatters and glass cascades across the bar; its tinkling meshes with the crashes and booms and screams that shoot across the city.

'Get down!' I drag Walter to his knees behind the bar.

There's less chance of being hit by shrapnel here, but the bottles are vibrating and shaking around us: booby traps of glass and flammable alcohol. And we aren't just facing ordinary bombs – the kind that

3

blow up with a blast of fire and smoke. These are alchemy bombs. They do the fire and smoke thing too, of course, but they're loaded with spellwork and magic tokens that burst like confetti through the streets.

'We've got to move,' I hiss, grabbing Walter's shoulder. He sways a little but doesn't argue as I yank him towards the back room. There hasn't been an air raid for years, but I still remember the survival tips. Find the smallest room, or get into a cupboard or under a solid desk . . .

We roll forward, away from the bar. There's a back room for storing the more expensive spirits and wines, but neither of us has a key. No barman in his right mind would let a couple of scruffers into his storage cellar.

I whip my head around, searching for the safest exit, and old Walter takes his chance to wriggle free. He stuffs himself into a cranny beneath the sink, moaning and singing a folk song as if it might drown out the crashing of bombs across our city. I'm about to argue, to pull him away, when I realise he's picked the safest place in the building. The sink is hard and heavy, shielding him from any shrapnel that might blast through the windows. It won't help much if the bar scores a direct hit – but then again, neither would the storeroom.

There's a jolt, a crash, and screams erupt from down the street. Walter swears, scrunches his eyes like a child in a storm, and raises his voice:

Oh mighty yo,
How the star-shine must go
Chasing those distant deserts of green . . .

As Walter sings, the shadows wash back and forth like the tide. I pull backwards, wary of touching anything controlled by an adult's proclivity magic. I'm not old enough to know my own proclivity yet, and I've got no way to defend against a drunken adult's power. Who knows what Walter's capable of in this state?

I force myself onto my feet and sprint for the door. There's nothing else I can do for Walter, and there's only room for one body under the sink. But I'm a scruffer – a homeless kid from the dodgiest streets of Rourton – and I know where to hide when the bombs crash down. The sewers.

*

I survived my first bombing when I was four. It didn't mean much to me at the time: it just seemed like an overexcited thunderstorm. My mother held

5

me tight, clutched me beneath the bed in our ramshackle apartment and whispered stories about the Magnetic Valley. Her arms were squishy and damp. My older brother was there too, pretending to be brave as he refused our mother's arms. I remember his breath hitching whenever a bomb fell too close.

I survived my second bombing when I was nine. The king must have decided that Rourton's people were getting restless, because it's unusual to bomb the same city twice within so few years. Perhaps we've got more dissidents than the other cities in Taladia. I wouldn't know; I've never been outside Rourton's walls.

Anyway, the night of my second bombing, I was walking home with my mother from the market. It was still evening, not time for curfew yet. My mother had bought me a honey biscuit for my birthday. I carried it home in a possessive fist, so tight that the corners crumbled in my palm. It came from Mr Corring's bakery stall, which was the centrepiece of the market with its shining lanterns and aroma of cakes, cookies and sugar buns.

'Just this once, Danika,' my mother said, as she handed Mr Corring his coins. 'You know we can't afford treats. Try to make it last.'

I nodded solemnly, already planning how to do

just that. I had a secret box beneath a floorboard at home – a cardboard soap pack I'd nicked from someone's rubbish – and I knew I could stash my biscuit in there. If I rationed myself a few crumbs each day, I could make that honey sweetness last for weeks.

When we were almost home, I tightened my grip around the biscuit. My brother would try to steal it, I knew. He would be waiting in the apartment doorway, waiting to see what I'd picked for my birthday treat from the market. My father would be in the bedroom, reading a book by lantern light. But my mother could distract my brother, perhaps, and I could slip past with my biscuit.

'Could you . . .?' I whispered.

My mother looked between me and the building, then nodded. She understood. She always understood. 'Wait here, Danika. I'll take care of it.'

So I stood in the streetlight outside our building, while she went ahead to distract my brother. I remember standing alone in that street, clutching that precious biscuit in sweaty fingers.

That's when the bomb hit. That's when my family burned. And I just stood there, terrified and useless, as that damn biscuit crumbled in my fist.

*

THIS IS MY FIRST BOMBING SINCE THAT NIGHT, THE first in seven years. I'm a scruffer now: no paperwork, no identity documents, and no money to bribe new copies from the authorities. I'm no one. I've lived on the streets, begged for food, scrimped and saved and worked my way through the dodgiest jobs in downtown Rourton. I've been cold. I've been alone. But I've survived it all, and I'm not prepared to die tonight.

The king's bombs took my family. I won't let them take me too.

CHAPTER TWO

DOWN IN THE DARK

I SLIP INTO A DESERTED ALLEY. THERE SHOULD BE RATS here, or a stray tomcat at least, but the animals of Rourton aren't stupid. They hear the bombs coming and they get out of the way. I'm not as fast as a rat, perhaps, but I can hide like one.

There's a sewer manhole near the end of the alley. I sprint towards it, inhaling smoke and light from distant fires. My city is burning for the first time in years and I don't want to imagine what else might be pouring into Rourton's skies. Alchemy bombs, with their cocktail of magical shrapnel, are not the sort of weapons you can predict. Their effects can be hideous or beautiful, plain or elaborate. Creating them is an art form practised only by the king's most cherished supporters.

It's strange to think how innocently they started: a long-ago failure to transmute lead into gold and silver. But alchemy isn't a natural power like proclivities. It's a created art, shaped and expanded by human hands. Now alchemy is used to taint metals with magic – and sometimes, to hurl down that magic from the sky.

Alchemy bombs have been known to blast a house to shreds and then bloom a jungle of flowers from the rubble within hours of the attack. They've melted entire apartment buildings into quicksand, sucking down anyone who attempted a rescue mission. And when my family died, the bomb painted our street with shining stars.

But why now, why tonight? Why is the king bombing us when winter has already beaten us into quiet subservience? His wars still rage on several of our borders, and people in Rourton are too afraid to resist. Many pray for the royals to protect us from Taladia's enemies. There is no reason for this bombing – no reason except to beat us down, to remind us to accept our place.

Or perhaps, to remind us to accept our losses.

Thousands of our soldiers are away in foreign lands, fighting and dying to expand King Morrigan's realm. As soon as I turn eighteen, I will be conscripted into his army. Five years of compulsory service – if you're lucky enough to survive – before they dump you back in your city of birth. And here in Rourton, some are starting to question the reasons for these wars. People are muttering. Whispering. *Questioning*. Why does the king need to conquer more lands? Why must their loved ones be taken?

They speak quietly, of course, but there are always rats in Rourton. And I guess that's why the bombs are falling.

I wrench up the manhole cover, breaking my stubby nails on the metal. As I climb down the shaft, the rungs flake with rust and one even snaps beneath my weight. My foot slides down with a rush of panic and I bang a shinbone against the lower rungs. More pain, but I can handle it. I clench my eyes shut for a second, blow the air from my lungs, then continue downward.

The air stinks of grime and faeces. It's thick and woolly, like I'm breathing dirty blankets. I shake my head and splash down into ankle-deep liquid. The sewer is dark, of course, but faint light trickles down when I pass beneath a drain. Echoes of streetlight and fire from above.

I'd never admit it aloud, but lately I've been tempted to run. It's suicide, of course – there are always announcements about refugee crews getting caught – but life in Rourton is a constant ache. The older I grow, the more I realise how a scruffer's life can scar you. No home, no future. Just the streets, the cold, and the ache in my belly. And I'm sixteen years old, only two years from adulthood. Only two years from removing my neck-scarf, revealing my proclivity and being conscripted into the king's army. Once I start looking old enough, it will become risky to go out in public. If any guards spot me, they'll drag me back to their station to be tested with a bloodline charm. Name, parentage, date of birth . . . all spelled out in blood and silver.

I don't want to join the army. I don't have a problem with fighting – it's part of life here – but I do it on my own behalf. Not on behalf of kings and councils who take our lives to conquer distant lands.

As I squelch along, I turn over Walter's words in my mind. *'There's gonna be a meeting tonight, in the sewers . . . Some of the scruffer kids are putting a crew together . . .'*

'A crew of teenagers,' I say aloud. The very idea sends a rush through my veins.

But it doesn't make sense. You can't build a refugee crew from kids. They'd be dead within hours of fleeing the city, if they got out at all.

There are stories of successful crews. They're rare – once or twice a decade, perhaps – and no one knows if they're true. *Fairy tales*, most people call them. Fairy tales and nonsense. But the stories spread, like litter in the gutter, and even the king can't quite stamp them out. When a rumour bursts free, the city comes alive with gossip and whispers. *How did they do it? What was the trick that kept them alive?* And if you add all the stories together, this is what you get:

Five adults.

If you take more than five, it gets risky – too many bellies to fill, too many people to hide from the king's hunters. Larger crews never make it through the forest, let alone the wilderness beyond.

Each of the five should have a different magical proclivity: five pieces of a jigsaw, slotted together to form a crew. And people's proclivities don't develop until the end of puberty – which is why a teenage crew would never work. Even if some of these scruffer kids know their proclivity already, it's taboo to reveal them to anyone else. That's why we wear neck-scarves until we're eighteen.

To reveal your proclivity early would be . . . wrong. Humiliating. Dirty. It would be like exposing your naked body to the world. So how are they hoping to design a balanced crew?

My father explained it to me when I was younger and I asked why teenagers all wore neck-scarves.

'Your proclivity is part of who you are, the part of nature that links to your magic,' my father said. 'Younger teenagers haven't earned the right or gained the maturity to declare their proclivities to the world. They haven't learned to use their powers safely. To show their markings early would be . . .' He shook his head. 'It'd be unforgiveable.'

'But what is a proclivity marking?' I said, leaning closer upon his knee.

He showed me the markings down the back of his neck: a twisting line of black that reminded me of claws. 'My proclivity is Beast.'

I traced my father's markings with my fingertips, thinking of how the stray cats followed him through the streets. 'What other proclivities do people have?'

'It varies. Some are more common than others. Rain, Wind, Bird, even Darkness itself . . .' He paused. 'Everyone's magic is like a radio message, but not everyone's radio is tuned to the same frequency.'

'What about Mother? Does she have a proclivity too?'

'Oh yes.' My father smiled then, looking a little wistful. 'Her proclivity is Daylight.'

I think of that conversation now, as I slosh through Rourton's sewers. My mother loved the sky. Every dawn she would throw open a window and coax gentle curls of light inside to wake our sleeping

14

forms. There's no sky down here to remind me of her. But I can hear the bombs falling – muffled echoes through the earth – and that's enough to trigger my memories. I can't picture my mother's proclivity mark, but I can hear her death. Again and again, with every whistle and flare of tonight's bombing. With every crash, I hear her die.

The mud is getting thicker now. My boots stick a little with every stride, as though the tunnel wants to suck me down into the dark.

'Hurry up!' a girl shouts.

I freeze. The voice has come from up ahead, just around the next corner in the tunnel. It echoes through sludge, bouncing off mildewed walls. You have to be careful in the sewer, because all sorts of dodgy people hide down here in the dark. I don't mean scruffers: no matter how poor we get, we'd only come down here in an emergency. I mean the robbers, the bashers, the scum who'd slash you with a knife as soon as look at you.

Don't get me wrong, they're not all violent. Sometimes you'll find a sad old man drooping in a sodden tunnel with his mind driven hollow by the years. But on the whole, it's safer to stay away. Not to mention the stench down here, or the risk of disease. Nothing about the sewers is inviting, really . . . unless you've got a good reason to hide.

15

A reason like a secret meeting to plan your escape from Taladia.

I push forward, trying to keep quiet. Every movement sloshes a stinking slurp of sewage in the dark. I pretend that it's just muddy water, a river of bubbles and natural muck, and splash onward towards the voice.

'Everyone here?' This voice sounds like a teenage boy: dark and gruff, but with the faintest hint of a whine on the final syllable.

'You know we're here, Radnor, so drop the silliness,' the girl says. 'I'd imagine that even *your* family taught you to count.'

The girl's voice confuses me a little. She doesn't speak with the coarse accent of a downtown scruffer. Her *R*s are too muted, her *A*s carry a posh lilt of 'la-de-dah' that suggests she's a richie from a wealthier part of Rourton. But I've never seen a richie hang out in the sewers.

'Just making sure,' snaps Radnor. 'We've got to move the plans forward, take advantage of this bombing. We'll never get another chance like tonight. But if we're gonna do this, Clementine, you'd better shut your face and learn to take orders.'

'Take orders from a scruffer?' says the richie. 'Are you mad?'

There's a louder boom from the city above.

16

The explosion must be close, because this time the entire tunnel shakes and sewage jostles around my shins. The conversation halts for a second, as everyone waits for the aftershock to die away.

'This crew is under my command,' Radnor says. 'I'm already doing you a favour by letting you tag along, and I don't reckon you've got –'

'Letting us tag along? *Letting us tag along?*' Clementine's voice grows shrill. 'I'm sorry, did you miss the part where I offered you enough cash to roll across Taladia in a golden carriage?'

I slosh forward carefully. One of the speakers must have a lantern, because the light throws patches around the corner. I can see shadows on the wall shifting against the smudge of lantern-light.

'Hate to be a party-pooper, guys, but can we get to the point?' says another boy, sounding amused. 'This whole debate's getting a bit old. Don't get me wrong – you've picked an awesome spot for a fight, but only if you're gonna get down and dirty with a round of mud wrestling.'

I recognise this boy's voice: Teddy Nort, the famous pickpocket. Born and raised on the streets, Teddy makes his living with fingers like snakes and a grin that could charm the king himself into letting slip of his purse. He's pretty notorious in downtown Rourton, and I know his tone as well as any other scruffer kid around. But Teddy's the last person I'd expect to risk his life on a refugee crew, and my gasp echoes like a slap on the tunnel walls.

'What was that?' Radnor says.

There's a splash of footsteps and light swings around the corner to greet me. There's no point running now, and nowhere to hide – not unless I want to dive headfirst into a river of sewage, anyway. So I do what my instincts tell me to do. I create an illusion. I focus upon the shape of my own body, where I can feel my limbs and heartbeat and head and toes. Then I force a spark of power along those body parts, hold my breath, and – with a burst of cold air that pinches each vein – I paint myself into the dark of a sewer wall.

An unfamiliar boy splashes forward, holding up the lantern to glare at me through the dark. He doesn't see me at first, fooled by my illusion, but the effect fades like melting ice and he spots me. 'You're a spy!'

The illusion is completely gone, and I'm wishing I'd never conjured it. I'm not very good yet; my personal record is about three seconds. Hardly anyone has the ability to cast illusions – it's just a freak genetic thing, like having blue eyes or being a fast runner – but I've always tried to keep my ability a secret. The authorities don't like it when scruffers show signs of unusual powers, so it's safer to pretend to be as average as possible. And unfortunately, since the whole *point* of an illusion is deception, it's the sort of ability that makes people suspect you're up to something dodgy.

I fling up my hands to show I'm unarmed. 'I'm just a scruffer,' I say. 'I'm not a spy or anything.'

The lantern boy is tall, with a thick neck and small eyes. There's a wisp of hair on his chin, as though he's trying and failing to grow a beard.

'Come on.' He grabs my arm tightly enough to leave a bruise. From the sound of his voice, I realise this must be Radnor.

I could twist free if I wanted to – I've been in enough street fights to know an enemy's vulnerable points, and Radnor's nose is within reach of my other elbow. But there are at least two other figures around the corner, maybe more, and I'm not stupid enough to take them on alone. Besides, I don't want to fight this crew. I've got something very different in mind.

I follow the boy's pressure on my arm, sloshing through the stink until we're round the corner. The tunnel opens into a sort of intersection between pipes. It reminds me of an old song, about meeting the devil at the crossroads to sell your soul. But

I doubt even the devil would be keen on sampling the aroma of Rourton's city sewers.

I hear Clementine's voice next. 'Who are you?'

I squint, trying to make out faces in the dark. There are three other kids here: two blonde girls, about sixteen years old, and a scruffer boy whose freckles are visible even in the flicker of Radnor's lantern.

The freckled boy, of course, is the pickpocket Teddy Nort. The girls are twins, almost identical. Hair falls in golden curls over their neck-scarves. They wear a pinkish stain on their lips and their fingernails catch the light with sparkles of bronze polish. Richies. They look like they belong in a High Street boutique, not crawling around the sewers like a couple of scruffers.

'I'm hiding from the bombs,' I say, trying not to look too nervous. Sometimes, to avoid a fight with another scruffer, it helps to pretend you're more confident than you feel. Walter once told me we're like fighting dogs: it's better to raise your hackles than tear a hole in each other's necks. 'I was working late, so I missed curfew.'

Silence.

I know what they're up to. They want me to get nervous, to rush to fill in the silence and give something away. But I refuse to budge. I clench my fists

20

behind my back. Then I pick one of the blonde girls and stare at her, waiting to see who'll blink. The girl bites her lip and looks down.

'Right,' Radnor says. 'And why the hell should we believe that? This sewer system is huge. The odds of you just stumbling across our meeting are –'

'She's a spy!' says the more forceful twin, Clementine. 'The king's hunters must be onto us. They're sending undercover operatives to catch us before we leave the city!' She raises a horrified hand to her lips. 'They'll make an example of us, won't they? They'll use our executions to scare the rest of the city into obedience.'

I glare at her. 'I'm not a spy, all right? I swear it.'

Radnor crosses his arms. 'Prove it.'

'How?'

There's another pause, as everyone tries to dream up some means to test me. Eventually, Teddy Nort gives his lips a thoughtful twist. 'How'd you know about our meeting?'

'I was hiding –'

'No, you were eavesdropping.'

I hesitate, weighing up my options. I've never been much good at lying, but I've heard Teddy Nort's a master at it. If there's one thing I've learned on the streets, it's not to bet against a gambler at his own game.

'All right,' I say. 'Look, I swear it's just an accident I found you. But I was working at the Alehouse when the bombs started. There's an old scruffer called Walter. You might've met him if you work the bar scene –'

Radnor cuts me off. 'Yeah, I know him.'

'Well, Walter told me about the meeting tonight. He said he wanted to join your crew, but you only wanted teenagers. And when I stumbled across you down here, in the sewers . . . you can't blame me for being curious.'

The others exchange glances.

'Why teenagers, anyway?' I add. 'You know you'll never make it to the Valley. Hardly any adult crews survive, let alone teenagers.'

Teddy grins. 'Yeah, but we're fresher, aren't we? The new generation. We're gonna take down the king's hunters like they're toddlers scrapping in the Rourton gutters.'

I stare at him, unsure whether he's serious. It's hard to tell with people like Teddy, who use bravado as their de facto language. He could be sending up Radnor's control act, or he could be just as cocky as his words suggest. Then he winks, and I know he's fooling around.

'You must have a plan,' I say. 'You're too young to have proclivities yet – or at least, too young to reveal them. How are you going to cross the forest or get up through the mountains without being caught . . .?'

'We've got a plan,' Radnor says. 'But I'm not sharing it with some random girl who just happened to gatecrash our meeting.'

'Gatecrash, eh?' Teddy perks up. 'Like a party? This place could do with some entertainment. I wasn't totally kidding about the mud wrestling . . .'

'Oh, for heaven's sake,' Clementine says. 'The last thing we need is another filthy scruffer around. Can we just dispose of this girl and get on with it?'

I scowl. That's all we are to the richies: filth and rubbish, things to be dumped in the backstreets and ignored. To be fair, though, she's got a point about me being dirty. There hasn't been a decent rainstorm for days, and – even on the nights I snare a bed in a cheap boarding house – I rarely have access to a shower.

'Why are *you* part of this, anyway?' I ask her.

'Yeah, I was wondering that too,' says Teddy Nort. In response to my questioning look, he adds, 'I only got sucked into this suicide mission about twenty minutes ago, so I'm just as confused as you.'

Radnor scowls at him. 'Sucked into a suicide mission? You *begged* me for a spot to save you from that manhunt, Nort. You said it was time for me to cough up and repay my –' He stops abruptly, as though he's just remembered that he has an audience. 'Anyway, you can't stay in Rourton now.'

Teddy shrugs, and offers me another cheeky wink. 'Meh. Sucked into a crew, on the run from the guards, what's the difference?'

I roll my eyes. He's such a ridiculous figure, puffed up with winks and bravado and hands that can nick a richie's coin purse in seconds. There's a moment's pause before I remember my original question and turn back to the richie twins.

'So,' I say, 'why are you two so keen to risk your lives on a refugee crew?'

The quieter twin opens her mouth, and I half-expect the squeak of a mouse. But to my surprise, there's a solid ring of determination in her voice. 'We don't want to live here any more,' she says. 'We want to escape, just like the rest of you.'

Teddy snorts. 'Oh, come off it. I bet you eat breakfast off golden platters. What've you got to run away from?'

Clementine turns upon him with a furious sneer. 'None of your business, scruffer boy. We're offering a great deal of money for our places on this crew, which is more than I can say for *some* people.'

'All right, keep your knickers on,' says Teddy, holding up his hands. 'If you've got a gold platter phobia, I'm not gonna judge. Never liked gold much myself, you know. It's bloody heavy to lug around when its previous owner is chasing you down High Street.'

I feel the corners of my lips twitch, but Radnor doesn't look too amused.

'That's enough, Nort. And you,' he adds, turning to me, 'you're not wanted here. Clear off and find another spot to hide from the king's firecrackers, won't you?'

'No,' I say firmly. 'I want to join your crew.'

Silence.

Clementine gives a derisive laugh. 'Oh, you've got to be joking.'

'Why not?' I say. 'You've only got four people. Everyone knows the best balanced crews are made of five.'

'We've already got a fifth member,' says Radnor. 'And you'd better clear off, or he'll smash your face in for trying to steal his spot.'

I squint down the tunnel. Have I somehow missed another figure in the dark? No, there's only the four of them: Teddy, Radnor, Clementine and her quieter twin. I can hear each of them breathing, harsh and hollow, in the stench-thickened air.

'Who's your fifth member?' I say.

'None of your business.'

'Look, I can be useful.' I take a deep breath. 'My name's Danika Glynn, and I'm a scruffer like you. My parents died when I was a kid – I know how to live rough on the streets. I've got skills. I could be useful.'

I glance pointedly at the richie girls, hoping Radnor and Teddy will know what I mean. Those girls' only contribution will be money, but scruffers have more diverse skills. What good is money, anyway, when you're on the run in Taladia's wilderness?

'Skills,' repeats Radnor.

'I'm an illusionist,' I remind him. 'You saw what I did in the tunnel before.'

Silence.

'An illusionist?' says Teddy Nort, looking eager. 'Really? Oh man, you should've joined my pick-pocket gang! We'd get rich with an illusionist. Imagine what we –'

'Forget it,' says Radnor. 'Just being an amateur illusionist isn't enough to buy you a spot on my crew. What other "skills" have you got?'

I hesitate. 'Well, I can climb walls pretty well. I can scrounge, too, and I'm not afraid to get my hands dirty.'

'We've already got those skills,' says Radnor. 'We've got scruffers on the crew and we don't need another mouth to feed.'

'I can get my own food.'

Radnor laughs coldly. 'Out there, in the wild? You're a city scruffer, not a traveller.'

I open my mouth to retort, but close it again. He's got a point. I've never been outside Rourton's walls. The only real trees I've seen are decorative, growing in the richies' front gardens. And even those are pruned into unnatural shapes, wrinkled and disfigured by the city's pollution.

Of course, I've seen trees sprout from alchemy bombs. They can shoot up in mere hours, unfurling roots across the rubble to ensnare their victims' corpses. But I doubt this memory will equip me for trekking through a real forest.

'What about you?' I say. 'You haven't been outside Rourton either, I bet.'

'*We've* got a plan.' Clementine sounds, if possible, even haughtier than before. 'I wouldn't expect someone of your status to understand, but it's amazing what you can achieve with a little economic leverage.'

'What are you gonna do, bribe a tree?' I say.

Teddy Nort snorts, then hides his amusement by faking a coughing fit into his sleeve. I suppose he isn't keen to alienate himself from the rest of his crew. That's fair enough, really; if I were about to risk my life on a long, perilous mission with only four companions, I'd do the same. Of course, the point's moot, since *I've* alienated myself from Clementine already. It isn't looking likely that I'll escape the city with this crew, but I figure it's worth one more try.

'I thought you were keen on being fresh,' I say, 'being the new generation. Why not try a crew of six instead of five?'

'She's got a point there,' says Teddy. 'And come on, Radnor – she's an *illusionist*! I've been looking to recruit one for years . . . Imagine the pranks she could've played on richies while I nicked their diamonds.'

Radnor shakes his head. 'We've already got a crew of five.'

'Well, who says we can only have five?' says Teddy. 'Can't hurt to shake things up a bit more. And hey, the guards won't suspect us if we look too big to be a refugee crew.' He grins. 'Maybe they'll reckon we're licensed traders or something. I'll be the richie merchant and you lot can be my servants. It'd make the trip a lot more fun.'

I try to imagine Teddy Nort, of all people, as a licensed trader. All I can picture is him stealing coins from his customers' pockets.

'Don't be stupid, Nort,' says Radnor. 'We've already got a good plan, and we're not screwing it

28

up at the last minute for the sake of some random scruffer girl.' He glares at me, then points down the tunnel. 'Get out of here, and don't even *think* about following us.'

I want to argue with him but it's pointless now, because Radnor has decided he doesn't want me. Even if I manage to bargain my way onto the crew, I doubt we'd make it out of Rourton alive, let alone all the way to the Valley. Crew members have to respect each other, without any backstabbing or distrust, if they want to survive.

'All right,' I say, in the poshest richie accent I can muster. 'Send me a wire if you change your mind. My address is in the golden directory.'

It's a stupid jab at Clementine, of course, because only the wealthiest richies can send or receive telegraphs – and I don't have *any* address, let alone one in the golden directory. I know I'm being immature, even as I say it. But it's enough to make Teddy Nort grin, just for a minute. I can't help feeling pleased that at least one of them seems to want me on the crew.

Then I head off down the tunnel, sloshing muck up my legs with every step. There's no point making friends with Teddy Nort – not when he's about to flee the city. I keep remembering Radnor's comment: *'We're not screwing it up at the last minute.'* It sounds like the crew is leaving soon, maybe even tonight.

And if that's true, it's a solid bet they'll be dead by morning.

CHAPTER THREE

THE CITY WALL

BACK UP ON THE STREETS, I FOLLOW A SHADOWED alleyway. There's no point thinking about the refugee crew. They don't want my help, and they don't want me. Full stop. End of story. Like everything else about life in Rourton, it's better to make myself forget.

The bombing's over now. I hear voices in the distance, and the crash and crumble of damaged walls collapsing into dust. Smoke pours up into the night, bathing Rourton in a sea of starlit grey. It stinks of ash and scorched debris.

The smell of fire brings back too many memories. Another night. Another bombing. My feet like lead upon another street.

When I was little, my mother told me stories of the Magnetic Valley. It's forbidden to speak of it, but everyone knows – everyone whispers its name in hope. That's what Walter's folk song was about, his drunken ramblings in the Alehouse as the bombs began to fall. Now, the words come back to me: a taunt of dreams that can never come true.

Oh mighty yo,
How the star-shine must go
Chasing those distant deserts of green . . .

The Magnetic Valley is where refugee crews run to, where our dreams carry us on the darkest nights, in the coldest alleyways. It's a boundary of green meadows, a doorway into another nation that lies beyond Taladia. In the Valley, the king's magically powered planes and war machines are as useless as toys. Its hillsides are lined with magnetic rocks, which interfere with magic.

And according to our legends, the nation beyond is a paradise. It's one of Taladia's only neighbouring lands where our king has not waged a war. I don't even know the name of the country, but if even half the stories are true, I'd give my right arm to live there. Supposedly there's enough food and warmth and shelter for us all. The people's leaders don't bomb them, don't send hunters to pursue them through the wild. Beyond the Valley, I could be safe. Safe, for the first time in my life.

But for now, I'm just a scruffer in a city of flames.

As the smoke thickens, my eyes start to water. I reach into my pocket for my handkerchief – a shred of stolen fabric from a clothing factory's scrapheap – but it's disappeared. I must have dropped it in the sewer somewhere. I wipe my eyes on a sleeve, but the grit feels like sandpaper. I haven't had a chance to wash my clothes for ages. So I pick up the pace and try to ignore the dribbles running down my cheeks.

At one point, there's a scream. It's a few blocks away, so I can't see the source, but it sounds husky: an old woman, perhaps. Has she returned home to find her house gone, her family lost amid the blood-streaked rubble? Maybe an alchemy bomb has replaced her home with wild flowers or a lake of rippling silver. There's wailing now, a chorus of grief as her neighbours take up the call. I grit my teeth, grind each foot into the cobblestones and try to ignore them. There's nothing I can do to help.

I hesitate at the intersection. I don't know which way to turn. It's too late to find a bed in a hostel tonight; they all lock their doors at curfew. The thought of a night on the streets – now, when the world is a blur of death and flames and screams – is enough to turn my stomach. I can't do it. I can't stay here and listen to my family die over and over again.

There's another scream, this one from the opposite direction, and I make up my mind. My encounter with Radnor's refugee crew has cemented something in the back of my skull. A feeling I never knew was brewing there . . . not until now, on the intersection of Rourton's alchemy-bombed roads. I can't do this any more.

I *refuse* to do this any more.

I refuse to spend my life in this grimy city, scavenging for food and sleeping in doorways. I refuse to reach my eighteenth birthday here, to be conscripted into King Morrigan's army and shunted off to fight on behalf of the monarch who killed my family.

I'm going to escape from Taladia. I'm going to find the Valley. And if Radnor's refugee crew won't take me, I'll do it alone. Tonight. This is my chance. The city is in an uproar. People are battling fires, searching for their families, or – if they're lucky – cowering in bunkers and waiting for dawn. Any obedience to the monarchy's curfew has gone out the window and no one will notice a scrawny teenage girl. If there were ever a perfect night for escaping Rourton, this is it.

I have no real possessions, beyond what I'm wearing. The clothes on my back and my mother's silver bracelet, which is secured up high above my elbow. It's a liberating thought. It means that I've got nothing to worry about or protect, nothing to retrieve in the jumble of a post-bombing frenzy. No possessions, no friends, no family. I can head straight for the city walls and make a good start on my journey before the night ends.

I cross the intersection and start towards the edge of the city. There's a thick plume of smoke and ash to my left, so I veer towards it. If anyone is looking out their window, hopefully they'll assume I'm just a local girl running home to make sure her family survived. In all this haze, it would be hard to make out the ragged clothes and unwashed hair that mark me as a scruffer.

Closer to the city outskirts, I see more signs of the bombs' destruction. There's a huge crater in the middle of a road, where white snowflakes fall upwards and melt into the dark sky. A few streets later, I stumble across what used to be Rourton's library. The building is gone, but broken books and papers flock like seagulls in the night. Thorny vines unfurl across the rubble so fast that I can actually watch them grow. I stumble forward, searching for signs of survivors, but of course there's nothing. No one ever survives an alchemy bomb.

There's nothing I can do.

The night my family died, the bombings were caused by a woman from Gimstead, a smaller city west of Rourton. She managed to whip a few dozen scruffers into an attack on their city's hunter head-quarters, trying to steal some food for the poorer children. Three guards were killed in the raid – alongside five or six scruffers. The whole block ended up on fire, and a lot of valuable paperwork was lost. Criminal records, court reports and the like.

The palace can't let that sort of thing go unpun-ished. That's the sort of thing that sparks more than fires. It sparks courage. Revolt. Maybe even revolutions. And so King Morrigan sent his bombs to punish every city north of the wastelands.

I understand why the woman in Gimstead did it. It was a cold winter and people were starving. It must have been hard to watch the king's hunters on patrol, wolfing down bread and casserole. I might have done the same thing, if I were cold and desperate and brave. But this doesn't stop a part of me from hating that woman, whose lust for food got my family killed.

In the early days, when I was just adjusting to life on the streets, I used to lie awake behind a stack of rubbish bins and hope that the bombs got her too. Then I would hug my torso, hating myself for thinking it, and wait in silence for the night to end.

*

WHEN I REACH THE WALL, THE SKY'S STILL SMOKY. I keep my head bowed low, hoping to shield my face. The wall is imbued with picture spells: a magical surveillance system for the city's edges. If you act too suspiciously, your picture can later be gleaned from the alchemical recording – and sooner or later, you'll swap city walls for prison bars.

The easiest way to escape Rourton is to join a licensed trading crew. Then you can travel legally out the gates in a cart carrying pots or food on the way to another city. But a scruffer girl like me has better odds of flying to the moon than finding employment with traders. They'd think I was a crook: a pick-pocket like Teddy Nort, hoping to steal their wares.

That leaves two options. Under the wall, or over it.

Going underneath is impossible. The wall's foundations were strengthened by people with Earth proclivities, who coaxed the ground to swallow a barrier as deep as it could go. The wall has stood for hundreds of years, and will doubtless last for hundreds more. I don't have the magic to fight against that. I don't even know what my own proclivity is yet, let alone how to counter someone else's.

Lately, I've sensed an odd itching at the back of my neck and down my spine. It must be the start of my markings, as I move towards adulthood and my proclivity begins to emerge. But until it fully develops, I have about as much magic as a five-year-old. Nothing that could bust through a wall of magically enhanced stone.

So I can't go through the gate and I can't get under the wall. That leaves one option: going over the top. I know that it's been done before, so there must be a way. Somehow, while the smoke's still swirling, I've got to find it.

On this side of the wall, I can only hear shouts and wind and the crackle of flames. But on the far side, if I strain my ears, I can just make out a faint chirping. Crickets. I recognise the sound from the city market. Sometimes traders sell them, for the times when you're starving enough to eat anything that might pass as meat. Now, though, their chirps don't sound like food. They sound like freedom.

I begin to climb. There's no time to worry about the wall's picture spells. By the time they identify me, I'll either be free or dead. The wall is made of huge stone bricks, each half a metre tall. They're roughly hewn, split by trenches and valleys that must seem an entire continent to the ants upon their surface. The valleys are too shallow for my fingers to grip but there are gaps in the mortar, worn away by decades of neglect. The king prefers to fund guards and weapons, not bricks and mortar. On a normal night, this wall would be crawling with guards, infesting the turrets that punctuate the wall every hundred metres. They'd stare up and down with metal binoculars and carry rifles on their shoulders. On a normal night, I'd be shot from this wall in an instant.

But this is not a normal night. Half the turrets are deserted – even the king's own guards are afraid of bombs. Perhaps they were given prior warning, or simply fled when they spotted the biplanes approaching. The guards who remain are too far away to make out a shadowy figure upon the bricks. Their spotlights are focused inward, highlighting the spectacle of Rourton's burning streets.

About four metres up the wall, I stop to take a breath. It's hard, sweaty work, even in the chill of a northern night. The smoke might be a good disguise, but it's also hot and gritty. I continue climbing. One, two, one, two. My lungs throb in time with the upward swing of my limbs. Scruffer kids are good at climbing, since we often need to make quick getaways. It's illegal to sleep in people's doorways and the richies are allowed to get rid of us however they see fit. We're just vermin to them. Scooting up the side of a building can be your only hope to escape a whack from someone's fireplace poker – or worse, their proclivity.

The wall begins to shake. For a wild second I think it must be another bomb – that the planes have returned and our city is under attack again, just when survivors are gathered outside to assess our losses. Then I realise. This vibration isn't the wild crash that comes from a bombing. It's a mechanical rattle, like power travelling along a wire.

Someone is opening the city gate.

I whip my head around, staring along the wall. I'm high enough to see over the roofs of nearby buildings, and I can just make out the gate through the smoke. It's a vast slab of iron about a hundred metres away. As I watch, squinting through the haze, it trundles out towards the world beyond. What are they doing? Why are they opening the gate at this time of night? I shift my weight, trying to fight the growing numbness in my fingertips. There's a group of figures near the gate. The guards are easy to pick out, because their copper breastplates gleam beneath the streetlights. The others, I realise quickly, aren't just normal traders. They're foxary riders.

That explains why the guards are willing to let them out at this hour. Foxary riders mean trouble and I bet the guards will be glad to see the backs of them – especially with all the chaos caused by the bombs. Foxaries are great, coarse beasts that resemble massive foxes but are ridden like horses.

They were created decades ago after someone with a Beast proclivity mated different creatures together. With breeding, magic and a bit of illegal experimentation, he created the first foxary. Originally they were used to pull wagons and carts, inspired by sled dogs in the far north. Then some crazy trader decided to mount them directly.

Foxaries are tough: hard to kill and even harder to control. The beasts can run for days, carry huge weights and even live off tree-bark, if need be. If your proclivity isn't Beast, there are only two ways to ride one: with its trust or with a knife bridle. Most riders rely on the latter, using metal blades and whips to keep their mounts under control.

Like I said, foxaries mean trouble.

King Morrigan could stamp out the riders if he wanted to, but he finds it more useful to turn a blind eye. Foxary riders are hired by wealthy traders as mercenaries, to guard the richies' possessions while they're on the move. If anyone threatens you on the road, a foxary's jaws will do a lot more damage than horse teeth.

Someone shouts from the gate. The situation changes so fast that I hardly realise it's happening until the fight has begun. Guards leap towards the foxary riders, raising pistols to fire, trying to stop them leaving . . . Someone is already manning the machinery, and the gate begins to close again with a mechanical groan . . .

A gust of wind blasts above the buildings. It clears the smoke for a moment and I steal a clearer glimpse of the figures by the gate. The foxary riders are smaller than I expected, and wearing neck-scarves to disguise any proclivity markings. Teenagers. And there are five of them . . .

A flash of gold curls reveals one of the twins: either Clementine herself, or her quieter sister. She tumbles backwards, falling from her foxary's back to avoid the blast of a guard's pistol. The riders are Radnor's refugee crew, disguised as foxary mercenaries to sneak out of Rourton.

It's a brilliant plan – no one would suspect that a bunch of refugees could afford such a disguise. But even brilliance isn't enough to survive King Morrigan's guards and somehow the plan's gone wrong. If they're captured, they will die. They'll be hauled off to the guillotine and beheaded at dawn, in the same market square where traders sell tea-leaves and crickets sing their way into cooking pots.

I have to do something. I can't just hang off a wall and watch the guards take them. The thought of Teddy's grinning head beneath a guillotine, or that quiet twin sobbing as they lead her to the blade, makes me feel like vomiting. I'm a hundred metres from the gate; if I can just distract those guards, get them to chase me into the wilderness, maybe in the confusion we can all get away . . .

There's an empty turret above and to my left, with no signs of human life through the guardrail. I've been climbing at a diagonal without realising it, inching along the wall to find the safest hand-holds. I struggle up the rest of the wall and throw my body over the rail. There's a rifle stand but no gun in sight. I guess the guard from this tower was clearheaded enough to take it, even while fleeing the bombs.

A wooden crate squats in the corner, half-concealed by shadows and smoke. I shove up the lid with a grunt and scan the contents through watery eyes. A hessian lunch bag. A box of matches. A pair of climbing picks: the portable handholds guards use to scale the city walls quickly.

And two emergency flares, ready to blast into the sky.

CHAPTER FOUR

DIVERSION

I STUFF THE LUNCH BAG INTO MY COAT. THE CLIMBING picks go into my sleeves, ready for quick access. I hesitate for a moment, then thrust one of the flares down my trouser-leg. The cylinder is cold against my thigh and its fuse scratches my skin, but I've run out of pockets and it might be useful later.

The second flare won't survive long enough to worry about 'later'. I position it on the turret floor, pointing up into the sky. The fuse isn't very long – a metre at most – and I tug on it uselessly, half-hoping it might extend like a coiled ball of wire. But it just flops to the side, frail and thin upon the stones.

'All right,' I whisper. 'I can do this.'

I open the matchbox, trying to control the

trembling of my fingers. There are only four matches inside. I strike my chosen match against the side of the box, fingers tensed. Nothing happens.

'Come on,' I mutter, and try again. Nothing. For a second I'm afraid the matches have been ruined by mildew or rain. I can hear screaming from the gate now and the faces of Radnor's crew flash through my head. Even though they're a hell of a long way from being my family, all I can think is: *I can't let them die. Not again.*

The match sizzles into life. I almost drop it in surprise, but clench my fingertips tighter and cup my other hand to shield the tiny flame from the wind. It seems so fragile, compared with the bombing fires tonight. But this fire is going to save lives rather than destroy them.

I press the match against the fuse. It catches immediately: a rush, a whoosh and then a sparkling trail of flame runs along the wire. I leap across to the turret's edge and thrust the climbing picks into the crumbling mortar between a pair of bricks. Then I'm over the edge, clambering down the far side of Rourton's wall. It's much quicker with the picks to help me, and I'm slipping and huffing down the wall like it's just another richie's rooftop.

I glance towards the gate and see that it's still half-open. The gate is strong but it's also slow. As

45

I watch, a pair of figures tumble out into the night. Two foxaries, each with two riders dangling from their backs. Two more foxaries burst past them, wild and riderless. Then one last foxary, a single rider on its back, and I'm counting to five in my head with a wild rush of hope. But there are guards behind them, spraying bullets towards the riders, and one of them is about to –

Psshreeeikkkk!

The flare screams into life above me. It's a fireball upon the turret, squealing and spinning and shooting flames into the night. This is a specially designed guard-tower flare, designed to imprint a golden tattoo upon the sky, but its flames whiz out of sight above the distant trees.

Then there's a smash of light and sound.

I slip several terrifying metres, but manage to slam one climbing pick back into the mortar. The jolt leaves me breathless, hanging from one arm. Agony tears through my shoulder and I know I've dislocated it. This isn't the first time I've suffered a dislocation – and this doesn't hurt as badly as the first time – but still, my eyes water. I can barely keep myself from screaming in tune with the flare. I thrust the other pick into the mortar and redistribute my weight onto the uninjured arm.

Then I twist towards the gate. The guards have

stopped, panicked, and turned towards the flare. It must be an important emergency signal – something that isn't just fired on a whim – because they're suddenly as jumpy as seeds in a toasting pan. Some run back inside the city, while others head in my direction. The foxary riders have vanished into the trees, a fact that sends a surge of hot triumph through my body.

But there's no time to celebrate. The guards have spotted me now – some are pointing up at the wall, loading their rifles. I scramble down even faster, favouring my bad arm. The guards are still too far away to shoot me, but they're getting closer every second.

Finally, with a reckless leap, I yank my climbing pick from the wall. It's a four-metre fall, but I angle my body towards a pile of leaf litter. I crash down with a shriek of pain, all the breath knocked from my body. I don't have time to check for injuries. There's a second of lying startled in the leaves before I'm up and staggering into the woods.

The guards are only fifty metres away. I plunge through the foliage with shaking legs. I keep tripping, thwacking my numb limbs into trees, but it doesn't really hurt. The fall has shaken me badly; it feels like my body is a puppet, and I'm a very inept puppeteer who's struggling to make its limbs work properly. I'll feel the bruises tomorrow – if I live that long – but for now I'm grateful that the pain's been put on hold.

My breaths are cold and sharp. I can't keep this up forever, and I can hear the guards drawing closer. I've got to find a hiding place, a way to disguise myself until they blunder past me in the dark. My only luck is that they're city guards, not used to the foreign environment of Taladia's woodland. They're probably just as lost as I am. If they were the king's hunters, I'd already be dead.

I plough through a thicker crop of trees, struggling not to break too many branches. The last thing I need is to leave a clear trail. A few years ago, a crew of five adults spent almost a week on the run before the hunters caught them. Their only mistake was breaking too many branches. How unfair is that? You struggle halfway across Northern Taladia and then get blasted to scraps because you snapped a few twigs on the way.

Hunters aren't like city guards. They're trained for canopies, not cobblestones. They can read your trail like they're tracking a deer, and they know how to handle the wilderness. When a refugee ends up dead in Rourton Square, you can bet it was a hunter who dragged him back in from the wild. I won't have long until the hunters are sent for – but in the meantime, I'm going to play this hand for all it's worth.

Then I spot it. A ditch full of dirty water, frosted over by the chill of the night. The thought of diving into that water – cold, muddy, maybe diseased – makes me hesitate for a second. But I can survive being cold and sick. I can't survive a bullet through the throat. So I clamber sideways and plunge into the pit.

It's cold. The shock is worse than falling from the wall, worse than slamming into tree-trunks or slipping down a furious richie's roof-tiles. It's like being whacked with a mallet. Every cell in my body screams, and maybe my mouth is screaming too, but all that escapes my lips is a torrent of froth.

I can't help it. I thrust my head back above the surface and suck down a desperate breath. The guards aren't in view yet, but I can hear them trampling towards me through the trees. I empty my lungs, then suck down the deepest breath I can manage. It's not much – my lungs feel as limp as wet fabric – but there's no time to try again.

I plunge below the waterline, crouching in the mud at the bottom of the ditch. The muck and leaf litter should be enough to hide my body. I clench my eyes shut after a few seconds, because the floating grit makes them sting and I can't see anyway. Any sounds from the surface are distorted, rippling like a dodgy radio wave.

When I was little, my father had a radio. It was a huge wooden box with copper knobs and strange wires poking from its back. Normally only richies can afford such technology but my father worked as a rat-catcher at the alchemics factory, using his Beast proclivity to stop rodents from chewing the wires. He won his radio in a staff lottery. It was a reject from the batch, with a wonky receiver that made the newsreaders' voices fizz and crackle. It only worked for a few hours at a time before we had to wait for the alchemy to recharge.

Sometimes, when we couldn't afford coal for the fire, my father would herd our family into the living room and say, 'Tonight is the night for a grand ball.' We would don our finest clothes – I still remember my mother's dress, as blue as the morning sky – and position ourselves on the living room floor. Then my father would switch on his radio, twiddle the knobs to find a music station, and we would dance the warmth back into our bodies.

The distorted crackle of that radio comes back to me now for the first time in years. The ditch water has that same fuzzy quality, that blurring in my ears. But instead of waiting to dance, I wait to die. My lungs hurt already.

I force myself to count to ten – a long, slow, torturous count.

One. Two. Three.

I need to breathe . . .

Four. Five.

Just a little sip of air . . . That's not too greedy, is it? That's not too much to ask?

Six. Seven. Eight.

I think my body is going to explode. The guards must be gone by now. They were tearing through the woods at such a pace, and I can't hear crashing overhead, so perhaps they've been and gone already and the gurgle of muddy water meant I never even knew . . .

Nine.

Almost there . . . Almost . . .

Ten!

I burst upwards like a flare, a sodden firecracker from a turret of ditch water. I suck down air with a horrible rattle, again and again, until the ache in my lungs subsides and the panic in my skull begins to fade.

Then, and only then, do I stop to look around.

CHAPTER FIVE

UNDERGROWTH

THERE'S NO SIGN OF THE GUARDS.

Broken branches hang, splintered, from nearby tree trunks. The guards have been and gone, oblivious to the girl in the water beneath them. Against all odds, I have escaped.

This realisation is almost enough to knock me senseless again. I've just broken through every shackle that held my life in place – the laws, the city walls, even the guards – but this is not the time for a victory dance. The hunters will be summoned soon, and I'm in danger. More danger than I've ever faced before.

I pull my dripping body from the ditch and shake myself off. I wring the water from my coat, from my sleeves, from my trousers and hair. I even risk removing my neck-scarf for a second to squeeze it dry. I feel incredibly exposed. It's like standing naked in the woods, divulging something very private to the trees. I know no one is nearby – the trees are silent, except for the crickets and the wind – but breaking the taboo feels *wrong*.

Then I snort, and clap a hand across my mouth to silence myself. I've broken enough laws to be shot on sight, but I'm worried about exposing proclivity marks that haven't even developed yet? It seems so stupid, now, to worry about taboos and modesty. Anyway, better to break the taboo than catch hypothermia. The water is too cold to leave it streaming down my neck.

Once I'm no longer dripping I set out into the trees. I need to find a safer place to hide. The guards will summon the king's hunters soon, and I haven't got the speed or knowledge to outrun them. My only hope is to bunker down for a few days, somewhere with fresh water and maybe even food nearby, until the hunters give up or look elsewhere.

Taladia is a huge country. One little scruffer girl can't be worth a massive search, right? They'll have to give up sooner or later, when they're summoned to deal with some more important case of rebellion or refugees.

Radnor's refugee crew is out here too but they've got a head start and they're riding foxaries. A human guard has no hope of outrunning a beast like that. Then again, the foliage is so thick that the foxaries' bulky bodies might be a disadvantage. Just like the city's slow-closing gate: too big and strong to move swiftly. I guess there's something to be said for being small.

As I crunch through the leaves, the cold sets in. The water is practically frosting over on my clothes. Fabric chafes like sandpaper in my armpits, and the flare in my trousers is even worse. With every step, its fuse scratches the soft skin of my thighs. Has the water ruined it? Maybe it will work once it's dried out. I'm half-tempted to toss the flare away, but it's the closest thing I have to a weapon. And it's more than that. The flare reminds me of what I did up on the turret, the way I blasted its sibling into the night. The memory feels foreign, like the actions of a stranger, terrifying but thrilling.

I fish the flare out of my trouser-leg and clutch it in my hand. If the guards find me, perhaps I can use it to scare them off. I bet a lighted flare could do some damage at close range. That threat might buy me a few seconds, before the guards realise the flare's been soaked.

I keep on walking. I don't know where I'm going

yet, and I'm too exhausted to think of a plan. Most refugees follow the main trading route south. I'm guessing that's Radnor's plan, since he's disguised his team as foxary riders. But I have no idea how to find the road, and in the meantime I'm as lost as a richie in Rourton's sewers.

The Valley lies far to the southeast, nestled in the Eastern Boundary Range. But I'm not stupid enough to head east right away. The Range is too high and desolate for even a biplane to cross in one piece. It's why the people on the other side remain safe from our king: the Valley is the only gap in their borders.

Besides, I'm not even sure which way *is* east. Left or right? Forward or back? All I can see here is darkness.

After a while, the silence begins to worry me. At least when the guards were chasing me I knew where they were. Now, though, I have no idea whether I'm being watched. I can't see smoke from Rourton any more – I've travelled too deep into the forest. The canopy is thick and bushy enough to block out most of the moonlight. All I can hear is the rustle of the leaves, and once the cry of a distant owl.

The world is black. I am alone.

Now that the terror of the chase is over, and my numbness from the freezing water is fading, I'm rewarded with a surge of pain from my shoulder.

It's sharp and hot, still injured from my slip down the wall.

To ignore the pain, I recite my times tables in my head. My parents were obsessed with education. They wanted me to learn my way out of downtown Rourton, I think. And so the tables come back to me in a rush, echoed in my mother's sing-song voice like a lullaby: *Five times three is fifteen, five times four is twenty, five times five is twenty-five* . . .

Five.

There are five other teenagers in these woods tonight. I wish I could find them. But the forest seems endless: a sea of black that rolls across the horizon as if to reach the very edges of the continent. There's nothing in the world except this forest, this night, and the nervous hitch of my breath in the dark.

Five times six is thirty . . .

If I found them somehow, if I joined them, we would be a crew of six. That's assuming that they're all still alive and haven't been captured by the guards. Not likely.

Eventually, I can't stand the pain in my shoulder any longer. I fall to my knees in the mud and shove a bundle of twigs between my teeth. I have never re-set my own shoulder before, but the blacksmith did it for me once and I think I remember the

56

process. And this dislocation isn't as bad as the first time; my tendons have already been stretched by the old injury.

It helps that I can't see. The darkness allows me to disconnect from my fear. I wrap my hands around a raised knee, intertwine the fingers and stretch back my neck. For a moment, I can't bring myself to move. I just sit there in the darkness, half-convinced that I'm already dead. But the stink of rotting leaves is too potent and my skin is still cold with the remaining ditch water. This is real. I have to do this.

I thrust my shoulders forward. There is a click and the mouthful of twigs muffles my scream. I spit out the twigs and force myself to my feet.

Finally I find a hollow log half-submerged in mud and leaf litter. Well, I trip over it. After a few moments of stunned pain and silence, I remember to breathe again. Then I stumble along to an opening at its end, use my fingers to trace its length in the dark and shove myself inside like I'm stuffing a sausage. My shoulder still burns, so I'm careful to keep that side of my body facing upwards. There's a scatter of frantic claws at the log's far end, suggesting I've startled a rodent from its lair.

It's not a very good hiding place – in fact, it's painfully obvious, and I probably smashed a clear path for my pursuers while I blundered through the night. But at least it's a shield from the wind, and from the shine of a hunter's lantern.

And so, inside my log, I wait in silence for dawn.

✳

I WAKE SLOWLY, DAZED AND DISORIENTATED, struggling to remember how I ended up in this tube of rotting wood. My body is numb, except for my aching shoulder, and some kind of sharp wire is poking into my belly. The fuse of a signal flare. Slowly, I remember my desperate journey last night.

I must have dozed for several hours. It's now early morning and sunlight filters down through cracks in the log. I hear a noise. A crunch.

Footsteps.

I hold my breath. How have they found me?

The footsteps crunch closer. A shadow blots out the light coming through the cracks in the log, as through someone is looming right above my hiding place. I slide a climbing pick from my sleeve and grip it in my hand. It's not much of a weapon, but at least it's sharp. If this hunter is going to kill me, I'm going down with a fight. Then I focus on the shape of my body, the weight of my limbs, and try to conjure an illusion to hide myself. It will only last a few seconds, but it might be enough –

Too late. Something rips away the top of the log, peeling back the bark as though I'm a walnut to be shelled. Light floods across my face; I blink, eyes stinging, and slash out wildly with the climbing pick.

'Hey, whoa!' says a familiar voice. 'If I'd known the party games were gonna be *that* full on, I would've brought my croquet mallet.'

It's Teddy Nort.

I peel myself upright out of the log. Teddy has taken a few steps backwards, holding up his hands in self-defence. Even now, he's grinning like a madman. I wonder whether maybe he is one.

'What's going on?' I say.

'Wanna drop the pointy thing before we get all heart to heart?'

I realise I'm still brandishing my climbing pick in his direction, and stuff it back into my sleeve. My shoulder is much less painful than last night, but it's still tender. 'Sorry. I thought you were a hunter.'

'Forget it,' says Teddy, waving a forgiving hand. 'I'm used to it. Wouldn't feel like a proper morning if it didn't involve someone poking knives at me.'

Knowing Teddy's reputation, that's probably true.

'So,' I try again, 'what's going on?'

'Well, it's morning. The sun is shining down, plants are using its energy to grow new cells, birds are hunting for worms . . .'

'You know what I mean! Where are the others?'

'The others?' Teddy claps a hand to his head, as though he's just remembered their existence. 'Oh, right, *those* others! Well, I dunno exactly. We stayed together for a while, but it was dark . . .'

'And you lost them?'

Teddy nods.

'You don't look too worried,' I say.

'They'll be all right. They're riding foxaries, aren't they? A few overfed Rourton guards aren't gonna catch them anytime soon.'

'What about the king's hunters?'

'Yeah, well, we've got a decent head start,' says Teddy. 'If we meet up with the rest of the crew quick enough, we should be able to outrun them for a while.'

I frown. 'Meet up? But how will you find –'

'Piece of cake.' Teddy pauses. 'Well, not literally a piece of cake, but tell you what, I could sure do with a chocolate cake right now.'

He looks so hopeful, as if expecting a cake to fall out of the sky, that I can't help smiling.

'What?' he says. 'For all you know, my proclivity could be Bakery Treats.'

'I don't think bakery treats are part of the natural balance.'

'Why not? It'd be a better proclivity than Dirt,

anyway.' He gestures for me to follow him through the thicket. 'Come on, we'd better hurry if we want to meet the others.'

'You were serious, then, about finding them?'

'Does this look like the face of a liar?'

Yes, I think instantly. 'In case you hadn't noticed, Teddy, this is a big patch of forest. How are you planning to find four people in the middle of it?'

'Same way I found you, Danika Glynn.'

'What?'

Teddy pulls aside a clump of branches, revealing a clearing. In the centre, atop a pile of boulders, lies the furry bulk of a foxary. Teddy gives a little bow and inclines his hand. 'After you, my fair lady.'

I stare at the beast. I've never seen a foxary so clearly. Occasionally one shows up in Rourton's marketplace, but in a thickly barred cage that makes it almost impossible to get a decent view. Up close, the creature is magnificent. It's the size of a large pony, with claws that could carve my head like a melon. The jaws are huge, lined with teeth that become visible when its lips twist up to breathe.

'This is Borrash,' says Teddy. 'He's a foxary.'

'I'd noticed.'

The creature lies at ease, sprawling on the rocks beneath a patch of open sky. Its fur sticks up oddly, as though statically charged, and it makes weird little grumbling noises. Even from a few metres away, though, the stench of its body crawls down my throat. It smells oddly familiar: like the musky dirt of an alley cat, or a hostel that's been infested by rats.

There are no knives, no bridle, no chains nearby. For a second I think it's snarling at us – about to pounce, maybe. Then I realise it isn't snarling; it's purring. It's sunning itself on the rocks, soaking up the sunlight like an enormous hairy lizard.

'All right, Danika?' says Teddy.

I nod, determined not to look afraid. 'How are you controlling it?'

He grins. 'That's my little secret.'

I glance between the boy and the foxary, trying to figure Teddy out. He's too young to reveal his proclivity markings or speak of his proclivity to non-family, but maybe his power has already developed. It's the only explanation I can think of. His proclivity must be Beast, just like my father's. He doesn't need a bridle or knives, because his magic communicates with this creature naturally. They're probably even friendly, understanding each other's needs and wishes in a symbiotic bond.

Well, that's how the proclivity relationship is *supposed* to work. Since this is Teddy Nort we're talking about, he's probably planning to fleece the thing of all its energy and steal the fur off its back for a jacket.

'*This* is how you found me?' I say.

Teddy looks pleased with himself. 'Foxaries have a pretty good sense of smell. I saw what you did with the flare – how you saved us – and I knew you'd head into the woods. So I stuck old Borrash here onto your scent trail and here we are.'

I wrinkle my nose. 'My scent trail?'

Teddy fishes something from his pocket, holds out his fist and unfurls his palm. He's holding my handkerchief: the scrap of fabric I lost during the bombings. 'Yeah, easy. I just got Borrash to sniff this and off we went.'

Too late, I remember Teddy's reputation as a pickpocket. 'You thieving little –'

He holds up a finger. 'Nuh-uh. I'm not guilty this time. You dropped it and I found it when you were gone.'

'If I'd dropped it in the tunnels, it'd be covered in sewage.'

Teddy laughs and passes me the handkerchief. 'All right, Danika, I plead guilty. I nicked it. Just testing you.'

I should be furious. How are we supposed to survive if we can't trust each other? But for some reason, it's hard to stay angry with Teddy Nort. Maybe it's the silly expression on his face or the fact that I'm not too attached to my handkerchief, but his act of thievery seems harmless.

'You're not gonna chop my head off with that pointy thing hidden in your sleeve, are you?' he says.

I sigh, indicating my forgiveness. 'Let's just get moving, before any hunters show up.'

We head towards the foxary. As we walk, I can't help reflecting that if he'd stolen something more valuable – such as my mother's bracelet – this would have ended quite differently. I wear the bracelet up high above my elbow, making it difficult to spot beneath my sleeve, but still . . . if anyone could manage to nick it, it would be Teddy Nort.

I frown at Teddy, and watch as he waves one of Clementine's glittery hair ribbons beneath the foxary's nose. Did he *know* that my handkerchief was worthless, that he could steal it without upsetting me? He's spent a lifetime sussing out pickpocket victims and deciding how much he can safely steal. I bet he's good at reading people, and he's not as stupid as he likes to pretend. Maybe he was reading me in the sewers, deciding what he could steal without dropping himself into my bad books.

But Radnor rejected me from the refugee crew. If Teddy thought he'd never see me again, why would he care about my reaction to his pickpocketing? Why not steal my bracelet instead of a stinky old handkerchief?

'Coming, Danika?' says Teddy.

I mentally shake myself, refocusing on the situation at hand. He's already sitting atop the foxary's back, waiting for me to join him. The creature is snuffling forward, ready to hunt down Clementine's scent.

'Yeah,' I say. 'Sure, I'm coming.'

I place a hand on the foxary's back. Its fur isn't soft; it's hard and bristly, like a toothbrush. As I swing my body into position, keeping my weight off my healing shoulder, I feel its muscles tense to accommodate my weight. The fur prickles through my trousers, sticking little spikes into the underside of my thighs.

Teddy twists his neck around and grins. 'Not worried about riding this old fleabag, are you?'

'Nope.' I shake my head. 'I'm not worried.'

And it's true, in a way. I'm not worried about this foxary any more, not when it's being ridden by someone with a Beast proclivity. The only risks here are claws and teeth: weapons that I can see coming, threats I can duck and avoid.

What worries me more is another type of threat. Words, lies, manipulation. And I'm worried that the boy in front of me, with his cheerful grin and slippery fingers, might wield these weapons a lot more effectively than claws.

CHAPTER SIX

PERIL IN THE FOREST

WE RIDE FOR MOST OF THE MORNING, LETTING THE foxary guide our jumbled route through the trees. The sensation of muscle and bone moving beneath me feels odd, and I'm not sure where to put my hands. I don't want to yank out any fur, but I'm sure as hell not holding Teddy Nort for support. So I plant my palms on the creature's sides and try to lean with its movements. At least my shoulder feels less painful, so I know I popped it back into place successfully.

The foxary careens left or right with a swish of the breeze, as though each whiff of distant scent brings directions to his nose. Teddy seems able to predict these sudden turns; his body bends aside to accommodate the twists of fur and muscle beneath us. Unfortunately, I'm not so naturally in tune with the creature's movements. With every change of direction, I feel as if I'm about to slip off into the undergrowth.

'Comfortable?' says Teddy.

'Yeah, not too bad,' I say. 'You should install some cup holders, like the richies have in their carriages.'

'Shame we haven't got any cups,' says Teddy. 'Or anything to drink. Or anything to eat, come to think of it.'

I remember the hessian bag that I stole from the guard turret. During the chaos I shoved it into one of my coat pockets, and I doubt its contents survived their dunking in the ditch. But my stomach is starting to rumble and even the soggy remains of a guard's sandwich seems appetising. 'Hang on, I might have something . . .'

The bag is stiff and frosty from the ditch water. I use one hand to balance myself on the foxary's back, while the other cracks the bag away from the pocket's lining. With a combination of teeth and my free hand, I open the drawstring and peer inside.

'Anything?' says Teddy.

'A few slices of apple, cheese and something . . . I can't quite see . . .' I jostle the half-frozen cheese aside, hoping to discover a chocolate cake, just to amuse Teddy. But what I find is even better. 'Oh, *yes!*'

'What?'

'Honey-spice nuts,' I say, relishing every syllable.

I've tasted these nuts once before, when I found a discarded food hamper in a richie gift shop's rubbish bin. The food was only slightly stale and – apart from some mouldy crackers – perfectly safe to eat. Alongside the honey-spice nuts, there was crumbling shortbread, a fancy wooden eggcup with a chocolate egg and a tiny pot of strawberry jam that lasted me months. Every morning, I would allow myself a lick of sweetness upon the tip of my pinkie finger.

'How the hell did you afford honey-spice nuts?' says Teddy.

'I didn't buy them,' I say. 'I stole this stuff from the turret last night, when I set off the flare.'

Teddy laughs. 'Maybe I should recruit you as an apprentice burglar.'

The foxary seems to be heading in a fairly straight line, so I risk removing my other hand from its body. Using my knees and calves to balance, I divide the food into two shares and pass half to Teddy.

'You'd better make it last,' I say, trying to ignore my rumbling stomach as I tip my own share back into my pocket.

But my words are too late; Teddy has already tossed his handful of nuts into his mouth. With a couple of satisfied crunches, he lets out an 'mmmmm' of appreciation and swallows the lot.

'Hey, we might not get food again until –'

'Calm down, Danika,' says Teddy. 'You think we're gonna set out into the wilderness without supplies?'

'Well, no, but –'

'The others have loads of food strapped to their foxaries. I bet those richie girls brought caviar and truffle cakes. When we catch up to them, it'll be better than the time I broke into that High Street bakery.'

This comment sends an odd twinge into my chest. I want to point out that we might not *find* the others, or that they might not be alive to be found. But Teddy seems so confident, so happily certain that everything will turn out fine, it's hard not to get swept up in his enthusiasm.

'All right,' I say. 'But I'm not part of your crew, remember?'

'You are now,' says Teddy. 'I reckon as soon as Radnor knew you were an illusionist, he secretly wanted to recruit you – but he was stuck with that rule about five crew members. He just needed a better excuse to recruit you and now you've given him one.'

'Like what?'

'Well, now we owe you our lives.' Teddy pauses. 'That flare was a pretty decent show, by the way, although a couple of coloured fireworks would've livened things up.'

I snort. 'I'll keep that in mind for next time.'

For the next twenty minutes or so, I fight the urge to scoff my food. I've spent so long saving every morsel for when it's most needed that I can't bear to squander all my food in one meal. But as morning burns away the fog from the trees, my belly's grumbling shifts into an uncomfortable gnawing. It tugs at my insides until I finally admit defeat. I choose an apple slice from my pocket and suck on the cold flesh, trying to make it last.

'So,' I say eventually, 'why are you leaving Rourton?'

'I thought a trip sounded like fun,' says Teddy.

'No, seriously. Everyone knows about the great Teddy Nort – that you're the best at escaping the guards, at covering up your crimes . . . You seem to have a pretty charmed life. I don't see why you'd risk it all to join Radnor's crew.'

'Maybe I was just bored.'

I consider this for a moment, then dismiss it. Even if he's reckless, Teddy isn't stupid.

'A lot of people believe that joining a crew is suicide,' I say. 'Most people who try to escape Taladia end up dead.'

Teddy doesn't answer. I think back to the conversation in the sewers, words that echoed through the tunnel while bombs crashed down above our heads . . .

'Radnor said you were on the run, that you begged him for a spot on the crew,' I say. 'But the guards are *always* after you. What the hell did you do that's bad enough to –'

Our foxary stops walking.

This isn't a slow, meandering halt. It's sharp and abrupt, and sends my forehead into the back of Teddy's shoulders. His muscles tense and I know instantly that something's wrong. I peel myself back up and twist around to view the trees. There's no sign of anyone nearby, but the foxary's muscles are so tightly strung that I feel them retract beneath me. It feels like sitting on a loaded slingshot, the string stretched back, just waiting for the shooter to let fly. 'What's going –'

Bang!

The bullet whizzes past my shoulder. Before I even know what's happening, there's a violent jolt beneath me and we're off, smashing through the trees. I'm almost thrown off the foxary's back, but fear makes me squeeze my arms and calves so tightly that I could rival a barnacle for gripping power.

'Hold on!' shouts Teddy, just as another bullet squeals through the foliage.

'What?'

'Just do it, Danika! We're about to –'

The rush of speed steals his words away. It doesn't matter, though, because I realise what's happening as the foxary's muscles retract into another squeeze beneath me. The creature runs like a spring, sucking up all its strength and then exploding forward with a crash. I duck my head low, struggling to avoid the whip of branches as we careen between tree trunks.

'It's a hunter!' I say. 'There's no way a city guard could –'

'I know! Can you see how many there are?'

Until now, it hasn't occurred to me that we might have multiple pursuers. I twist my neck around, squinting through the mess of brown and green and blustery air. There's a flash of green – the royal uniform of King Morrigan's hunters – but it vanishes quickly between the trees.

'Left!' shouts Teddy.

His warning has barely registered when the foxary throws itself sideways, ducking to the left of a massive tree trunk. It's a close call and we just avoid smashing into the bulk of wood. My right leg crashes against the side and agony shoots up through my knee. I let out a cry. Every instinct tells me to grab my leg, to squeeze the wound and numb the pain, but letting go now would mean death. I clamp my eyes shut instead and silently order myself: *Ignore the pain, Danika. It's not hurting, it's just a race. It's just a race, and if you let it hurt you're going to lose . . .*

I force my eyes open and twist back around, fighting for a better view of the hunter. He must be riding a foxary of his own, or some other beast with enormous speed – how else could he keep up with us?

Then I feel the gush of wind rise up behind us and I realise. This man is not riding an animal. He rides the wind itself, meshing and floating and flickering along its power currents. His proclivity is Air, perhaps, or Wind – either way, it's given him enough speed and power to keep pace with a foxary. This man is no amateur, no unpractised recruit. He's a professional killer. And he's going to blast our bodies into mulch on the forest floor.

We twist through the trees; the foxary's muscles clench and release like a piano accordion. I fall forward onto Teddy's back a few times, smashing my face against the hard bone of his spine, but with a gasp and a wrench of my own muscles I manage to regain my balance. Everything is a blur – brown, green, trees, wind, leaves – and all I can think is that I'm going to die. Any second now, we'll smear ourselves across a tree-trunk, or a bullet will blast through my head in a spray of blood and darkness . . .

We burst into a clearing.

Screams. People scatter, foxaries snarl and I just glimpse the remains of a campsite as we smash through the middle of it.

The hunter gushes out of the wind behind us, solidifying in an empty space in the middle of the clearing. He smiles, raises his pistol and begins to curl his finger around the trigger. I watch every click of his knuckles, every bend and strain of the tendons in his finger . . . His fingertip touches the curve of metal, the knuckles stiffen . . .

Then someone runs through the wreckage towards us and the hunter explodes into flame.

CHAPTER SEVEN
THE CREW

AT FIRST, I THINK I MUST BE DEAD. MY BRAIN CAN'T register what my eyes are seeing – the flaming body can't be real. The hunter must have pulled the trigger. Maybe this is what dead people see: delusions, unexplained fires, screams that echo like claws across their skulls . . .

The hunter's scream dies. His body falls.

My knee burns with pain, my head throbs and each breath barks up my throat with a ragged scratch. This isn't a delusion. There's nothing hazy or dreamlike about it. It's raw, it's brutal and every second hurts.

I turn slightly, surveying the ruins of the clearing, and realise that we've found the rest of Radnor's crew. Two foxaries are chained to a tree behind the crumpled remains of the crew's campsite. The blonde richie twins, Clementine and her sister, gape in shock at the destruction. Radnor himself wears a bloody bandage across his forehead. But my eyes are drawn to the bulky figure before us, hands outstretched, still ready to lunge at the smouldering corpse of the hunter on the ground. His features are obscured by smoke from a burning stick in his hands.

'Who are you?' I whisper.

Radnor steps forward. 'This is Hackel. Number Five in our crew.'

As the smoke clears, I get a better look at the newcomer. He's huge and strong, muscles bulging beneath his cloak. If I hadn't known about Radnor's teenager-only rules for the crew, I would have guessed Hackel was in his twenties. He glares so hard at the fallen hunter that I expect another fireball to shoot out of his eyes. But he just drops the stick and kneels beside the body.

Now that the shock has worn off a little, my senses shoot into overdrive. The stink of burning flesh, the hot sting of smoke in my eyes . . . It's enough to make my stomach heave, and I want nothing more than to run into the trees and never look back, never think of this horrific scene again. But I can't show weakness now, not in front of the refugee crew that could mean my survival. So I clench my fists, tell myself to ignore the stench and try to breathe through my mouth.

Hackel grabs the hunter's burnt wrist. Flakes of something fall away – I don't know whether it's fabric or flesh. Hackel examines the forearm, but obviously doesn't find what he's looking for, because he drops it back into the dirt. Then he reaches around the man's neck. I want to stop him, to tell him that this is barbaric – he's already killed the man once, he doesn't need to throttle him too.

But Hackel isn't trying to throttle him. He just pulls a silver chain from the hunter's neck, black and dingy with soot. There's a quiet clink as he examines the metal charms that hang from the chain. *Alchemy charms*, I realise with a start. I've never seen them up close before, since only the wealthiest of richies can afford such trinkets. The charms have spellwork imbued into the silver, ready to be deployed against the bearer's enemies.

Hackel pockets his trophy, rises to his feet and exits the clearing in silence.

It takes a moment for me to find my voice. 'What . . .?'

'He's going to check for more hunters,' says Radnor. 'If you were followed by one, there might be more just behind us.' He glances around the ruins of the campsite. 'We've got to move. That scream, and the smoke . . .'

Radnor doesn't need to finish his sentence. We all know other hunters will be here soon. Even if they didn't know our location before, they do now. By killing the hunter with his Flame proclivity, Hackel has set off the equivalent of a flare to guide them through the trees.

'What are we doing with this scruffer?' Clementine points at me in apparent distaste. 'We already have five people on our crew. We should leave her here to draw the hunters. She could be a useful distraction, buy us some time.'

I stare at her. 'I saved your lives last night.'

Clementine sniffs. 'And we're all grateful, but that doesn't entitle you to jeopardise them now.'

'Hey, hang on a second!' says Teddy. 'This girl could be useful – she's got skills. You saw how she climbed that wall. And she's an *illusionist*! Just think, if she trains a bit and gets better at illusions, she could hide us from the hunters.'

Clementine looks ready to argue, but visibly swallows back her annoyance. She turns to Radnor with a raised eyebrow, as though seeking support from the crew's leader.

Radnor frowns at me. 'What's your name again?'

'Danika,' I say. 'Danika Glynn.'

'What other skills have you got?'

I straighten up, trying to hide any pain from the wound in my leg. This is not the time to show weakness. 'I can climb, I can run. I can fight a bit.'

'What else?'

There's silence for a moment as I struggle to think of an answer. 'My family died in a bombing raid.' I pause. 'My parents always told me stories of the Valley, like it was some kind of paradise. I'll do anything to get there.' I take a deep breath. 'I'm going to reach that Valley and I'm not going to surrender. I don't play to lose.'

Radnor eyes me quietly, as though weighing up a sack of flour at the market. Deciding whether I'm worth the price.

'All right, Danika Glynn,' he says eventually. 'Welcome to the crew.'

*

WE GATHER UP THE REMAINS OF THE CAMPSITE. THIS involves stuffing blankets and supplies into heavy packs, which Teddy buckles onto the foxaries. He murmurs as he strokes their necks and I wonder what he's telling them. Is he confirming their bond, offering them rewards . . . or threatening to skin

them if they don't behave? With someone like Teddy
Nort, it's hard to tell.

There are only three foxaries now: the one that
Teddy and I rode to the campsite and two others.
I don't know what happened to the other two –
perhaps they fled into the wild in the panic last night,
or maybe the Rourton guards shot them. Either way,
there's no time to ask for details. No time to tend
to wounds, to patch up the bloody mess across my
knee. All we can do is bundle onto the creatures'
backs, wrap our arms around each other and flee.

'What about Hackel?' I say, squashed between
Teddy Nort and a stack of supplies. 'How will he
catch up without a foxary?'

'Don't worry,' says Radnor. 'Hackel can take care
of himself.'

This much, at least, I don't doubt. The boy carries
a weight of power within his muscles and a tightness
to his face that I've seen before in Rourton's darkest
alleyways. Hackel's a basher, I'm sure. A thug for
hire, a killer. He's got that look in his eyes. Back
home, crime bosses and paranoid richies would have
paid him good cash to carry out their dirty work.
I wonder whether he's a real refugee or just a paid
bodyguard – hired by the richie girls, perhaps, to
keep them safe in the wild. Either way, he didn't
show any qualms about revealing his proclivity to

the rest of us. Only someone with a link to Flame could have killed the hunter like that.

I suck on the back of my teeth, feeling nauseated again as the image of the burning hunter blasts across my mind. I tell myself that Hackel had no choice; that the man was going to kill us all. But it doesn't purge my mental image of the man screaming as he burns.

'What are you thinking?' I say to Teddy.

He doesn't answer for a second and I wonder whether he's replaying the same scene in his own head. Then he forces a laugh. 'I was thinking about the Magnetic Valley. If you got someone with a Metal proclivity, would they get attracted by the magnets? Because I reckon that's what Clementine's proclivity is – and it'd be pretty funny to stick her to a hillside.'

I get an image of Clementine zooming through the air and sticking to a magnetic slope, as she spits out insults in her snobby accent. The idea is so ridiculous that it makes me smile. 'What makes you think her proclivity's Metal?'

'Well, she's brought enough jewellery to open a metalwork shop.'

I peer around his shoulders at the foxary in front of us. The two richie girls are hunched on its back, necks drooped as their animal traipses between the trees. Yet again, I find myself wondering why they've come on this trip. Maybe they thought there was something glamorous about fleeing the city, although I can't imagine what. I bet they weren't expecting so much cold or blood or pain.

I indulge in a silent moment of 'serves you right' at the twins' expense. Clementine was so confident last night, so certain that her parents' money would buy her out of any trouble. All these twins have known is luxury and part of me hates them for it. *This is what the real world's like,* I want to scream. *This is what it's like to fight, every day, to stay alive.*

The second twin glances back at me, just for a moment, and I see the puffy wetness of her eyes. She turns back and hides her face in her sister's shoulders, but it's too late; I've already seen. And what I've seen makes me feel sick with myself. She's just a terrified girl, as lost and alone as the rest of us.

And no matter what I tell myself, there's no point feeling superior. I'm no better equipped to deal with this forest than the twins are. There are no bins out here to scavenge food from, no richies to beg for a cleaning job or barmen to offer me under-the-table shifts in their alehouses. There are only trees and hunters and death.

'What's the plan?' I say, as the foxaries pick up speed. They've shifted into a tighter formation now, allowing for easier discussion.

'What d'you mean?' says Teddy.

'I mean, every refugee crew needs a plan to reach the Valley. Once we're out of these woods, we've still got a massive country to cross. What's our angle?'

'I thought we should take the merchant trader approach,' says Clementine, 'so we could at least travel in comfort. But unfortunately I've been outvoted by these –' She huffs out the first syllable of 'filthy', but catches herself. 'By my crewmates.'

'We're not following the road,' says Radnor.

I frown at the back of Teddy's shoulders. Since the Valley lies to the southeast, the traditional route for refugee crews begins with Taladia's main trading road: a vast belt that stretches right down the country's belly. It provides the safest route from north to south, leading travellers away from the most dangerous wilderness.

Following the road is risky, of course, because it's full of traders and it's the first place hunters will look for a refugee crew. But *not* following the road is even worse. Crews who are arrogant enough to travel away from the road always get lost. Taladia is a vast, wild place. Apart from the forests, there are snow-covered mountain ranges, endless deserts of baking sand . . . and of course, there are the wastelands.

'If we're not following the road,' I say, 'how are we going to find the Valley?'

Radnor smiles tightly. 'The river. It runs parallel to the road, just further east. Goes through rougher terrain, but there won't be as many hunters around – and it'll take us in the right direction.'

I'm about to respond when the foxary's muscles clench beneath me like a spring. I tighten my grip and struggle to keep my balance. Three, two, one . . .

The foxary shoots forward: a streak of red fur and musky stench on the breeze. We zig and zag between the trees, ducking beneath low branches and lurching sideways. The other foxaries are running too, yanking their riders forward with the same explosion of speed.

Clementine throws herself across her own animal's neck. 'What's going on?'

'They smelled something weird! Hang on, I'm trying to . . .' Teddy leans down into our foxary's neck, as though trying to inhale the creature's thoughts through its fur. 'They smelled something strange and they want to go and check it out.'

I'm not sure whether to feel relieved or terrified. 'Strange' is better than having hunters on our tails. But what if 'strange' is just some deadly trap the hunters have set for us? They know we're riding foxaries now – they could have laid a false scent trail, a way to lure the beasts into their nets . . .

'Right!' warns Teddy.

85

The foxaries hurl themselves to the right, changing direction as nimbly as leaves on the wind. Unfortunately, I'm not as agile as the creature I'm riding. I'm already sliding sideways and I barely manage to grab a fistful of fur before I'm flung left by the force of its turn.

'Argh!' I hang off the creature's side, one leg still hitched over its back. I dangle from one clump of reddish fur and the rest of my body threatens to smash against every passing log and tree-trunk as we hurtle through the forest.

Teddy twists around, alerted by my cry. 'What're you doing down there?'

'Admiring the view,' I snap, as I struggle to find a better grip.

I can tell Teddy's swallowing a laugh – I guess I must look stupid – but he manages to hold himself together for a second. He hauls me back up into a sitting position, just in time to avoid a faceful of prickly thornbush.

'Thanks,' I manage.

The foxaries slow, then bring us to a halt. Fur bristles beneath me, spiky with anticipation, and some strange instinct makes my own hair prickle down the back of my neck. For a moment I wonder whether it's my proclivity mark appearing but soon I recognise the feeling as nerves.

Clementine brushes a stray curl back behind her ears. 'Where are we?'

I sniff, hoping to pick up a hint of what drew the foxaries to this place. There's an odd tang to the air. It sends a lurch into my stomach – something about the smell triggers a terrible impulse to run. It's like a forgotten memory, just out of reach . . .

The realisation slaps me.

'Bombs,' I say quietly. 'I can smell burning metal.'

What I really smell – and taste – is a sudden memory of *that* night. The scent makes me hear those screams again, tells me that my family is burning before me and I have no way to save them. Again and again, I must watch them die. I must smell them die.

I slide down from our foxary's back. My feet aren't too steady and I almost slip when I land in the leaf litter, but I manage to catch myself just in time. I can't afford to look weak in front of the others. I'm already furious at myself for needing Teddy's help during the ride; Radnor probably regrets inviting me to join the crew.

'Yes,' says a voice. 'It smells like bombs.'

I turn around, surprised to hear an unfamiliar female voice. It's the quieter twin, the one whose name I've never managed to learn. She slips down from her own foxary, eyes downcast, hands clasped in front of her stomach.

'Dunno about you guys,' says Teddy, 'but I always thought bombs came out of biplanes. Don't hear any planes up there, do you?'

I glance up. The canopy is too thick to make out the sky; if one of the king's biplanes were overhead, we wouldn't spot it until it was too late. But Teddy is right about the noise. Those planes rattle and spit: hunks of metal that choke their way across the skies. The forest is too quiet for a biplane to be overhead.

I sniff again and then spin around to follow the source of the smell. After traipsing through a few metres of tangled undergrowth, I see it: a tiny wisp of smoke twisting up among the mess and roots of a nearby thicket.

'Hey, over here!' I whisper.

The others join me, hot and nervous in the thick of the trees. We push through the foliage, pulling aside leaves and twigs to squeeze our bodies further into the thicket. Even from here, I can tell that something's wrong – there's too much light ahead, as though something has smashed a hole through the canopy itself.

Finally, we thrust our bodies into the clearing.

'What the hell?' says Teddy, as sunlight hits his face.

I stare down, right at the source of the smoke. The burning metal, the crumpled glass, the shattered wings . . . and a scorched golden tattoo that marks the impact of a signal flare. The debris flickers oddly, as though an invisibility enchantment is still wearing off. It must be tainted with magical residue, to still be smoking so long after last night's carnage. This broken hunk of metal is no ordinary wreckage.

'Is that a . . .?' breathes Clementine, sounding horrified.

I swallow. 'Yeah. It is.'

This is one of the king's biplanes, scorched with the mark of a signal flare. And last night, by launching that guard-tower's flare, I shot this plane right out of the sky.

CHAPTER EIGHT
TREE-LANDS

THE ONLY SOUND IS WIND IN THE TREES. WE STARE AT each other. Then we stare back at the plane, stunned by the sight of a palace machine, broken and smouldering, in the middle of the forest.

'Those markings,' says Clementine. 'Our mother told us about the signal flares. Each turret has a unique tattoo, so guards in the other towers know which part of the wall has been threatened.'

I nod. 'My flare.'

Silence.

When it becomes clear that no one else is keen to look, I take a step closer. If there's a body in there, if I've killed someone . . .

'Don't look, Danika,' says Radnor. His voice is

calm, imitating the tone of a leader, but a twinge of uncertainty lingers in each word.

'What if the pilot's still alive?' I say. 'What if he's just unconscious?'

No one answers. I don't want to think what sort of injury could knock someone unconscious for the better part of a day. With a couple of shaky steps, I find myself at the edge of the wreckage.

I bend down, trying to ignore the stink of bombs – no, not bombs, just hot metal – and peer through the shattered window.

The cabin is empty. 'There's no pilot!'

'What?'

'There's no body or anything!'

I straighten up and find Radnor raising an eyebrow. 'A plane can't fly itself,' he says. 'And no one could just walk away from a crash like that.'

'Not unless . . .' I say. 'Maybe the pilot got out of the plane before it crashed. Maybe he had an emergency parachute, or maybe his proclivity was Wind or Air or Darkness or something, and he just floated down into the trees.'

'Oh, that's just fantastic,' says Clementine, glancing around with a nervous twitch. 'Another enemy to worry about.'

'Why was there a plane around, anyway?' says Teddy, frowning. 'I mean, if I had a plane I'd go for joy-flights too, but I reckon it was a bit dark to see much.'

'There were heaps of planes over Rourton last night,' says Clementine impatiently. 'Or have you already forgotten we got *bombed*?'

Teddy scowls at her. 'I'm not stupid, richie! But the bombing finished back when we were still in the sewers. Why the hell would a single plane hang around and check out the view?'

'To report on the damage?'

'There are hundreds of guards in Rourton – any one of them could report that stuff. I still don't see why this plane needed to hang around after the bombings.'

There is silence as we all mull this over. If this lone plane had its own, secret mission, and I shot it down before it could complete it . . .

Someone nudges me. I turn to see Clementine's quiet twin tilting her head as though to ask permission to pass.

'May I have a look?' she says, so shyly that I barely make out her words.

'Go ahead,' I say, and make space for her to squeeze between the trees.

She bends down to examine the plane, a frown upon her face. For a second I think she doesn't believe me – that she's about to search the cabin for the pilot's body. But instead she peers beneath a broken wing.

'Six bombs,' she says.

'What?'

She straightens up and looks at Clementine. 'There are still six alchemy bombs, ready to launch. That's the maximum these biplanes can carry, isn't it?'

We all nod. Even in years when the bombs don't fall, we're regularly treated to displays of biplanes soaring overhead. They're a constant threat to ensure we behave, so we make damn sure to learn as much about them as possible. Everyone knows these biplanes carry six bombs each: no more.

'So,' I say, 'this pilot was part of the bombing crew. He had a full load of alchemy bombs. But he didn't drop them on the city, and he waited around afterwards for . . . what?'

Radnor gazes at the smoking metal. 'Must've had a special mission. Maybe he was going to bomb the survivors, to take us out when we thought it was safe again.'

Silence. I feel a little sick. In the aftermath of the bombing, so many people were out on the streets. If this plane was waiting to launch a second strike . . .

'You might have saved a lot of lives, Danika,' says Teddy. 'Hey, we should throw a plane-smashing party! Can you believe it, what you've just done? You've taken out one of the king's own biplanes.' He grins. 'Anyone got a bottle of wine?'

The impact of his words hits me hard in the throat. 'Oh no.'

'What's wrong? Don't you see, this is awesome!' Teddy raises his fist in a pump of triumph. 'This must be the best blow that anyone's struck against the palace in decades.'

I shake my head, trying to hide the fear that's just taken seed in my gut. 'And don't you think the palace has noticed?'

Teddy's grin fades and he drops his fist. 'Oh.'

'We might've struck a blow against the palace,' I say, 'but we've also blown ourselves to the top of the palace's kill list.'

'Every hunter in the land is going to be gunning for us,' says Radnor tightly, glancing between the wreckage and my face. 'You're gonna be the most hunted person in Taladia.'

'Imagine the price they'll put on your head,' says Clementine. 'They'll plaster your face across the papers, on wanted posters . . . The scruffer who shot a biplane from the sky! Whoever catches you will win a fortune.'

'Trust a richie to think about money,' mutters Teddy.

'It was an accident!' I say. 'I didn't even know the plane was there.'

'You think the king will care?' says Radnor.

Clementine throws up her hands. 'Well, you can't come with us! This trip is already dangerous enough, thank you very much.'

'Danika saved our lives!' says Teddy. 'Anyway, we already had hunters after us. What difference will a few more make?' He gives a cocky grin. 'We can get away from a few overfed palace buffoons.'

'A few overfed buffoons?' says Clementine. 'I'm glad you think this is so amusing, but I refuse to treat this journey like a game. If we stay with this scruffer girl, Nort, we are all going to die.'

'Bit melodramatic, don't you reckon?' Teddy says.

I gaze down at the remains of the plane. It still doesn't feel real. How could I, a runty little scruffer kid from Rourton, destroy a palace biplane? Clementine is right. I'll have half the kingdom after me, all eager to set an example of the fate that awaits traitors. As long as I stay here, I'm a danger to the crew.

'I'll go,' I say. 'I won't be responsible for the rest of you getting caught.'

'They're gonna kill us if they find us, anyway,' says Teddy. 'I reckon your illusion skills are the best hope we've got.'

'If they're busy chasing me, maybe they'll leave the rest of you alone. This could be your chance to get out of the forest, to find the river . . .'

'Forget it, Danika,' says Teddy. 'They'll be after all of us now. You set off the flare to help us escape, remember? They probably reckon we planned it all together.' He brightens. 'Hey, do you reckon the papers will run my old mugshot from the jewellery store heist? I reckon I look pretty dashing in that one.'

Clementine shakes her head. 'They won't be able to identify us. It was dark, and –'

'The city wall is lined with picture spells,' says Radnor. 'They'll have images of all our faces by now.'

A breeze eddies across the ruins of the plane, twisting smoke into the air. We all know what Radnor means. Rourton is a hive of rats: of whispers and rumours and dealings in the dark. The guards need only flash my picture around the dodgier end of town, and I can think of a dozen scruffers who'd sell my name for a fistful of coins. It won't be hard to identify the richie twins, either, and as for the infamous Teddy Nort . . .

We can never go back. If we set one foot back in Rourton now, we might as well sign our own death warrants. The realisation tightens in my stomach like a fist.

'You should get going,' I manage. 'The smoke's going to draw the hunters this way.'

Radnor nods. 'Come on, everyone.'

'Her too?' says Clementine sharply, tossing her head in my direction.

'No, I'll stay here,' I say. 'I mean, I'll head off in another direction, and maybe –'

Radnor shakes his head. 'No, you're part of the crew now, Danika. I want an illusionist on my side. Anyway, this is my crew and I make the rules. We don't leave anyone behind, and we don't betray each other – no matter what.' He gives Clementine a stern glare. 'If we can't trust each other, we're not going to survive.'

Clementine doesn't look convinced, but she nods. I hesitate before I do the same. Then I swing up onto Teddy's foxary and tighten my grip on its fur.

This is going to be a long ride.

CHAPTER NINE
ILLUSIONS

WE TRAVEL FOR MOST OF THE DAY. MY LEGS CRAMP, MY shoulder aches and my wounded knee throbs. I wrap the knee in some spare fabric from the pack behind me: a pale blue skirt, which shimmers prettily when we pass beneath sunlit gaps in the canopy. At least, until my blood soaks through and turns the fabric crimson-brown.

'That was one of my favourite skirts,' hisses Clementine, when she spots my choice of bandage.

I want to point out that opportunities for sparkly skirt-wearing don't look too promising in the near future, but remember the need to get along with these people. They're my crew now, too.

'Sorry,' I say.

Clementine's mouth is open, ready to snipe at me again, but my apology catches her unawares. She closes her lips, gives a tight nod and looks away. I'm not sure whether this means I'm forgiven or whether I'm just not worth her time. Either way, it's better than fighting.

As we ease into the afternoon, my stomach begins to complain. Up until now, fear and adrenaline have kept it full enough. But after hours of riding and no signs of pursuit, I'm too tired for adrenaline. I feel like a washcloth with all the water squeezed out. I'm not alone, either, because Radnor keeps sucking on his bottom lip and – every few minutes – Teddy's stomach offers a grumbly soundtrack for the ride.

'What food do we have left?' says Radnor.

I look at him, surprised. He has always seemed so in control of this mission: the very image of a determined crew leader. Surely he would have planned the food supplies back in Rourton?

'Leaves,' says Teddy helpfully. '*Lots* of leaves. I reckon we could set up a decent scam selling leaf soup, if there were any richies around to buy it.'

'No, seriously,' says Radnor. 'I want a rundown of our current supplies.'

'Most of the food was on Maisy's foxary,' says Clementine.

Maisy. So that's the name of the quiet twin. I remember seeing her fall off her foxary during the struggle at the city gate – obviously one of the others picked her up, but her foxary is gone. And of all the foxaries, we've lost the one that carried the food. The knowledge sends a cold shudder into the base of my spine. I know what this means. We all do. There's even a jump-rope rhyme about it in Rourton: one of the grim little ditties that scruffer kids sing to keep distracted on cold nights.

'*And if a crew does not keep fed,*' I recite quietly, '*you know that crew will soon be dead.*'

'That's not the version I learned,' says Teddy.

'Oh yeah? What's your version, then?'

Teddy holds up a hand in a grand gesture, as though he's an opera singer about to perform. '*And if a crew does not keep fed, they'd better nick some richie's bread!*'

I snort. 'Even *you* couldn't find anyone to pick-pocket out here.'

'Hey, who knows? Maybe ravens and earth-worms have a secret economy going. There's always someone around to nick stuff off, if you know what you're doing.'

I try to imagine Teddy pickpocketing an earth-worm, then give up.

'Why'd you put all the food onto one foxary,

anyway?' says Teddy, turning to Radnor. 'I would've thought it was safer to spread it around.' He pauses. 'Not that I'm advocating safety regulations. You wanted to walk on the wild side, right?'

Radnor shakes his head. 'This trip is dangerous enough. I'm not about to add more risk for fun.'

'So why'd you put all the food on Maisy's foxary, then?'

'I didn't,' says Radnor, looking annoyed. 'That was Hackel's idea. He's being paid to lead us to safety – he's supposed to be an expert at this.'

Realisation hits me like a slap. Radnor may have started this crew, and he may be its official leader, but he's not the one calling the shots. Hackel is the true organiser. And he isn't just an ordinary hired basher.

'Are you saying Hackel's a –?' I begin.

Radnor nods. 'Yeah, he's a smuggler. He's made his living smuggling black-market stuff across the country – rare metals, mostly, and stolen goods – but he says he's taken people too. Refugee crews, just like us.'

'He was certainly expensive to hire,' says Clementine. 'And he *insisted* that we use foxaries as our disguise. Do you have any idea how much it cost to buy those foxaries and load them secretly with supplies?'

'A lot?' I guess.

Clementine nods. 'More than you'd see in a thousand lifetimes, scruffer. Maisy and I poured our life's savings into this trip. That smuggler had better not get himself killed or we'll have paid him for nothing!'

'So it's Hackel's plan to follow the river?' I say.

Radnor nods. 'It's the route he uses for his black-market transport, for smuggling stuff across the country. He promised it's safer than the road.'

'Just like he promised us it would be better to pack each foxary with a different type of supplies,' says Clementine, looking distrustful. 'And *that* didn't end well, did it?'

'Could've been worse,' says Teddy. 'I mean, we could've lost the foxary that was carrying this sparkly blue skirt, and that'd be a real tragedy.'

'It's not funny, Nort,' snaps Clementine.

'I'm not trying to be funny. If a hunter catches us, we could get away by chucking fancy waistcoats in his face.' Teddy turns to grin at me. 'What do you reckon, Danika?'

'Well, it'd have the element of surprise,' I say.

By the time we find an adequate campsite, the lower half of my body feels ready to drop off. The constant tensing of the foxary's muscles, the throbbing of my knee, and the jostle of movement at the base of my spine are all enough to send me slipping down into the leaf litter with a moan.

Radnor chooses a secluded clearing hidden within a thick patch of forest. We're near the edge of a creek, which churns and gurgles with the promise of fresh water. There have been no sounds of pursuit and the foxaries seem relaxed, so I'm guessing this clearing is as safe a campsite as we're going to get.

For about twenty minutes, no one really moves. We slouch against tree trunks, resting our heads against the bark and exhaling weariness through each flare of our nostrils. It's heading into evening now – the sky above our clearing looks grey – and the air is colder than ever. Each day brings winter closer and this isn't a good time of year to be trekking across Taladia. But there's no use moaning now. We're out here in the cold, and all we can do is grit our teeth and *survive*. That's the real trick to a successful refugee crew. There's no magic answer. All you can do is survive, and then survive again, day after day, until you reach the Magnetic Valley.

'Do you think it's like the song?' I murmur.

I'm so tired that I don't even realise I've spoken aloud until Teddy Nort answers. 'What are you on about?'

'You know, that song about the Valley,' I say. *'Oh mighty yo, how the star-shine must go, chasing those distant deserts of green* . . . Do you think the Valley's really like that?'

'Well, I don't reckon there'll be much more star-shine there than we've got in Taladia,' says Teddy. 'Hope not, anyway. It's hard enough to sleep without a whole load of light pollution.'

I smile in response, but can't help taking note of the last sentence. The great Teddy Nort has just admitted he has trouble sleeping. I doubt it's guilt about pickpocketing that keeps him awake . . . but what else could it be?

'All right, crew,' says Radnor. 'We'd better set up camp while we've still got light.'

We divvy up the chores in a vaguely equal fashion. Radnor will unpack the sleeping sacks, Clementine will start a campfire and Teddy will take care of the foxaries. I head down to the creek to gather water with the twin called Maisy. She's painfully shy, too timid to speak unless you ask her a question. Even then, she barely allows her voice to rise above a whisper. In my head, I nickname her 'Mousy'.

'So,' I say, as we fill an assortment of jars, 'why'd you and Clementine decide to run away?'

Maisy doesn't answer. She fiddles self-consciously with a strand of hair that isn't quite long enough to stay tucked behind her ear. She reminds me of a little ghost, a wisp of a girl who belongs in a pretty dress shop or a library. Not out here, in the rough and mud of the forest.

'I'm not gonna bite, you know,' I say.

She looks up. 'I know.'

'I'm guessing you haven't met many scruffers before,' I say, 'but we're not all thugs and criminals. I mean, it's not like I'm gonna beat you up if I don't like the answer.'

Maisy's jar shatters on the rocks.

She looks horrified. 'Sorry! I mean . . . I . . .'

Before I can respond, Maisy scurries off back towards the campfire. I pick up my water jars, then realise I'd better clean up the broken one first. No point leaving the hunters with a pile of glass to mark our trail. I scrape up the larger shards, then scoop a few fistfuls of creek water to wash away the shiny dust that remains.

'Hey, Danika,' says a voice.

I jump and almost break the remaining jars. Then I realise that it's just Teddy, waving me back towards the campsite. 'What's wrong?'

'Radnor wants you.'

I gather the jars and follow him back through the trees. I can't imagine what Radnor wants with me – is he angry that I've upset Maisy? Perhaps she ran back to the campsite in tears and dobbed on me for interrogating her. The idea sends a cold twist into my belly. I'm lucky to be travelling with this crew at all; if I screw it up now, I'm dead. There's no way I'll make it to the Valley on my own.

But as it turns out, Radnor isn't mad at me. He's clutching a rough hessian sack, which must have been stuffed inside one of the larger packs. 'Danika,' he says, 'do you think you can use these?'

I take the sack cautiously and peer inside. I have no idea what to expect – hopefully not a ravenous litter of foxary pups – but it turns out to be dull metal plates.

I pull out a plate, frown, then turn to Teddy. 'You nicked someone's family silver?'

He holds up his hands in protest. 'Hey, would I do a thing like that?'

'Yes,' I say, in unison with Clementine.

'Well, I've got nothing to do with this stuff – it's not worth much, I reckon. All dingy and cheap. I don't even reckon that's silver.'

'What is it, then?' I turn the plate over, examining it more carefully. As far as I can tell, it's just a tarnished disc. It wouldn't look out of place in a richie's dinnerware cabinet. But it seems too heavy for its size, a disproportionate bulk of cold metal.

'It's a magnet,' says Radnor.

I almost drop it. 'A magnet? Like the rocks in the Magnetic Valley?'

He nods.

I stare in shock at the disc in my hand. Magnets have been illegal for over a century, ever since the palace started seriously investing in alchemic machinery. 'I didn't think there were any magnets left in Taladia.'

'That's what the palace wants you to think,' says Radnor, 'but this is an old set that survived the purge. They belong to Hackel. He uses them for smuggling.'

'How'd he get hold of them?' says Teddy, an eager glint in his eye. 'I thought I did a good job robbing the High Street jewellers, but imagine who you'd have to rob to get a set of magnets!'

'I don't know where he got them,' says Radnor. 'Another smuggler, probably. What matters is we've got them now, and I think they might save us from the hunters.'

I stare at the sack. 'What's this got to do with me?'

'Isn't it obvious?' sniffs Clementine.

'Not unless you want me to play discus, no.'

'You can use them to amplify your illusion powers,' says Radnor. 'The magnets should trap your magic, you see. If we set them up around our camp, and the magnetic energy bounces your power between each plate . . .'

I bite my lip. 'I told you I'm not very good yet. I started growing illusionist powers just a few months ago; my illusions last only seconds.'

'Should be enough, though,' says Radnor. 'You just need to start the effect, and trap it in the magnetic circle. So long as no one moves the plates, they'll just ricochet the illusion between them.'

'Worth a shot, I guess,' I say.

I try to look confident, but I've never tried anything like this before. Mixing magnets and magic is dangerous. That's why the king doesn't dare invade the Magnetic Valley. According to stories, the landscape is too unpredictable; it could amplify his troops' powers . . . or backfire and destroy them. I wouldn't want to fly a plane with alchemy bombs above the Valley. You might explode into a riot of burning flowers, or melt your plane's wings into waterfalls.

I cross to the edge of our campsite and press a plate into the dirt. The earth is hard and frosty, but I wriggle the metal a little and squash it down with the palm of my hand. Then I move along several metres and plant the next plate, then the next. Soon, our campsite is surrounded by a pentagon: five magnetic plates, humming with invisible currents that should react to any hints of nearby magic.

'Ready?' I say to the others.

Clementine steps aside, as though she's about to exit the circle. I don't blame her; who knows what effect my illusion will have inside a circle of magnets? But I reach out to stop her, ignoring her snarl as I dare to grab her sleeve.

'You've got to stay here,' I remind her. 'If this works, anyone outside the circle will lose sight of us.'

'Don't you dare touch me, scruffer,' she says.

I release her sleeve. Clementine sneers at me but doesn't move.

'When you're ready, Danika,' says Radnor.

I take a deep breath and bend down beside the nearest magnet. It's cold beneath my fingers, but if I close my eyes I can almost sense the power that hums inside it. My illusion power is still weak and mostly untamed, but the magnet slams against it as though it's made of metal itself.

I picture our campsite: every detail I can remember. The sleeping sacks among the leaves. The shapes of my companions. The stink of sweat and foxary musk in the evening air. I grab my illusion power – just like clenching a fist or sucking in my stomach – and imagine that the clearing is empty.

Nothing happens.

I open my eyes and glance around the circle, just to be sure. Nothing. Clementine crosses her arms, clearly not impressed.

I wet my lips. 'I . . .'

'Try again,' Radnor says.

I shut my eyes and try to refocus. But I'm suddenly very aware that the others are judging me. This is my chance to prove my worth to the crew. My fingers feel twitchy enough to slip off the magnet, and it's impossible to concentrate when –

I take a steadying breath. I can do this.

The campsite unfolds inside my mind: a wavering image, conjured from memory. I hold onto it for a long moment, filling in every little detail. Sleeping sacks. My crewmates' bodies. The sound of human breath on the air.

And then, with my mind as my paintbrush, I slowly re-colour the memory. Instead of humans and sleeping sacks, I picture chinks of light beneath the canopy. Tumbling leaves and the hiss of breeze. A thicket of branches and a scrabble of bird claws. The faintest scent of rot in the undergrowth . . .

A hot spark stings my hand and I yelp. I yank my skin away from the magnet and open my eyes, half-afraid we'll be blasted into dust.

'Nice job,' says Teddy, sounding impressed.

I glance around the circle. Everyone's limbs still seem to be intact and the campsite itself is safe and secure. But there's an odd ripple in the air, a gust of unnatural wind between the magnets.

My illusion is skimming around the circle, again and again, keeping us hidden from those outside. 'Hey, it worked!'

'I should certainly hope so,' says Clementine.

When everyone has satisfied themselves that the magnets will hold my illusion, we settle down for the night. The only food in the packs is a loaf of bread, which Radnor distributes between us.

'Shouldn't we save it?' I say.

He shakes his head. 'No point. It's not gonna last long anyway. If everything goes to plan, we should find the river tomorrow and get out of this forest.'

'And there'll be something to eat at the river?' says Teddy.

Radnor shrugs. 'Fish, maybe. Water plants.'

I think of the slimy riverweed that hawkers sold in Rourton's market. Richies would buy it sometimes for their pet fish: tiny creatures that lived in glass bowls and were purely for decoration. I always felt a bit sorry for those fish, endlessly trapped, swimming in circles with no hope of escape.

Clementine prods her food with distaste. 'This bread is stale.'

I bite into my own chunk. It's a little chewy, maybe, but it's better than a lot of bread I've eaten over the years. There are sesame seeds across the top and crumbs gather in a satisfying clump on the backs of my teeth. I wonder what Clementine is used to eating, if she can afford to look down on decent bread like this. Maybe her family were the type of richies to throw away perfectly good food. Maybe I've even scrounged bread or biscuits from their bin, never knowing the girls whose scraps would fill my belly.

The foxaries seem happy to strip bark and branches from the trees. It's a shame human stomachs aren't tough enough to thrive on that sort of food, or this bread would just be the entrée to a feast. As it is, I try to eat slowly, but my chunk is gone in a couple of minutes. I lick my fingers afterwards, straining to gather any hint of salt or crumbs among the dirt.

As the sky darkens, we settle into our sleeping sacks for the night. I'm careful to lie on my back and keep weight off my healing shoulder. The sacks are lined with thick fleece: warm, durable and very high quality. I would have killed for a sack like this back in Rourton, especially on the coldest winter nights.

'I'll keep first watch,' says Radnor. 'Any volunteers for the midnight shift?'

'We don't need to keep watch. We've got an illusion to hide us,' says Clementine.

Radnor shakes his head. 'Better safe than sorry. We need to know if any hunters come near – just in case they stumble into our circle by accident, or overhear us.' He pauses. 'Or if Danika's illusion fails during the night.'

All I want to do is bury myself in my sleeping sack and pretend the world beyond our cosy campsite doesn't exist. But it's my responsibility to volunteer. After all, the others are putting their lives into my hands by trusting my illusion. The least I can do is try to keep them safe. So I raise my hand and Radnor promises to wake me when it's time.

Considering what I've experienced today – the burning hunter, the plane crash, the horrors of our chase through the forest – I don't expect to sleep. I figure I'll be kept awake by nerves, or the horrible memory of that dying hunter's scream. But exhaustion wins out and somehow I manage to slip into the dark.

CHAPTER TEN

THE KITE

WHEN RADNOR WAKES ME, THE SKY IS BLACK. THE only light comes from a cloud-streaked moon and a speckle of starlight above the trees.

'Midnight,' he whispers. 'Your watch, Danika.'

I fight back a groan and silently curse myself for volunteering. But I don't want Radnor to see any weakness – at this point, losing my spot on his crew would mean death. So I force a confident nod, pull myself out of my sleeping sack and tiptoe to the edge of our campsite. At least my knee feels noticeably better; perhaps the wound is healing beneath its bandage.

Behind me, I hear a rustle of fabric as Radnor lowers himself down to sleep. The forest is quiet, but not silent. There's a whisper of night breeze in the canopy and the buzzing song of distant crickets. A couple of rats venture out from the bushes, but they scarper as soon as they smell the foxaries. I don't blame them. I'll admit the beasts look almost nice when they're sleeping: huge bulks of fur, streaked orange beneath the moon. But still, it's hard not to focus on the claws.

Minutes fade into hours and clouds shift across the sky. I wish we'd decided to keep watch in pairs, because it's pretty lonely by myself. I stare at Teddy Nort, half-hoping he'll wake up and we can have a chat. Then I want to smack myself for being so selfish. Sleep is a valuable commodity and I have no right to steal it from Teddy. Being well-rested might help to keep him alive.

There's no real way to keep track of time – I've never owned a watch. But after years of living on the streets, I've learned to sense things. I can roughly tell by the chill in the air and the shift in the darkness how long it will be until morning. At this point, it seems years away.

Then I see it. Something moves across the sky: a rumple of wings, perhaps. But it's not alive. It's a flap of fabric on a string, silhouetted against the stars. I stand up abruptly, staring through patches in the canopy. It's a kite.

Some of the richie kids owned kites in Rourton – they flew them in summer, up above the smog and filth of the city streets. This isn't as large or decorative as the richie kites I've seen, but it's the same basic shape: a diamond on a string.

'Radnor!' I hurry across and shake his shoulders.

He looks dazed for a moment, but recovers within seconds. Then he's sitting up, alert and charged, as though we're under attack. 'Where? What?'

'Up there,' I whisper, pointing.

He frowns and squints. 'Is that a kite?'

'I think so.'

We cross to the edge of our campsite, angling for a better look. It's hard to see much through the trees, but the kite is only about fifty metres away. Whoever is flying it must be hidden in the forest and close enough to attack us if they stumble across our camp.

Radnor grabs my sleeve. 'Don't step outside the circle, Danika.'

'But what if it's another refugee? Shouldn't we go and check?'

'No. It's not a refugee.'

'How do you know?'

Radnor gives the kite a dark look. 'They'd be a suicidal refugee to fly a kite around here. Who's stupid enough to draw the hunters in like that?'

I don't respond.

'That thing is a trap,' says Radnor. 'A trap for *us*, to lure us out into the open.'

'What if it's Hackel?'

Radnor shakes his head. 'Hackel's not an idiot. Anyway, where would he get a kite from in the middle of the forest?'

'Good point.'

'I bet it's the hunters,' Radnor says. 'They're trying to make us curious, make us do something stupid. Maybe they think we're so desperate for supplies that we'll risk going out there.' He gives a bitter laugh. 'It's not like they'd have high opinions of a scruffer crew's intelligence.'

As we watch, the kite dips lower in the sky. It moves jerkily, as though its owner is reeling it in against the pull of the wind. Soon it dips below the trees and out of sight, leaving an empty patch of stars.

'So, we're not leaving the circle, then?' I say.

'We're staying put,' says Radnor. 'But I'll keep watch for the rest of the night. You should go back to sleep.'

'It's my watch,' I protest, frowning. 'You've already been on watch tonight – you're the one whose turn it is to rest.'

Radnor shakes his head. 'It's my job to lead this crew, Danika. I'm not letting you guard alone while the enemy's so close.'

It takes a moment for his meaning to sink in. After all we've been through, Radnor still doesn't trust me. I scowl. 'I'm capable of keeping watch, you know.'

'Maybe you are, maybe you're not,' says Radnor. 'And if you want to stay up too, that's your choice. But I'm guarding this camp tonight, no matter what, so you'll just be wasting sleep-time for nothing.'

I almost plant myself in the dirt, determined to stay on watch beside him. But I've spent too many years on the streets to underestimate the value of sleep. In Rourton, if you try to fight the tiredness, you die. I've seen it before: kids passed out behind rubbish bins, too cold and weary to haul their bodies out of the frost. They should have rested earlier, when they were still alert enough to find a safer nook or cranny. I always helped them into a doorway, gave them any scraps I had left, but sometimes kids died without anyone spotting them in time. In Rourton, tiredness is a carnivore. All you can do is force yourself to stay rested, try to keep fed and hope it doesn't catch you.

'Fine,' I say through gritted teeth. 'But if you change your mind, wake me up.'

Radnor nods, but I know it's a lie. He'll never wake me now; it would be a sign of weakness, revealing he's not the super-tough leader he likes to pretend he is. I've only known Radnor for a few days, but I'm starting to suspect he's as stubborn as I am.

Maybe even more stubborn, actually. Because I'm not stupid enough to throw away my chance of survival just to make a point.

I slink back to my sleeping sack and wriggle into the fabric. It's warm and snug, and doesn't take long to absorb the heat of my body. Then I close my eyes, slow my breathing and try to think of the Magnetic Valley. I try to picture green hills and distant cities and earth that keeps the king's own army at bay. But all I can picture is a kite fluttering across the dark.

*

IN THE MORNING, I'M THE FIRST TO WAKE. I GLANCE around the campsite and see that Radnor has dozed off. For a second I'm furious – what if we'd been attacked? – but then I see the bags beneath his eyes and sigh. He obviously needed the sleep.

I stagger down to the creek to wash my face. As soon as I step beyond the circle, the image of my crew vanishes behind me. I'm secretly a little proud of my illusion's staying power, even if the magnets had much more to do with it than my skill did. The foxaries growl as I pass and my stomach growls back at them.

'Hey, fellas,' I whisper. I'm not afraid of the foxaries, but I'm not stupid either, so I keep at least a metre away from their mouths as I pass.

Down at the creek, I dip my hands into the water. It's icy this morning and it bites my fingers. My skin is reddening already, stinging from the frost. I pull my dripping hands away and shake them, then thrust the fingers into my mouth and suck, trying to warm them up again. The only result is numbness, which I suppose is an improvement on pain. It's not worth washing my face this morning, I decide. The last thing I need is a frostbitten nose.

I peel the bandage from my knee and clean my wound, which is healing fairly well in the circum-stances. I stuff my hands into my trouser pockets, rub them against my thighs through the fabric and hurry back to the group. It takes a few false tries to find our campsite, since it's still shrouded by my illusion and the trees all look the same.

We knew yesterday, when we finished the bread, that there'd be no more food for a while. Even so, it's hard to accept that I won't get breakfast today. In Rourton, getting a meal is never impossible. The meal might be some cheap fried crickets, or stale crackers from a richie's rubbish bin, but at least there's always *something* to eat if you're desperate.

Out here there's only the frost, and crackling leaves and twigs that taste like soggy cardboard.

I force my numb fingers to move and grab a fistful of leaves from the ground. Then I stoke the fire into life and boil some water in an old billy can. The water takes forever to heat up, but eventually I'm rewarded with a faint spiral of steam to defrost my hands. I toss some leaves into the water and stir them with a stick.

'What're you doing?' says Teddy. He's sitting halfway up in his sleeping sack, propped on his elbows. His nose is bright red. My own must look the same; it certainly stings enough.

'Making tea,' I say.

Teddy sniffs the steam and pulls a face. 'Tea or leaf soup?'

'Aren't they the same thing?'

Teddy shrugs. 'Can I have some?'

I scoop out a serving of tea and lean over to hand it across. Teddy sits up properly, sniffs the tea and takes a sip. I sit in silence, waiting for the verdict.

Teddy pulls his face into a pompous scowl, raises one eyebrow and speaks in a perfect imitation of the richie girls' posh accent. 'I do say, Miss Glynn, you have evoked a fine bouquet of natural aromas.

This seems a rather fine beverage, best served with a gourmet banquet of sticks and tree-bark.'

I snort and throw a fistful of leaves at him. They eddy down pitifully, about a foot away from my own body.

'Ooh, I'm terrified,' he says. 'A leaf-throwing monster is after me.'

'Hey, leaves could be deadlier than they look.'

Teddy gives a pointed gesture at his jar of leaf tea. 'Oh, believe me, I know.'

I try to look grouchy, but can't help snickering at the distasteful wrinkling of his red nose when he risks another sip. 'That bad, huh?'

'Well, better than nothing,' says Teddy.

I sip my own tea. It tastes like leafy water, but at least it's warm. I roll each mouthful around my tongue, trying to defrost my body and soothe my growing hunger.

'We'll get some proper food today,' says Teddy.

'How?'

'I dunno, we'll rob a farmhouse or something. There's gotta be a little cottage in these woods. I mean, if there's not, then a hell of a lot of storybooks have been lying to me.'

I picture a toddler-sized Teddy Nort wrapped up in bed while his parents read a bedtime story. It's almost impossible to reconcile this image with the brash boy in front of me, who'd sooner rob a woodside cottage than listen to sweet little stories about it. Teddy Nort is such a legendary figure among Rourton's scruffers that it's odd to think he hasn't always been there. The legends make it seem as if he just sprang from the cobblestones: Rourton's infamous teenage pickpocket, fully formed and ready to cause mayhem.

Once everyone's awake and had a sip of tea – with varying attempts to hide their distaste – we load up the foxaries to head on our way. Maisy's fingers have turned red in the cold and swollen up like sausages. We knot Clementine's extra clothes – silken blouses, cashmere socks and designer skirts – like overgrown gloves around Maisy's hands.

'Thanks,' she says, looking miserable.

'It's just her bad circulation,' says Clementine. 'Maisy always gets fat fingers in winter – even at home by the fire.'

I can't help feeling a stab of pity. No matter what I think of the spoiled richies, it's obvious that Maisy's in a lot of pain. After a life of privilege, it can't be easy suddenly to be thrust out into the cold.

I gather up the magnets that surround our camp; as soon as I've moved the first one, it feels as though something snaps inside the air. The circle is broken and my illusion is gone.

'Where are we going?' I ask Radnor as we mount our foxaries.

'To the river. We should reach it this afternoon, if everything goes to plan.'

'We've already found a creek,' says Clementine. 'Why do we need another one?'

Maisy leans close to her sister's ear and whispers something.

'We don't want a creek, we want the main river,' says Radnor impatiently. 'Hackel said we could follow it to find our way south, instead of using the road.'

'Yes, well, there's no need for that tone,' says Clementine. 'And Maisy just reminded me, anyway.'

For the next few hours, we do nothing but ride. As the sun rises higher, it burns most of the fog away from the trees. Even so, the day is bitterly cold. I hope it doesn't start snowing, because that means clearer footprints. The last thing we need is to help the hunters find our trail.

I'm starting to feel more comfortable on the foxaries now. My thigh muscles still ache from their unnatural positioning, but I'm learning to read the beasts' movements better. I can sense, from the throb of a muscle or the twitch of a limb, when the creature beneath me intends to change direction.

Around lunchtime, the trees start to thin out. We must be nearing the edge of the forest, because there are no more clusters of dense foliage or even clearings. It's just uniform, endless woodland: all the same, all completely dull. That's okay though; I like dull. I've had enough excitement in the last few days for a lifetime.

'Hey!' says Clementine. 'What's that?'

We stiffen. At first, all I can see is a bunch of scraggly trees – no different from a million other patches of woodland around here. Then I see the pair of human bodies sprawling in the leaves.

CHAPTER ELEVEN

STREAM'S HANDS

I STOP BREATHING. THE OTHERS DO THE SAME. THE foxaries must sense our tension because they freeze still and silent, except for the faint quiver of muscles preparing to sprint. Are these hunters? Are they sleeping? Are they awake, lying in wait, baiting a trap for us with their own inert forms?

As the seconds pass, I stare as hard as I can at the bodies. There's no sign of movement – not even the gentle rise and fall of a torso. Are they breathing? Their uniforms are emerald and gold, a mark of palace majesty that looks almost perverse out here in the muck of the woods. *Hunters.*

'They're dead,' whispers Maisy.

'How do you know?'

She shakes her head, looking pale. 'They're not breathing. And they're lying on their faces.'

She's right. It's hard to tell, because of all the dead leaves, but the hunters are lying facedown. Their bodies don't move, not even when a breeze ruffles dirt across their backs. If they're not dead, they're very good actors.

I slip down from the foxary's back. It takes a moment to de-jellify my legs after the morning's ride, but I manage to reach the two hunters' bodies without falling on my face. The bodies are stiff and pale, hands contorted into desperate fists by their sides. I take a deep breath and prod one of them with a stick. No response.

'They're dead,' I confirm.

The others dismount and lead their foxaries forward. Radnor glares at the bodies, his expression flitting between worry and satisfaction. I glance at the richie twins, half expecting them to squeal or cover their eyes, but they must have stronger stomachs than I expected. They just stare down at the bodies, eyes hard, mouths drawn into identical straight lines.

Teddy Nort, of course, heads straight for the loot.

'Look at this!' he says, hauling up a pair of packs from beside the bodies. 'Do you reckon there's food in these?'

Five minutes earlier, I would have jumped a mile high at the thought of food supplies. But now I feel queasy, staring down at the corpses of hunters who wanted us dead. How has this happened? How have our hunters become the hunted?

'Who killed them?' I say.

There's a pause.

'Maybe they killed each other,' says Teddy. 'You know, had a fight or something.'

I bend down to examine the bodies, trying to keep my emotions in check. I've seen my fair share of bodies but even so, it's sickening to see these hunters' corpses up close.

There's no sign of injury on their torsos or their limbs. But the hair at the napes of their necks is clotted with blood. I poke the hair aside with my stick, revealing perfect bullet holes in the backs of their necks. The shots have travelled right through their proclivity tattoos, skewering the image of a flame on one and a mountain on the other. I've never seen a mountain tattoo before, but maybe this man's proclivity was Earth.

'Do you think . . .' Clementine begins, sounding hopeful. 'Do you think maybe it was Hackel?'

Radnor shakes his head. 'Hackel doesn't use guns. He can kill people with Flame.'

I stare at the wounds, perfectly drilled into

the base of each hunter's skull. Their bodies lie facedown, as though they were kneeling when they died. I can picture it now: the impact of the shots, the bodies falling forward . . . It's too perfect. Too precise.

'This wasn't a murder,' I say, quietly. 'This was an execution.'

Clementine looks up from the bodies. 'Then where's the executioner?'

No one answers.

*

FOR THE NEXT FEW HOURS, WE RIDE. THERE'S NO TIME to search the hunters' packs and count our new supplies. We just load the packs onto Radnor's foxary and head off into the trees. Whoever killed those hunters could still be close by. Our only option is to put as much distance as we can between ourselves and the bodies.

We hear the river before we see it. It gushes up ahead, like the static of my father's radio. As we approach, the world seems to grow lighter. At first I'm confused – what does a river have to do with daylight? – until I realise there are no more trees ahead. This is the edge of the forest, and we are nearing the next stage of our journey.

We ride out between the last of the trees and find ourselves at the edge of emptiness. At least, that's what it looks like until my eyes adjust to the sudden flood of light. Everything is dappled grey, the same colour as the winter sky. Then I realise it's a sea of rocks – boulders, really. At our feet, the earth slopes sharply downwards: an escarpment tilting into their midst. There are occasional splashes of green, as though a few shrubs or vines might be hidden in this field of stone, and a vast river cascades below us to mark our path. But on the whole, I feel like I've landed on a plate of greyish porridge.

No one speaks for a minute. We all just stare across the expanse, agog at the idea of crossing this world of stone.

'That's a lot of rocks,' I say eventually. 'Are you sure this was Hackel's plan?'

Radnor nods. 'He said to follow the river – that's his smuggling route. This is the only major river around here. And he warned me about this place.'

'He did?'

'It's called the Marbles,' says Maisy.

We all stop and stare at her. It's so uncharacteristic for her to speak up in a conversation, I think my mouth actually opens a bit in surprise.

Maisy reddens, then looks down at her feet. 'I read about it once, in a geography book.'

'The Marbles?' says Teddy, brightening up a little. 'I like marbles. Worth their weight in silver, I reckon, if you know what you're doing.'

I bet he does. I imagine Teddy in an alleyway, holding illicit gambling matches with his fellow pickpockets. If the scruffers in Rourton aren't betting on cards or street-ball, there's a good chance they're betting on marbles. It's a common way to make a living – or lose one – on the streets back home.

Then I silently chastise myself. I shouldn't be thinking of Rourton as 'home'. I will never see those city walls again.

'Imagine the games you'd have out here,' Teddy says, a hungry glint in his eye. 'You could roll a big boulder down the hill, and bet on whether –'

'How is Hackel going to find us?' Clementine interrupts. 'We paid good money for him to guide us, you know.'

Radnor points into the distance. 'Somewhere out there, beyond the Marbles, there's a town called Gunning. Hackel said if we got separated, he'd meet us there. He'll look for us in the town market at twelve every day for the next couple of weeks.'

'Gunning?' Clementine says. 'Never heard of it.'

'It's a pretty dodgy town, I think,' says Radnor. 'A lot of smuggling deals happen there. They used to make illegal pistols – that's why it's called Gunning.'

Teddy looks up eagerly, a glint in his eye. 'Sounds like fun.'

'Well, we've got a long way to go first,' says Radnor. 'Come on. I want to find a good campsite before tonight.'

As we descend into the Marbles, the wind slaps strands of auburn hair across my cheeks. I feel a little uneasy. Over the last couple of days, I've started to feel almost safe beneath the canopy. At least we had trees to hide us from the hunters. In the Marbles, there are no trees. We will be exposed.

At the bottom of the slope, we meet the river. It is wide and noisy, funnelling between walls of ragged boulders. Its banks, hemmed by stone and water, provide just enough room to manoeuvre the foxaries. This part of the journey would be easier on foot; some rocks leave little space for the beasts to squeeze past without touching the water. The foxaries aren't keen on wading; when Teddy tries to steer them into getting their paws wet, they twist away like angry cats.

As the hours pass, I find my skin getting damp and cold. The river churns up mist, just enough to condense beneath my sleeves. 'At least it's not snowing,' I say aloud.

'I wouldn't mind some snow,' says Teddy. 'Snow balls could be pretty good weapons if the hunters rock up.'

'Give them frostbitten noses?'

'Something like that.'

When the sun is sinking behind the boulders, Radnor looks worried. This place all looks the same: rocks, rocks and more rocks. I'm starting to suspect I hallucinated the streaks of green when I looked down at this slope from the forest, because there's almost no foliage – apart from occasional clumps of brown thistles.

Worst of all, there's nowhere safe to camp. If we sleep in a cluster of boulders, it'll be almost impossible to set up a decent magnetic circle because the ground is so uneven. But if we opt for a bare stretch of rock, we'll be too exposed.

We press onward, constantly searching the riverbanks, but there's no sign of a handy cave to shelter in. This part of the slope is too fragmented, cluttered with shoulder-high chunks of rock. Judging by the view this morning, there should be larger boulders ahead, but we've got no hope of travelling that far tonight. With every step, the daylight seems to fade further away. I stare ahead, running my gaze across the gnarled landscape. There must be something, anything . . .

'Excuse me,' Maisy says shyly, 'but I think we should try up there.'

I follow her sideways glance, up away from the bank. It's hard to tell from this low angle, and in the evening shadows, but the rocks all look the same to me.

'I think that's limestone,' says Maisy, when no one else speaks. 'It's a lighter shade of grey, see? Limestone's quite soluble, for a rock, so it often forms strange shapes. Lots of caves are made of it.'

Radnor looks ready to argue and I can't really blame him. The river is our guide, our sustenance and our only link to Hackel's plan. None of us wants to stray from its banks.

'Can't hurt to look, can it?' says Teddy. 'For all we know, there might be a five-star boulder resort up there. With caviar cakes, even, or those little chocolate truffles they have in gentlemen's clubs.'

'When have *you* been inside a gentlemen's club, scruffer?' says Clementine. Then she seems to consider this and scowls. 'Never mind, I don't want to know.'

We dismount and lead our foxaries up into the rocks. The sides of the river are steep. My legs are numb from a long day's riding, so I skid a few times on piles of pebbles. Our foxaries are happy to get away from the water, so they strain ahead with forceful necks and bright eyes.

I traipse over the top of the rocks and get a clearer glimpse of the landscape beside us. Huge rocks grasp up like open fists, the residue of a broken plateau. The formations seem ready to shelter us, providing a hundred craggy overhangs.

'How did you know?' I say to Maisy. 'About the limestone, I mean?'

She twists her fingers together, like she's been caught misbehaving. 'I like to read.'

I think of the other times she's shown little glimpses of understanding. When we found the crashed biplane, it was Maisy who thought of looking underneath to count the bombs. And this morning, she was the one who knew this place was called the Marbles. She might be timid, but I'm starting to suspect that Maisy knows a lot more about the world than she lets on.

We move between the rocks carefully. It's not quite as cramped as the riverbank this afternoon, but the foxaries can still barely squeeze between some of the formations.

'Over there,' says Radnor. 'Under that ledge.'

We follow his nod towards a patch of gravel to our left. A pile of boulders looms above it, blotting out most of the sky. It's not exactly a cave, but it's the best hope of shelter I've seen all evening. We set up camp as far beneath the ledge as we can. I'm not sure whether my illusion can reach right up to hide us from biplanes, so it seems safest to keep under-cover.

When our camp is set up, Teddy arranges the magnets in a circle. I summon an illusion to hide us in the night. Then we wrap ourselves in sleeping sacks and prepare to open the dead hunters' supply packs. What might be hidden inside? We've been waiting for this moment all day; I can't help imagin-ing chunks of bread, canteens of soup, maybe even an apple or two if we're lucky. At this point, though, I'd settle for a baked rat if it looked edible.

Radnor opens the packs and I gasp. The supplies are even better than I'd let myself hope. Each pack contains a massive sack of oats: if we ration carefully, we could live off porridge for weeks. There are two paper bags of dried fruit – apples, fried banana chips and even raisins. There are rocky flour cakes: baked to a dull brown and ready to sustain a hunter as he hikes across Taladia. And finally, there is a bottle of strange amber liquid, which resembles syrup. We all taste a speck on our fingertips and decide that it's made from apricots. The sugar sends a little rush across my tongue.

Just for tonight, we decide to forget about ration-ing. We've earned a feast. I drizzle apricot syrup across a flour cake, relishing the mess of savoury crumbs and sweet nectar between my teeth. Then I suck a ring of dried apple and even crunch down a fistful of oats with raisins. Making a fire would be too risky, so there's no hope of hot porridge, but we fill a large bowl with oats and water to soak overnight.

'It should turn mushy, like cold porridge,' says Maisy.

I stare at her, wondering why a richie girl would ever eat cold porridge. Surely she's always had hot water and stoves at her disposal?

'Our cook at home made something similar in summer,' Clementine explains. 'She soaked oats in fruit syrups with dates, or apple and cinnamon.'

Eventually we finish eating. I feel a little sick. After days of hunger, my body isn't used to such a feast. But the sickness is tempered by a glorious feeling of fullness. This mightn't have been the fanciest meal in history, but it must rank among the most satisfying.

Teddy stretches, pats his belly and grins. 'Ready to turn in?'

It isn't my turn to take a watch shift tonight; Teddy and Clementine are chosen to cover half the night each. I set up my sleeping sack on the edge of the campsite, where I can just steal a glimpse of stars around the edge of our rocky ceiling.

But no matter how long I stare, fingernails in my palms, there is no sign of a kite upon the sky.

CHAPTER TWELVE

UNANSWERED QUESTIONS

IN THE MORNING, WE GORGE OURSELVES ON SUMMER porridge. It's cold and gluggy, but a dash of apricot syrup turns the mush into a treat. The sugar in the syrup gives me enough energy to mount a foxary with a smile on my face.

Unfortunately, our happiness at the food supplies does not last. We spend the day travelling, winding through the Marbles' barren landscape. Occasionally there is a patch of open rock, where the foxaries are free to stretch their legs. We cover a lot of ground in these sprints, which is good, because I'm starting to hate this place. It's just so desolate. So lifeless. An endless sheet of grey.

Even the lack of pursuit is starting to worry me. There must be hunters looking for us, and maybe even the unknown person who killed the men in the forest, but all we see are boulders.

When the sun goes down, we camp in a tiny cove on the edge of the river. The deeper we travel into the Marbles, the larger the rock formations seem to become. There are more hiding places now, more campsites to plant our nightly circle of magnets. Sleeping on the riverbank provides a constant sound-track: a gurgle of water that lulls me into sleep.

Another day passes and another. Nothing changes. We follow the river. The wind gets colder, perhaps, and the nights come earlier, but these are just normal signs of winter. My physical wounds are healing well, but my thoughts grow more and more uneasy. By the fourth day, there is still no sign of our pursuers and somehow that scares me more than any actual fight I've seen.

'We must have lost them,' says Radnor, looking pleased. 'Hackel was right after all. They'll look for us on the trading road, not out here on the river.'

The others agree and dig into their porridge with a relaxed sort of looseness in their grins. But I'm not so sure. I can't stop thinking about those dead hunters in the forest, the ones whose food we are eating. Someone killed them. No, someone

140

executed them. And that someone was on their way to the river.

Every night, I volunteer to take a watch shift. At first, the others refuse to let me, so I make up a story about how I can sense my illusion weakening in the early hours of the morning. It's a load of rubbish, of course – once the magnets have got hold of my illusion, I can't feel the power link at all. But no one knows much about illusionists, so the others seem to buy it.

'All right, Danika,' says Radnor. 'You'd better take the second watch.'

And so I spend half of each night watching the sky, waiting for that mysterious kite to reappear. It's stupid and I pay for it three times over when my limbs get jittery or I almost slip off my foxary the next day. Back in Rourton, I would never have risked such sleep deprivation. But this isn't Rourton, and the rules are different now. I no longer know what I should be doing to survive.

It's the fifth night when I see it.

The shape is distant – maybe a kilometre away – but it's silhouetted against a full moon. A flap of fabric, the shape of a stretched diamond. I sit bolt upright, fists clenching. There's no hope of seeing the flyer from here; there are too many boulders to see more than a couple of metres away. But I can see the string, the kite and the stars. And now I know for certain.

Someone is following us. Is this the person who killed the hunters? Is the kite-flyer another hunter himself, trying to lure us out with this strange bait? Or is it another refugee crew? Surely we can't be the only crew to engage a smuggler and find this secret river route. But if our pursuer is also a refugee, why would he – or she or they – risk everything by flying a *kite*? It's a flashing beacon to the hunters.

'Radnor,' I whisper, and shake him awake.

He moans a little, but pushes himself up onto his elbows. 'What?'

'It's back.'

Radnor doesn't need to ask me what 'it' is. He rolls out of his sleeping sack and follows me to the edge of our campsite, where I point towards the shape upon the sky.

'I want to go and check it out,' I say.

Radnor shakes his head. 'Forget it, Danika. No one leaves this circle at night, got it?'

'What if it's another refugee? They might need our help.'

'It's *not* another refugee,' says Radnor. 'It's a hunter trying to trick us. If you go out there, you'll die.' He pauses. 'And even if it *is* another refugee, they're suicidally stupid to be flying that thing around. I'm not going to burden my crew with another liability.'

His words sting. Is that all I am to him – a liability, tossed into his hands at the last minute? He speaks as though I've ruined his plans by tagging along, ruined his perfect crew of five. But really, Hackel isn't here at the moment and I'm the one providing the illusions. I've earned my place in this crew, haven't I?

'This is an order, Danika,' says Radnor. He pauses, and doesn't continue until I meet his gaze. 'You are not to leave our campsite to follow that kite. Ever. If you try it, I will kick you off this crew.'

'You need my illusions.'

Radnor shakes his head. 'Everyone on this crew is expendable. Your illusions are useful, but we can survive without them.'

I imagine being kicked off the crew, out here in the middle of the Marbles. I have no idea how Radnor is navigating, apart from following the river. But the river will run out eventually, and then I'll be left alone. No food, no companions, no plan for survival.

'Don't wake me again, Danika,' says Radnor. 'Not because of the stupid kite, anyway. If you want to weaken your own reflexes by staying up night after night, be my guest. But you're not dragging me down with you.'

He stalks back to his sleeping sack, slides into the fabric and shuts his eyes. But I doubt he'll sleep again tonight. He'll pretend, of course, but I'm sure he's secretly watching me. He doesn't trust me, not entirely.

I run a hand through my hair, take a shaky breath, and return to my guard post. The kite is still there, taunting me. I just want to know who's flying it. Is that too much to ask?

✳

THE NEXT DAY, WE TRAVEL ON. RADNOR DOESN'T mention the kite or our late-night conversation. He just shovels down a flour cake, helps load up the foxaries and waves us on our way.

I'm sharing a foxary with Maisy today. Teddy has informed us that the beasts are tired of carrying the same people, so he wants us to 'mix it up a bit' to keep them happy. He rides with Clementine. Radnor, of course, has a foxary to himself. I guess there are some perks to being leader, apart from having the power to chuck people off the crew.

For the first few hours, no one really talks. It's a little awkward; Maisy is so timid and I'm half-afraid to make any sudden movements. What if I startle her into falling off and into the river?

When I was riding with Teddy, we used to talk quite a bit. He'd keep me entertained with stories of his assorted burglaries: how he stole a six-foot wedding cake for his gang-member's birthday, or fleeced a richie socialite of her diamond ring. In turn, I told him anecdotes from working in Rourton's bars: the dodgy customers, the drunken proposals, the embarrassing secrets that people admitted when they were off their faces. Neither of us mentioned the bad things – the bombs, the deaths, the days of starvation. When you're a scruffer, those things go without saying.

But I'm not so sure about talking to Maisy. All I've gleaned about the twins is that their surname is Pembroke, their family is wealthy and Clementine blew all their savings to fund this trip. Our lives have been so different up until now. I imagine Maisy sitting in a mansion on High Street, nibbling on custard pastries and syrup cakes while music plays from a top-notch radio. What did she do all day? Then I remember what she's said about reading.

'So,' I say, 'you like reading, right?'

Maisy nods. The movement sends her blonde ponytail bobbing up and down in my face.

'What sort of stuff did you read?' I say.

She gives a little shrug. Then, after a few awkward seconds of silence, she says, 'Lots of things. I like to learn about the world.'

'Why?'

'I thought I'd never get to see it,' says Maisy. 'It was nice to explore outside for a bit, even if it was only with words.'

I frown. Maisy sounds as though she's been trapped or something. But most richie girls have plenty of money they can use to explore Rourton; they like to wander up and down High Street and buy perfume from the boutiques, or sit around giggling in high-class restaurants. They must still accept the curfew, of course, and the city wall's limits – but within those boundaries, money is freedom. Maisy could have bought herself a chance to explore, if she'd wanted.

Then I realise. That's what she's done.

Instead of buying perfume and coffee, Maisy and Clementine have used their riches to fund this trip across Taladia. Is that why they ran away? To see the world? But it doesn't make sense. No one would risk death or starvation or dehydration, or any other number of perils that arise on refugee journeys, just to go sightseeing.

Perhaps they're escaping from army conscription. But richies get all the plum jobs in the army; they'd never have been shunted onto the frontline with the scruffers. And besides, the twins can't be older than sixteen – it's not as though conscription is an urgent issue. Who in their right mind would flee a life of luxury two years early?

Maybe they're *not* in their right minds. Maybe having so much money does something funny to your brain. I want to ask more directly: 'Why the hell did you run away?' But the last time I tried interrogating Maisy, she broke a water jar and ran off like a startled mouse.

I struggle for a gentler way to phrase my question. 'Well, now you've seen the world. What do you think of it?'

'It's better than . . .'

'Better than what?' I prompt.

But Maisy just shakes her head and looks down at our foxary's neck. A few minutes later we stop for lunch and that's the end of the conversation.

As we ride on into the afternoon, I start to notice a strange itching on the back of my neck. If we were back in Rourton, I might assume I'd been bitten by a rodent or something, but there's nothing here to bite me – not unless one of my companions has developed some very strange sleepwalking habits, anyway. I've spotted a few moths and dragonflies, and once a tiny lizard on a rock, but our foxaries' scent seems to frighten other animals away.

I raise a hand to touch the itchy spot and I'm surprised to feel a series of bumps growing on my neck. They feel like welts, sensitive to the touch.

My proclivity mark is starting to develop.

This is *not* a good time to develop my powers. The process can take days, weeks or even months – but those itchy bumps are always the first sign. I know that I'll soon feel tired and cranky, which isn't going to help me survive the journey to the Valley. It's lucky Radnor doesn't know what's happening, because I'm about to become an even greater liability.

Although, if my maturation is a fast one, maybe I'll become a liability to our enemies too.

CHAPTER THIRTEEN

HUNTED

In the late afternoon, when we're sagging upon our foxaries and dreaming up a new syrup-porridge-cake combination for dinner, Teddy jerks upright as though someone's thrown him into a frying pan.

'What is it?' says Radnor.

At the same time, our foxaries freeze. Momentum sends me hurtling forward into Maisy, who falls across our animal's neck with a cry. Fur and muscles bristle beneath me. We all fall silent. The foxaries whip their heads around to our right, staring up at a skyline blocked by rock formations.

'They can smell something,' whispers Teddy. 'I reckon we'd better hide.'

149

We dismount and lead our foxaries towards a nearby overhang. It's a pretty pathetic hiding place, but at least it's safer than the riverbank. I fumble for the magnets, toss them into the neatest circle I can manage, and cast my illusion of empty air. The illusion quavers a bit – my circle isn't precise enough, so the power isn't bouncing between magnets properly – but it holds. For now, at least.

'Shhh,' whispers Teddy, as one of the foxaries begins to growl. He rubs it behind the ears and the noise fades.

There is a crunch to our left. I whip my head around to see a group of people approaching. They wear the emerald garb of palace employees, with knives and pistols dangling from their belts. Hunters. Their leader is a woman in her late twenties, with hair that curves in a sleek brunette bob around her cheekbones. She wears a dark stain on her lips and her fingernails look as long as claws.

The hunters travel along the riverbank, obviously on the lookout for prey. Are they looking for us specifically or just doing a random sweep for refugees and smugglers? Either way, they are only metres from our hiding place. My illusion quavers a little – I can see a ripple in the air between the magnets – but it still holds. I'm suddenly grateful for the lifeless rocks we've been travelling through, and their inability to hold our footprints.

Some of the hunters walk normally, but a couple travel through their proclivities. One man drifts above the rocks, floating. He keeps fading, then flickering back into visibility: a tumbling leaf on the breeze. His proclivity must be Wind. Another man floats on his back down the river, watching the sky. He almost collides with a boulder in the middle of the stream, but quickly dissolves into torrents that gush around the sides of the rock. Water.

It's lucky that none of their proclivities is Beast, because I doubt my illusion could stop them sensing a trio of foxaries at this close range.

'Anything?' says the woman coldly.

The Water hunter thrusts his head up from the river and gives it a shake. 'Nothing, Your Highness.'

'Your Highness?' mouths Teddy.

I shake my head, stunned. Is this woman a member of the royal family? It's illegal to print images of the royals, since King Morrigan's paranoid about secrecy and assassination attempts, so I wouldn't recognise one of his relatives if I saw one. But the king famously expects his younger kinsmen to serve their country for several years: military command, perhaps, or alchemy. It's supposed to set an example to the rest of us, proving the ultimate might of the king. If even our noblest aristocrats serve his causes, then what right do the rest of us have to complain?

If this woman is a Morrigan, she must have decided that her royal skill is hunting. That means she *chose* to serve as a hunter – not a commander, or a strategist on the council. That means she's good at this.

And that isn't good news for us.

'I've got nothing either, Your Highness,' says the Wind hunter, and I'm suddenly glad that we hid beneath this overhang. The boulders shield us from the breeze, enough to interrupt this man's ability to sense us.

'Perhaps I was mistaken and they took the main road after all,' says the woman.

None of the other hunters reply. They throw each other nervous glances, as though afraid to speak out of turn.

The woman turns to a short hunter with a huge scar across his cheek. 'What do you think, Argus?'

The hunter hesitates, then nods. 'Yeah, maybe they did.'

There's an intake of breath from a few of the other hunters and I know that Argus has made a terrible mistake. The woman pulls a matchbox from her pocket and strikes a stick into life. I barely have time to realise her proclivity must be Flame, before she sends a massive gush of fire towards Argus.

152

He twists aside just in time to save his face, but howls as the fireball scorches his shoulder.

'Do not question my plans again,' spits the woman. 'I *told* you that the brats would follow the river, not the road. I don't make mistakes, Argus!'

Argus is still screaming. The sound echoes across the Marbles, slapping against rocks and bouncing back to my eardrums. I want to clench my eyes shut, to look away, but even then I can smell the stink of burnt flesh.

'S . . . s . . . sorry,' he gasps, collapsed upon the rocks. 'I'm s . . . sorry, Your High . . . Your Highness.'

The woman stands over him, frowns, then waves a hand. 'I'll forgive you this time, Argus, because you are a valuable hunter. But you'd better repay me for my mercy.'

Argus manages a shaky nod. 'I'll kill 'em . . . I'll find . . . I'll find those br-brats and –'

'Yes, yes, you'll kill them. Very good,' says the woman. Then she gestures at the river. 'You may wash your shoulder if you wish, but do not take too long. We shall not be waiting for you.'

The hunting group continues up the river, beyond our hiding place and out of sight. As they pass, I notice one man wearing a chain of snakes around his neck. He croons at them as he walks, as if he's whispering poems into a lover's ear. I guess his proclivity is Reptile. It's a fairly rare proclivity and would be useless for most people, since it's much harder to find affordable reptiles than air or fire or birds. But if you're a richie – or even better, a palace hunter – it's probably a brilliant ability to have on your side. Snakes, lizards, poisonous crocodiles from the south . . . I wonder what other toxic creatures are concealed beneath his clothes.

When his companions are gone, Argus staggers into the water. He moans and whimpers as he soaks his shoulder, rolling and splashing around like a half-slaughtered sheep in the market. I'm worried that my illusion might fail or the foxaries might growl. But Argus seems too tangled in his own pain to pay much attention to nearby rock formations. When he finally leaves, face streaked with snot and tears, we all exhale.

'I can't believe she just –' says Clementine.

'Believe it,' says Radnor. 'That's what the palace people do. They kill without a second thought.'

I think of Hackel, on our own side, burning that hunter's face off. The king's hunters are brutal, yes, but maybe we are too.

'Who was that woman, anyway?' I say. 'And why would she want to become a hunter, of all things? I can't imagine the king's relatives traipsing around the Marbles for fun.'

'The royals are usually given safe roles,' says Maisy, nodding, 'far away from the firing lines. It's just a way to occupy their time and give them some experience at –'

'Ordering people's murders,' finishes Radnor.

'Have you read much about the current royal family?' I ask. I haven't kept up with politics in the years since my own family died. When you're scrimping and starving on the streets, the royal bloodline isn't exactly an urgent area of study.

'I'm not sure,' says Maisy. 'I think King Morrigan has a niece, about that woman's age. A duchess of some sort. Maybe that's her?'

'Well, whoever she was, she's bad news for us,' says Teddy. 'I reckon that hunting group's been sent after our crew – just us. Because we shot down that plane.'

'You mean, because Danika shot down that plane,' says Clementine. For a minute, I expect her to start harping on again about how I'm a danger to the crew, but she just bites her lips and looks at the sky.

We decide to stay where we are and set up camp for the night. It seems safest to let the hunters get as far ahead as possible and this ledge provides as decent a shelter as anywhere else. Sunset is only a couple of hours away and after days of hard riding, Radnor decides we've earned a break.

I rearrange the magnets to create a safer circle, while the others unpack our sleeping sacks and food. We eat an early dinner, then sit around awkwardly trying to make conversation. I wish Clementine had brought a pack of cards or something, as stupid as that would have seemed to me a few days ago.

It's funny: I should be treating my crew members like a family, but I have almost nothing to say to them. None of us has anything in common. Maisy and Clementine are too rich, too spoilt, to share any of my life experiences. Teddy is a thief and a liar, and Radnor is . . . well . . . I'm not sure. He's determined to be a good leader, but he doesn't seem to have much experience at it. He's the only one of us who knows Hackel's plan, who can lead us safely to the Valley. And he's the one who created this crew.

Even so, I feel like I know nothing about him. What does he want? Why did he decide to form this crew, to risk his life – and ours, too – on this mad dream of escape? If he's already got his proclivity, I bet it's something like Shadow or Night. Those proclivities are shameful in Rourton, signs that someone can't be trusted, and Radnor has stayed pretty secretive about himself so far.

Then again, hasn't everyone?

I glance at the twins. I still don't understand why

they've come on this journey, but I think I'm getting an idea of their personalities, at least. Clementine's proclivity is probably Gold or Gems or something – pretty and sparkly, but useless for survival. I'm not so sure about Maisy. I've never heard of someone having Books as their proclivity. But I can picture her as a little rainstorm, pitter-pattering shyly on someone's roof. Maybe her proclivity is Rain.

Teddy is Beast, of course, and Hackel is Flame: by far the most common proclivity. If Hackel lived permanently in Rourton, he'd probably work in the factory forges. As a smuggler, though, he can utilise fire for more brutal purposes.

That just leaves me. I can still feel the itch on the back of my neck, the sign that my proclivity is starting to develop. It's pointless to guess what it might be – I've been guessing and dreaming my whole life, just like every other kid, but it's never what you expect. People say that illusion skills don't have anything to do with your proclivity, but I don't know. I hope mine has something to do with the air. I've always dreamed of flying, travelling with the breeze. Knowing my luck, then, it'll probably be Mud.

No one feels like talking, so we decide to turn in for the night. I'm still exhausted from my lack of sleep, so Radnor insists I'm not allowed to take the first watch. It's Maisy's turn and she promises to wake me for the second shift.

'Sure you're up for this, Danika?' says Radnor.

It's so tempting to say 'no', to curl up in my sleeping sack and get an entire night of rest. But something troubles me about that kite, like an itch I can't scratch, and the thought of missing a chance to see it worries me more than another day of weariness.

'I'm sure,' I say, trying to sound as bubbly as possible. Actually, I probably sound more deranged than anything at this point, but the others just nod and settle down for bed. I guess that I've proven I can function without much sleep and that I'm a decent guard. Nothing's gone wrong during my countless shifts. Not yet, anyway.

When Maisy wakes me, it's past midnight. I can tell by the chill in the air, the clarified blackness that marks the early hours of morning. *The dying hours*, we say in Rourton. It's the time when the hunger gets you, when the cold bites hardest and scruffer kids die on the streets.

'You should've woken me hours ago,' I whisper.

Maisy shakes her head. 'You needed sleep more than I do.'

'Thanks,' I say.

Maisy's face is obscured by darkness, but I think she smiles.

I take my place on the guard rock. It's cold and hard, ready to freeze my bum off, but at least the chill should keep me alert. It's tempting to drag my sleeping sack over here, just as a shield against the night wind, but comfort means drowsiness. So I stay cold, hug my knees and watch the night.

As the hours pass, my head begins to droop. I force myself to my feet and pace a little, shaking life back into my body. There are pins and needles in my knee, and it almost feels disconnected from the rest of me. As I jiggle it quietly, careful not to wake the others, a flash of movement catches my eye from above.

It's the kite.

And tonight it's closer. It's only a hundred metres from our campsite, somewhere on the opposite side of the river. Boulders hide its owner. From here, all I can see is string and shadow upon the sky.

I hesitate. Our camp is protected by my illusion, isn't it? Even if something happens to me, the others will be safe. They'll be left alone to slumber until morning . . .

I pilfer a knife from the nearest pack, and slide it down the side of my boot. Then I clench my fists, summon my courage and step outside the magnetic circle.

Nothing happens. I exhale slowly. I don't know what I was expecting – for a dozen hunters to swoop down and gut me? But there's no sign of movement, no sounds of encroaching attackers. There's only the chill of the night, the gurgle of the river and the fog of my own breath upon the cold.

The water lashes my ankles, stronger than I expected, and for a horrible second I think it might yank my body out from beneath me. It's cold, too, so cold that I almost shriek in pain. But I grit my teeth and clench my eyes shut. I allow myself this one moment of weakness, steadying my nerves. Then I press onward. This kite has haunted me for days. It could be a danger to our crew; a trap just waiting to be sprung. And tonight, the kite is closer than ever. What if its flyer means us harm? What if he's working some unknown magic, out there in the dark?

When the water is almost at my chest, I reach the first boulder. I can't swim – there's nowhere to learn in Rourton, unless you're a richie with access to the private bathing pools – and the current grows stronger as I approach the deeper waters. My only hope of getting across is to use these boulders. If I tell myself they're just enormous stepping stones and this river is just a downtown street on a stormy day . . .

I haul myself up onto the rock, gasping at the smack of cold air. It's funny how cold water hurts when you first submerge yourself, but by the time your body adjusts, it's re-entering the outside air that really stings. My clothes are sopping and I wince a little at the noisy slosh of fabric as I hit the rock.

The next boulder is only a metre away. I balance on my knees and throw my upper body forward, extending my legs like a frog beneath me. With a huff – and a pang as my palms hit rock – I make it across. Then, before I have a chance to panic, I force myself to repeat the action.

Within a minute, I've lurched across three boulders and I'm halfway across the river. My legs get drenched, but I always manage to grab a handhold in time to save myself from the current. It's deep here – my flailing legs don't touch the riverbed – and the water is strong. It takes all my strength to haul my body upwards onto the next rock and the next . . .

I'm three-quarters of the way across when it happens. I miss my handhold and tumble into the river. There's a lash on my knuckles and sudden pain as I collide with the submerged bulk of the rock. Then froth and cold and my own shriek, gurgling beneath the water. The current drags me down-stream. In this moment, I'm more terrified than I've been in years. This river isn't just some basher scum in an alleyway or a richie with a fire poker. The river doesn't want to fight me. It doesn't even want to kill me. It just doesn't *care*. I'm as worthless as a leaf or an animal carcass. A piece of debris to be churned against the rocks.

My head slams into another boulder. There's a flash of black, then flickering white beneath my eyelids. Is this what it means to 'see stars'? But this pain doesn't feel like starlight. It feels like lightning. I struggle to get a grip on myself. I regain control of my hands, just for a minute, and lunge through the flurry. I don't know what I'm grabbing for – rock or empty water – but my fingers find the edge of the boulder.

I haul myself up: gasping, dripping, dizzy. And then I realise. This isn't just another pile of rocks. It's the bank of the river. I've made it to the other side. And thirty metres from my sodden body, a kite flutters across the stars.

CHAPTER FOURTEEN

THE PURSUER

I LIE ON THE RIVERBANK, FIGHTING TO REGAIN MY breath. My lungs seem to have forgotten how to fill and empty; they just ache. I twist over a couple of times to cough up water. Luckily the river is loud against the rocks, or I'd reveal my position with every choke.

After a few minutes, my body starts returning to normal. There's a rhythm to my breathing now, like the quiet cycle of a nursery rhyme. In my head, the words churn over again.

Oh mighty yo,
How the star-shine must go
Chasing those distant deserts of green.

My breath eddies into the rhythm of the folk song. In, out. In, out. I force myself onto my knees, then my legs. I'm a little unsteady, but the boulders provide support as I grope my way downstream.

We shall meet with the tree-lands
Then bet with the stream's hands
As star-shine's fair pistol shall gleam . . .

The night is quiet, but the river makes enough background noise to hide my footsteps. From behind a stack of boulders, I risk a cautious glance towards the kite flyer. He sits on a rocky ledge, silhouetted against the sky. There's a shadowed space behind him – a cave in the rocks, I guess, which he'll shelter in tonight. But for now he's out in the moonlight, coaxing his kite string down as though to end its flight.

He's younger than I expected. Too young to be a hunter. Seventeen or eighteen at the most, although it's hard to tell in the dark. His hair is dark, falling around his face in tendrils. He stares up at the stars, mouth closed, eyes bright and open. I inch closer.

The boy whips around, alert as an alley cat. 'Who's there?'

I shrink back behind my boulder. Then I swear at my own mistake; my shadow has been amplified by the angle of the rocks and moonlight. There's no way he could have missed its jerking retreat. Is he approaching? It's too risky to stick my neck out again. I can't hear anything, but maybe he's been trained to move silently. Maybe the palace is recruiting younger hunters to fool us somehow . . .

I slip the knife from my boot and point it outwards. If he approaches, I'll be ready. I'm not going to die like a mouse, cowering in the shadows without a fight.

Nothing.

A minute passes, maybe two. I force myself to keep as quiet as I can. Any second he might appear, armed with terrible weapons I've never dreamed of. Or worse, armed with spells and alchemy.

'I'm not going to hurt you,' the boy says.

His voice echoes from across the clearing. He hasn't moved from his position on the ledge. Why hasn't he moved? Maybe he's toying with me; he knows he can take his time. If he knows his proclivity, he might be able to move through the air or the rocks or even the darkness. Maybe I'm no safer here than I would be if he stood inches from my neck.

I tighten my grip on the knife, just in case. 'Why should I believe you?'

'Because I'm a refugee,' says the boy. 'Just like you.'

'You know nothing about me!'

'Yes I do. I've been following your crew. You're from Rourton.'

I peer around the edge of my boulder, trying to suss out his tone. He hasn't moved. 'Who are *you*?'

'My name is Lukas,' he says. 'I've been travelling for weeks now, from Norville. I just turned eighteen and I didn't . . .' He trails off, gesturing at his lack of a neck-scarf. 'I didn't want to join the army.'

'If you're a refugee, where's your crew?'

'Since when is it compulsory to join a crew?'

He has a point. If I hadn't joined Radnor's crew, I'd be a solo refugee too. Well, either solo or dead. 'What's with the kite?'

Lukas hesitates. 'It's hard to explain.'

'Try me.'

'Well . . . it helps me find my way.'

I venture from behind the boulder. I feel very exposed in the moonlight, but I want a better look at his face. It's too hard to tell whether he's lying, to know whether to trust him. 'How?'

'It helps me communicate with my proclivity. It helps me to see.' Lukas folds his kite gently and then winds its string around a reel. 'My proclivity is Bird. There aren't many birds around here but the kite attracts them.'

He twists to show me the back of his neck.

Proclivity markings run across the skin, creating a trail from his hairline to his jacket collar. From here, they just look like black splotches. They must be tiny birds, though, or maybe feathers. I step forward, angling for a closer look, but Lukas has already turned back around to face me.

'Why are you following our crew?' I say.

'I don't know. I guess . . .'

'What?'

'I guess it seemed safer to stick close by. That smuggler that was leading you, back in the forest, he looked like he could handle a pack of hunters.'

'Well, we haven't seen him for days, so I wouldn't get your hopes up.' I pause. 'Anyway, we've already got an oversized crew. Our leader isn't going to let you join as well.'

'I don't want to join,' says Lukas. 'But we're travelling the same way, aren't we? We're all heading for the Magnetic Valley.'

'So?'

'So what does it matter if I stick close by?' Lukas slips off his rock and steps towards me. 'No one else knows about me, right? It's just you.'

I hesitate, then nod.

'Well, doesn't that show I've got some skills? I know how to keep quiet, how to hide myself. I won't endanger your crew.'

'You're in more danger yourself if you stick near us,' I say. 'You were nearby in the forest – you must know that I brought down a biplane.'

His eyes widen. 'That was you?'

I nod. 'The king's hunters want us dead. If you've got any sense, you'll get as far away from our crew as possible.'

'And go where?'

'I don't know. Find another way to the Valley or something.'

Lukas shakes his head. 'I got lost days ago, and my original plan is wrecked. My only hope of finding a safe route is to follow the river . . . just like the rest of you.'

'What about your kite?'

'It's not enough.' Lukas sounds frustrated. 'There were plenty of birds back in the forest, but not so many out here in the rocks. Why do you think I keep risking it, night after night? I need to borrow their eyes and see the world from above. I *like* seeing the world from the sky.'

'I would've thought they'd be sleeping,' I say, thinking of the pigeons back in Rourton. They always disappeared at night, roosting in the nooks and crannies of the city. 'Or it'd be too dark for them to see your kite.'

Lukas shakes his head. 'Owls and nightjars can see in the dark. Anyway, the birds don't need to physically see it. This isn't . . .' He weighs the folded kite in his hands. 'It isn't a normal kite.'

I stiffen. If Lukas is rich enough to afford enchanted objects, he's not a normal refugee. I don't know what mysteries the kite holds – maybe it's been dipped in alchemy potions or weighted with an unknown spell – but I *do* know what it means for me. It means this boy is suddenly a lot less trustworthy.

Lukas seems to sense the shift in my mood, because he takes another step forward. 'It's just a family heirloom,' he says. 'My grandfather's proclivity was Bird as well. He passed it down to me when he died.'

I don't respond.

Lukas puts his kite down on the rocks, and holds up his hands to show he's unarmed. 'All the kite does is call birds, I swear. It doesn't have any other powers.'

'Why should I believe you?'

'If I wanted to hurt you, I wouldn't have told you the truth. And if I was working for the palace, why wouldn't I have attacked your camp days ago?'

'Because you're waiting for backup,' I say.

'If I need backup to attack a bunch of teen-agers,' says Lukas, 'my kite obviously doesn't have any hidden evil powers, does it? You can't have it both ways.'

A breeze filters between the rocks. It chills the damp fabric against my skin.

'Did you kill those hunters?' I say eventually.

'What?'

'We found two dead hunters in the woods. Someone executed them – shot them through the base of their skulls. Was it you?'

Lukas looks rattled. 'I don't even have a gun. You can check my supplies if you want.'

For some reason, I believe him. There's something about his eyes and the open spread of his hands that makes me trust him. Or maybe it's the way he looks genuinely shocked by the idea of plugging someone's neck with bullets.

'If you didn't kill them,' I say, 'then who did?'

'I don't know.'

Silence again. My throat feels a little dry now, husked out by confusion. Part of me wants to flee, to run back to my crew's camp and pretend I've never met him. The rest of me buzzes with curiosity. I want to know more about this boy called Lukas, this boy who is not afraid to risk his life by tossing a kite into the stars.

'I've got to get back to my camp,' I say. 'I won't tell them about you, not yet. But if you try anything dodgy –'

'I won't.'

Lukas steps towards me. When he enters a patch of moonlight, I get a better look at his body. He is hard and lean, built with the sort of rangy muscles that you never see on spoiled richie kids. But his face is strained, as though he's lost a bit of weight, and quickly. I wonder how long it's been since his food supplies ran low.

'What's your name?' he says.

'Danika Glynn.'

He nods. There is a pause. 'Well, Danika, I'm glad I met you. It's not every day you meet a girl who can bring palace biplanes down from the sky.'

Then he stands, gives a little smile and slips away into the night.

CHAPTER FIFTEEN

AMBUSH

I STRUGGLE BACK ACROSS THE RIVER, WRING OUT MY clothes and slip back inside our campsite's illusion. I'm glad that we chose to camp beneath the rock ledge, because it tells me where the rest of my crew lies hidden. There's no sign of disturbance and everyone seems to be sound asleep, so I sigh in relief. I return my pilfered knife to the pack and settle back onto the guard rock.

The rest of the night passes in odd time – fast, then unbearably slow, then fast again. My clothes dry slowly, ruffled by the breeze. I'm not sure what I'm waiting for. I want it to be dawn, but I also want the night to linger. Why? Maybe I'm hoping that Lukas's kite will fly again, that I'll get some kind of confirmation that I didn't just imagine him. It's surreal to think there's a boy out there in the dark, following our crew like a silent shadow across Taladia.

When dawn finally comes, we eat a breakfast of gluggy porridge. We're running low on syrup now, so Radnor carefully rations one drop for each of us. Its sweetness is so diluted that I can hardly taste it among the greyish slop of oats.

The morning is a cold one, but at least there's winter sunshine. It reflects off the rocks as we pass. We're back down on the riverbank today, since the higher rock formations are now too crowded to slip between. Maisy still wraps her hands in spare clothes, but when I ask about her fingers she reveals they're healing a bit.

'I think my body was just getting used to the cold,' she says.

Everything seems quiet and normal. We ride along, shaking warmth into our limbs, and the foxaries lick lichen off some half-submerged boulders. But I'm starting to feel uncomfortable, as though we're missing something important. The riverbank is narrowing, hemmed in by boulders and rock formations that grow higher with every passing hour. We're heading into the true Marbles now.

And if anything goes wrong, we're trapped. There's no way to climb up over these rocks in an emergency. It's like walking through a crack in the earth, with no ability to scale the sides and escape. The rock faces get higher and craggier, the river keeps leading us lower down the slope, and the foxaries' muscles tense.

'They don't like this place,' says Teddy.

Radnor gives a shake of his head. 'The riverbank's getting a bit narrow, that's all. They're worried their paws'll get wet.'

'Not just that,' says Teddy. 'Something doesn't feel right . . . the way the wind is blowing . . .'

I concentrate on the air around us, trying to figure out if he's right. I hadn't noticed it before, but maybe the wind is what's putting me on edge. It blows towards us like it's coming through a funnel or being blasted from a big industrial fan in one of Rourton's factories. But surely these rock faces should shield us from the wind?

That's when the wave hits us.

It gushes up from the river below, knocking us back in a tangle of screams and limbs. The foxaries make horrible sounds – choking, drowning – and the last thing I see is a snatch of empty sky. Then my head goes under. I flail instinctively, but there's no way to fight the torrent. Someone kicks me in the head, and I feel my own boots collide with flesh. Everything turns to white froth – in my eyes, my nostrils, my lungs . . .

Then the water recedes. We wash up onto shore, battered and gasping. I can't stop coughing as water crawls up behind my nostrils and my eyes sting. The others are crawling beside me, but the shock makes me selfish – or perhaps I'm just a selfish person – because at first, I don't even check that they've survived. I just cough and snort and haul my own throbbing body to safety.

At least, it seems like safety until I look up. That's when I see our attackers: two hunters, silhouetted against the sky. They're members of the crew we saw before, but they must have split up to cover more ground. Or maybe the royal woman decided to leave a pair behind, hiding in wait, just in case. Whatever the reasoning, it's worked. These hunters have found us and we're going to die.

'Hello, children,' says one of them. It's the man with the Water proclivity, the one who must have sent the wave. 'We're looking for a girl called Danika Glynn.'

I freeze. Around me, my crewmates do the same.

'That's me.' My voice is hoarse, battered by coughing, but I manage to straighten up onto my knees. If I'm about to die, I want dignity. I won't let these filthy hunters blast me aside while I lie gasping at their feet.

'You're quite a celebrity, you know,' says the hunter. He pauses, and then gives a nasty little laugh. 'Oh, but of course, you *don't* know, do you? You've been out here in the wilderness, without any access to newspapers.'

I push my palms against the rocks, take a deep breath and manage to get to my feet. 'What, you want my autograph before you kill me?'

'You brought down a palace bomber, you brat! The city wall's picture spells captured the whole thing – your face is on every wanted poster in the country. Did you really think we'd just kill you out here, in the middle of the Marbles?' The man laughs again. 'Oh no, we're going to make an *example* of you.'

My legs wobble but I refuse to fall. An example. I know what that means. It means a long, slow death in a city square – maybe even back in Rourton. They'll turn it into a spectacle with alchemy weapons. They might make a tree sprout out of my chest, ripping me open with its growing roots. They might fill my clothes with firecrackers or . . . .

'No you're not!' says a voice.

I whip my head around in surprise, because that voice's owner is the last person I'd expect to stand up to a hunter. It's not Teddy or Radnor or even Clementine. It's Maisy.

'Sorry, sweetheart,' says the second hunter, 'but you're not getting much say in the matter. You've had your fun, but this little runaway adventure ends right here.'

He swipes out with his fist, as though grabbing a handful of air. Then he hurls the air downward in Maisy's direction. I barely have time to realise he's the one who sent the wind, when I'm diving towards Maisy to knock her aside. His fistful of air will smash her like a bullet. But I'm not the only one who leaps – there's a crash, an eruption of cries, and I'm crushed in a heap of limbs on the rocks.

Someone's screaming and there are hands and feet everywhere. The mass lifts. Bodies roll away. For a terrible second I just see blood across my eyes, and I think something has blinded me. But it's not my blood. It's from Radnor.

Teddy and Clementine lie beside me, arms still flung over Maisy. Clementine keeps letting out little half-screams, as if she's not sure whether to shriek or cry. And when I follow her line of sight, I see Radnor. He's covered in red, dark red, a sticky crimson like toffee apples in the market. His shoulder is a mess of blood and exposed flesh.

'Radnor!' But before I can reach him, there's a wider blast of wind that rises up from the riverbank, and it throws us all sideways like twigs. I land with a painful thump on my own shoulder, but roll a few metres to absorb the impact.

The second wave hits.

It barrels down from behind us, sweeping our bodies into the river. There is so much water that the river floods the space between the rocks. There's no riverbank any more. There's just water, water everywhere, rushing up to hurl us downstream. I thrust myself above the surface, steal a huge gasp of air, and shout, 'Radnor! Maisy!'

Other heads burst up around me, but it's too confused and fast and within seconds I'm under again. Where's Radnor? If we don't stop the blood, he's going to die. He's going to bleed out right now, while the hunters play with us in this river.

There's a sudden wrenching at my lower back. It's like I'm a fish, yanked from the river by a hook. It hauls me up above the water, just long enough to manage another gasp for air. I strain to swivel my head and realise what's happened – one of the hunters has fished me out with long pole hooked onto my belt. He's yanking me up, away from my friends. The others are allowed to die in this river, but he's got other plans for me. I'm to become an *example*.

A body passes beneath me, pale and gasping and filling the water with clouds of red. It's Radnor. I fumble for the buckle and my belt slips free, snaking violently up through my trouser loops. A moment later, I hit the water. The hunter above me shouts, but it's too late – I'm back in the river and I don't intend to be hooked again. Not while my crewmates are still flailing down here, anyway.

I grab Radnor's ankle and try to haul him towards me, but the water is too strong. He slips away, and I'm left holding nothing but froth. We are tossed and turned, gushing downstream between the rock faces, and the world turns over and over until I see nothing but snatches of foam and sky.

Then I see the drop. I only get a quick glimpse – sometime in the middle of flailing sideways through the torrent – but it's enough to know we're going to die. We're heading for a steeper slope, practically a cliff, and the river gushes off its edge like a waterfall.

'Grab –' I manage, but then my head goes under. I thrust myself up again and shout, 'Grab onto something!'

There's a large boulder coming up, only metres from the edge of the fall. A few bodies are already clinging to it, and I see a glimpse of blonde hair, but there's no way to tell whether Radnor made it. I collide with the rock and manage to grab on, then push my head above the rapids to get a better look. Teddy Nort screams and for a second I think he's gone over the falls. Then I realise he isn't screaming for himself. He's screaming for one of the foxaries.

We watch, helpless, as a second foxary scrabbles at the edge. Teddy starts releasing his own grip, ready to go and haul the animal back towards us, but I seize his arm to stop him – if he loses his grip on the boulder, he'll go over too. There's another terrible scream, or a howl, and I'm not sure whether the sound comes from the foxary or from Teddy or maybe even both. Then the animal disappears over the edge of the waterfall.

'No!' Teddy shouts, fighting me.

My head goes underwater and I choke, but manage to thrust my mouth back up in a coughing fit. 'It's too late, Teddy!'

'Where's Radnor?' shrieks Clementine.

I glance around, but there's no sign of life in the water. Four members of our crew cling to this boulder – Teddy, the twins and me. Two foxaries are dead, and I can't see the last one; hopefully it managed to get a grip on the rocks somewhere behind us. Then I see the body below the surface, churning pinkish blood through the water.

'Radnor!' I lurch sideways, forgetting my own need to hold onto the boulder. But Teddy grabs the back of my shirt and holds me steady, forming a chain of bodies as I snatch Radnor's ankle and drag him forward.

There's a horrible shout from above. I know it's the hunters, and I know they could kill us at any second, but there's no time to look up. All I can do is haul Radnor's bleeding body towards me . . .

'Arrgh!'

Something falls from the sky. It's a body – a larger body, a fully grown man – and he crashes down into the river beside us. One of the hunters, but I can't tell which one. His head smashes against the rocks on his way down, and he disappears beneath the water. A few seconds later, a dark bulk passes over the edge of the fall and I know he's gone.

'What –?'

'Look!' interrupts Teddy.

I wrench my gaze upward. There is only one hunter left: the man whose power is Water. But he's grappling with a smaller figure, a boy whose fingers are alight with odd flashes of silver. *Lukas!*

As we watch, Lukas ducks to avoid a blow from the hunter. I can't tell what he's doing, or how he's summoning this magic – he must have more enchanted objects than just a kite. These flashes of silver, these bursts of light that claw at the hunter's face, go far beyond a simple Bird proclivity.

They're getting closer to the edge, now; my breath catches in my throat as Lukas teeters on the brink. The hunter is so much larger, with fists that could crush the throat of a teenage boy in seconds. But Lukas darts sideways and kicks out at the man's shins. There is a scream – of rage, maybe, or just terror – and the hunter topples over the edge of the cliff.

The river surges. It must be a final act of vengeance as the Water hunter falls, because suddenly I'm underwater. Froth smashes over my head, grinding me down into the rock. I lose my hold on Radnor, and almost on the boulder itself. Water floods into my nose, my ears . . . it forces open my lips and fills my lungs, batters against my eyelids . . .

Then it's gone. The torrent drains like water in a sink. I'm clinging to a boulder in an ordinary river, coughing and spluttering beside a group of bedraggled bodies. I manage to force my eyes open, to count them. Teddy. Clementine. Maisy. Me.

'Where . . .?' I take a shaky breath. 'Where's Radnor?'

No one answers. But we all turn towards the edge of the waterfall, knowing the terrible truth. In that last rush of water, all we could do was save ourselves. No one kept a grip on Radnor's broken body.

And now, our leader is gone.

CHAPTER SIXTEEN

LOST

WE THROW OUR SODDEN BODIES ONTO THE BANK. Someone is hyperventilating – maybe it's me, I don't know – and it feels like a drum is beating inside my skull. All I can do is breathe, in and out, in and out, and try to quell the horror that's strangling my gut.

After a few minutes, a gentle hand touches my shoulder. I flinch.

'Sorry,' says the voice. 'Are you hurt, Danika?'

I force my eyes open. It's Lukas. He must have clambered down the edge of the rocks. I suddenly feel a surge of guilt; he just saved our lives, but I'd completely forgotten about him.

'I'm fine,' I manage. 'You?'

He nods and helps me to my knees.

'Who are you?' says Teddy, staring at Lukas with a numb expression. He almost looks as though he doesn't care – and right now, I don't blame him. Radnor is dead. He's *dead*.

'I'm another refugee, from Norville,' says Lukas. 'I've been following your crew to find my way through the Marbles.'

'It's true.' I hesitate, then add, 'I think we can trust him. He's been following us for days, and he hasn't hurt us. And he just saved our lives.'

Teddy nods, apparently too stunned to feel suspicious. My stomach feels as cold as stone, and my fingers tingle where I last felt Radnor's ankle against my skin. He was just here with us, a moment ago. Alive. Breathing.

Maisy is staring towards the edge of the waterfall, as though hoping Radnor will magically pop back up into view. Clementine buries her head between her knees, bunching white-knuckled fingers into her hair.

After a long moment, we venture to the edge of the waterfall and peer over. There's no way down, not from here. The cliffs are too steep, too rough. If we all had Water proclivities, maybe we could melt into the river and ride it down. But since we don't, trying to descend would just mean death.

Even worse, we can see the river far below.

184

The river is supposed to be our guide, to lead us all the way to Gunning. But about fifty metres away from the base of the cliff, it merges into a messy swamp and disappears. Surrounding the swampland, there's only empty fields. No more Marbles, no more river . . .

And no idea how to find our way.

'We've got to move,' I say, when it becomes obvious that no one else is going to take charge. 'We have to get away from here, find somewhere to hide . . .'

Maisy looks around at me, face paler than I've ever seen it. 'Yes,' she says. 'You're right.'

The others don't argue. We move automatically for the next few minutes, traipsing back up the river to the original ambush point. Our lone surviving foxary clings to a ledge halfway up the rocks, but Teddy manages to coax it down with some gentle murmurs and hand signals. I wonder whether this foxary knows its friends are dead. I wonder whether the deaths caused Teddy physical pain, since he's so connected to these animals. When I remember Teddy's scream in the river, it seems all too likely.

We backtrack for a while, until we find a stack of boulders that are the right height to serve as stairs. Then we clamber up out of the riverbank, onto the higher plain of rock above.

'Where now?' says Teddy.

I shake my head. 'I don't know. Did Radnor tell the route to anyone else?'

'All I know is to follow the river,' says Clementine. 'But I never heard him mention a waterfall.' She lets out a low breath. 'We should have taken the trade road. None of this would have . . . I mean . . .' She pauses. 'It would have been so much easier.'

'If we'd taken the trade road, we'd all be dead.' Teddy looks grim. 'If a plan seems too easy, it's too easy for your enemies to figure out. I've learned that much from burgling.'

There is a long pause. Now that the initial shock is wearing off, the aches are beginning to set in. The river's battering has not been kind to our bodies.

'But now we're lost,' Clementine says. 'Radnor was the only one who knew the way.'

'I don't reckon Radnor even knew the way, really,' Teddy says. 'He was just going by what Hackel told him.'

'Hackel!' I blurt. 'We're supposed to meet him in Gunning, right? He'll know the way to the Valley.'

'Yeah, maybe,' says Teddy, 'but that's not gonna do us a lot of good if we can't find Gunning in the first place.'

I turn to Lukas. 'Any luck summoning the birds?'

He shakes his head. 'Nothing yet. I don't think there are any birds out here. It's all so . . . well . . .' He gestures across the endless marbles. 'So *dead*, I guess. Maybe down there in the fields I'll have more luck.'

I gaze over the edge of the cliff, thinking of Radnor. His body is somewhere below, beyond our reach. We can't even give him a proper burial.

'Come on,' I say, when it becomes obvious that no one else is ready to speak. 'We've got to keep moving.'

*

FOR THE REST OF THE DAY, WE TRAIPSE ALONG THE edge of the cliff, searching for a route down to the plains below. My body throbs and my mind aches. But there's no way down, nowhere safe to climb: just steep, crumbling cliff face.

We set up camp about twenty metres from the edge, inside a protective cluster of boulders. Our surviving foxary carries three packs – two large ones and a smaller one – but the rest of our supplies went over the fall. Mercifully, our magnets have survived the ordeal, but we've lost all the food and half the sleeping sacks. Teddy gives a bitter snort as he fishes through our supplies.

'Of all the packs to survive . . .' he mutters, holding up a sparkly evening gown. Clementine, at least, has the good grace to look as disappointed as the rest of us.

I use a knife to slice open the remaining sleeping sacks. It's a bit like gutting fish down the side, and bits of fleece spill across our campsite. But this way, each sack becomes a large blanket for two people.

Teddy slips beneath a sack and forces a grin. 'Just like those fancy mansions on High Street.'

'We'll need to find some food tomorrow,' I say.

Lukas crosses to a pile of boulders, arranged higgledy-piggledy in the shadows of a rock ledge. He squats and bends to peer underneath, as though he's dropped something.

I frown in confusion. 'What are you doing?'

'Looking for seeds.'

'Oh!' says Maisy. 'Of course – there must be rock-fig seeds under some of these boulders.'

'What?' says Teddy.

Maisy rises to join Lukas by the pile of rocks. 'In springtime, the Marbles are covered with rock-figs. The plants spread their vines and flowers everywhere. I saw a picture in a book once; it was beautiful.'

'So what? It's winter, not spring.'

'So rock-figs grow from seeds,' says Lukas. 'The seeds from last year's crop are scattered all over the place, waiting for spring. Most of them probably blew away months ago, but there are plenty under the rocks. That's all I've been eating for days.'

'Doesn't seem to have done you much good,' says Clementine, eying Lukas's underweight frame.

'Better than nothing,' I say, and join the others at the rock pile.

After twenty minutes of careful picking, we've amassed a handful of seeds. They're tiny and hard – half of mine get stuck between my teeth – and by the time I've finished, I'm hungrier than I was before. It's funny how that happens. If you don't eat anything for a day or so, sometimes you're lucky and your stomach will stop bothering you for a while. But if you sneak in a little snack, you've suddenly got a full-scale stomach uprising to deal with.

My belly gurgles impatiently, awaiting more food, but all I can do is scavenge for a few more seeds around the campsite. 'How did you know to look for seeds, anyway?' I say to Lukas.

He shrugs. For the first time, I notice the colour of his eyes: a vivid twist of green. 'I've spent a lot of time looking at the world through birds' eyes,' he says. 'You get a good idea of where seeds and stuff might be hidden.'

The evening passes in a haze of hunger and grief. I wish someone would start talking again.

Even mindless chatter would be fine – anything to break this silence. I keep hearing the scream of the waterfall, and feeling the touch of Radnor's ankle as he slips between my fingers. A flash of crimson in the water. I hug my knees and scrunch up my eyes, shielding my body against the night.

I've seen death before, of course. Back in Rourton, the winter took dozens of scruffers' lives. People froze in alleyways, or starved in the gutters. Sometimes I found their bodies: curled up and broken, like withered tree-limbs in the frost. A couple were people I knew. The old man who taught me which alleyways to scour. The girl who once traded me an apple for a stale chunk of bread.

And, of course, my family.

After all these years, I know how to push aside my grief. Tomorrow I will lock away these emotions, deep inside me, to deal with later. It's the only option, when you grow up on the streets. The only way to survive. But for now, it's all I can do to fight off the shake in my limbs and the ache in my bones.

No one has the energy to keep watch except for Lukas, who volunteers to take the whole night. Teddy gives him a distrustful look, until I sigh and offer to stay up with him.

'I'm not too tired, honestly,' I lie.

Teddy doesn't look like he believes me, but the twins are already asleep – or passed out – and he clearly can't fight his body's cry for rest.

About halfway through our watch, I turn to Lukas. I still can't shake the tingle from my fingers and I need a distraction. Anything to break the silence. 'How did you fight those hunters?'

Lukas pulls a chain from beneath his shirt. Half a dozen silver charms dangle from the end. I suddenly remember the hunter Hackel burned to death, and the necklace of charms that Hackel pilfered from his body. *Alchemy charms.* Portable spells, baked into the silver. My breath catches.

'Are they . . .?'

Lukas nods. He pulls the chain from his neck and shows me the charms. 'This one is dizziness,' he says, pointing to a tiny silver goblet. 'And this horseshoe means luck, and the padlock is for unlocking things. The rose can hide my scent from animals, which is why your foxaries never sensed me following you.'

'But they must have been so expensive!'

'My grandparents collected them, and they were passed down to me,' says Lukas. 'Just like the kite. My family used to be rich.'

'So, if you've got all these family heirlooms, why haven't you sold them off by now? You could buy a lifetime of food with those charms.'

Lukas shrugs. 'They were gifts from my family.'

'Sentimental value?'

'Something like that.'

I hesitate, then pull up my sleeve to expose my mother's silver bracelet. It slips down from my elbow to my wrist, and the metal seems to wink beneath the moon. 'I know what you mean.'

He smiles. And despite everything, I smile back. I think I'm starting to get a better idea of Lukas. He grew up a scruffer, just like me. Most scruffer kids would sell a fistful of silver in seconds for a bite to eat. But Lukas couldn't let go of this memory of his family . . . and neither could I.

I touch the nearest charm on his chain: a tiny silver star. 'What's this one for?'

Lukas smiles again. 'My grandma gave me that one personally. It doesn't have any powers – it's just a trinket.'

We sit in silence for a while, staring at the stars. Now that it's dark, the edge of the cliff looks like the edge of the world. I can't see down to the fields beyond, or the line of earth that marks our distant horizon. There's just twenty metres of rock, then blackness.

After a while, Lukas starts to fiddle with the clasp of his necklace. He opens it gently, then slips a charm off the chain.

'Here.' He hands me the tiny silver rose. 'I want you to have this, Danika.'

I frown. 'Isn't this what hides your scent from foxaries?'

'That's why I want you to take it,' Lukas says. 'If I'm going to join this crew, I want . . . well . . . I don't think I deserve your trust until I've earned it. And this is a first step in that direction.'

I roll the rose between my fingers. 'What do you mean?'

'Without that charm I can't abandon the crew or sneak away to betray you, can I? It wouldn't take long to track me down with the foxary – not out here.'

I hesitate. It feels wrong to take the charm, which is probably worth more than anything I've owned. And besides, it was a gift from Lukas's family.

'It's all right,' I say, feeling a little awkward. 'You fought off a pair of hunters to save our lives. I don't need this to trust you.'

He gives me a quiet smile. 'Thank you, Danika. I'm not used to . . .' His voice trails away, and he shakes his head as though to clear it. 'Look, if you don't need it to trust me, then consider it a gift.'

'A gift for what?'

'Just a thankyou gift,' he says.

There is a pause.

'All right,' I say. 'Thank you. It's beautiful.'

I hold out my wrist to reveal my mother's bracelet. Lukas smiles gently, takes the silver rose, and twists its metal loop through the bracelet. I pull my wrist back to examine it. 'How do I use it?'

'Close your eyes.'

I hesitate. 'Why?'

'It's how you bond with an alchemy charm for the first time. Don't worry, it only takes a minute.'

There's nothing fishy in his expression, so I shut my eyelids.

Lukas takes my hand and places it against the silver rose. 'Now just focus on hiding yourself,' he says. 'Pretend you're far away, where the beasts can't find you.'

I try to concentrate, but Lukas's fingers are warm against my wrist and it's hard to focus. I take a deep breath and tell myself that this is just like casting an illusion. I focus upon my desired result: hiding away, beyond a foxary's senses . . .

There is a sharp twang in the air. The silver rose heats up in my fingers, so hot that I almost drop it. 'Ow!' I open my eyes to see Lukas smiling at me. 'Did I do it?'

He nods. 'You've bonded with the charm now. The spell will be ready when you need it.'

There's a pause. I finger the rose, feeling a little

awkward. I wish I had something to give him in return. 'Thanks, Lukas.'

'You're welcome.'

I can't think of anything else to say, so I turn back to face the edge of the cliff. The moon is rising higher now; it casts just enough light to make out the world below. In the distance, I can see the horizon. And tomorrow, I hope, we might find a way to reach it.

*

THE NEXT DAY, WE TRAVEL PARALLEL TO THE EDGE OF the cliff. I feel oddly conflicted, torn between grief and a strange sort of lightness. The landscape makes me think of Radnor, which sends an ache through my gut. Boulders, cliff, sky . . . everything here seems to signal death. But at the same time, I find myself fingering the silver rose upon my bracelet. I'm not sure why – maybe I'm subconsciously afraid I'll lose it – but it's reassuring to roll its solid shape between my fingertips.

After a while, I realise that I'm wearing the bracelet around my wrist instead of my elbow. I automatically move to shove it back out of sight – but then I stop myself. I don't think my crewmates would steal from me. Not even Teddy.

It isn't until noon that Maisy spots a possible route down the cliff. We're rounding a large bend in the plateau, so we've got a decent view of the cliff face ahead. She gives a shy little cough to get our attention, then points towards a rough ledge of rocks that trails down the cliff.

'I think we found our ladder,' she says.

It's tempting to rush down into the fields, to escape from the Marbles' endless grey. There might be grain down there, or edible flowers. Even a pot of boiled thistles would be welcome at this point. But we force ourselves to travel slowly, to assess each footfall before we take the plunge.

'If we fall,' Teddy points out, 'then a field full of thistles won't do us much good.'

I know what he's thinking, of course. What we're all thinking. Radnor fell down into this place. Somewhere down below, in the swampland perhaps, his body lies alone.

It's hard to get the foxary to cooperate; it doesn't seem keen on descending such a narrow strip of boulders. I don't blame it, either; I'm having enough trouble with two legs, let alone four. But Teddy manages to coax it down with a little whisper, and a rub behind the ears. I can't help smiling at how they trust each other: the thief and the beast.

I sometimes hope my proclivity will be Beast too. It must be nice to have a guaranteed friend out here – although it would've been terrible for Teddy when the other foxaries died. That's the price of relationships, though. I learned that when I was just a kid, the night I watched my family burn. You get the benefits of companionship, of love and trust, maybe. But I'm not sure it's worth the pain that you get when they're gone.

About halfway down, Lukas stiffens.

'What is it?' I say, suddenly alert.

'I think I can sense . . .' He swivels around and breaks into a grin. 'Look, I knew it!'

In the distance, a flock of birds circle above the fields. They dive and swoop in perfect formation: a better crew than we'll ever be. Their dance is almost hypnotic. In other circumstances, it might seem nice to watch them for a while. But since I'm dangling halfway down a cliff – not the best time for bird-watching – I just turn back to the slope and look for somewhere safe to place my feet.

At the bottom, we stop for a rest. Our bodies still ache from the abuse of the river, and this trek down the cliff-side has hardly comforted our muscles.

'I think we should head back towards the swamps,' says Clementine. 'Where the river disappeared,

I mean. Perhaps there'll be a clue about where to go next.'

'What, like a big sign saying "This way to Gunning"?' says Teddy. 'We'll be backtracking our whole trip since the waterfall. That's another day's travel wasted.'

There's a pause.

'Does anyone have another idea?' I say. 'Can you remember *anything* Radnor said about how to find Gunning?'

Everyone shakes their head.

'All right then,' I say. 'Clementine's plan is the best we've got.'

The grass in the fields is tall and thick, about the height of our chests. It's dotted with boulder formations and occasional groves of scraggly trees. The trees don't bear any fruit in winter, but we're so hungry that we settle for chewing the bark. At least it keeps our teeth busy.

The further we walk, the taller the grass becomes. Soon it's at my eye-level, and then even higher. I feel like I'm back in the forest, unable to see any sign of a horizon. There's only foliage, all around me, and I've never felt so lost.

'If that woman finds us now, we're dead,' says Clementine, looking gloomy.

Lukas stiffens. 'Woman?'

'Yeah, there's some horrible woman leading the hunters,' I say. 'We think she's royalty, because the others kept calling her "Your Highness".'

Lukas looks uncomfortable. Almost self-consciously, he raises a hand to his charm necklace. 'That's Sharr Morrigan. The king's niece. She's got a reputation for being cruel.'

'How'd you know about her?' Teddy frowns. 'You're just a scruffer from Norville. The royals don't spend much time in the dodgy cities, do they?'

Lukas shakes his head. 'Everyone in my city knows about Sharr. She leads a platoon of hunters near Norville, and uses the city as her base.' He swallows. 'You wouldn't believe the things she does to people. Even to children, if they get in her way.'

We all fall silent, because we *can* believe it. We saw what Sharr did to her fellow hunter when he dared to question her plan. Blasting aside a few worthless scruffer kids would probably seem perfectly acceptable to someone like Sharr Morrigan.

By the time evening rolls around, we're still as lost as ever. The entire world seems a sea of grass. It whips my face with every gust of wind and blots out the sky.

The only relief comes when we find a grove of scrappy trees. I set up the magnetic circle and cast my illusion, then we wriggle our gutted sleeping sacks into uncomfortable positions among the roots. There's no real space to lie comfortably – the rocks and roots dig into our backs – but it's better than the grass. At least we can see the stars, since the trees' branches are so sparse in winter.

'That's the Warrior of the Northlands,' says Maisy, pointing out a constellation above our heads. 'And that one's called the Wolf.'

I squint at the stars, but all I can make out are dots. I've never seen much sense in constellations, but my mother used to like them. She always pointed out a particular formation through our uppermost window. Something called the Gun, I think, or perhaps the Pistol.

'Which one's the Pistol?' I say.

Maisy points to a formation. It's not directly overhead, so grass and branches conceal half the shape. But I recognise it now, the L-shaped cluster of stars.

'My mother always said to remember the Pistol,' I say. 'Said it was a good luck constellation.'

Teddy snorts. 'Yeah, because shooting people is really lucky.'

I think back to those evenings with my parents, clustered in our cheap apartment in Rourton. Before my father brought home the radio, we would pass the nights by singing songs and telling stories.

'My mother used to sing an old folk song – that one about the star-shine,' I say. *'Oh mighty yo, how the star-shine must go . . .'*

'Everyone knows that one,' says Clementine. 'It doesn't mean anything. It's just a stupid scruffer song.'

'I don't know it,' says Lukas.

We all turn to look at him.

'Really?' says Teddy, raising an eyebrow. 'It used to be a smuggler song, but I reckoned everyone in Taladia must have known it by now. Dunno why it caught on, really. I reckon that tune about the drunken caterpillar is catchier.'

A gust of wind blasts through our grove, and I turn my face sideways to avoid the dust. A couple of leaves flutter down onto our sleeping sack, and I'm suddenly grateful for the circle of magnets around us. These bare-limbed trees seem like a worse and worse hiding place by the minute. But I stare up at the stars, and think of my mother's voice.

Oh mighty yo,
How the star-shine must go
Chasing those distant deserts of green . . .

I don't realise I'm whispering the lyrics aloud, until Lukas gives me a smile. When I was a kid, on those first lonely nights after the bombing, I used to sing myself to sleep with the star-shine song. I guess my lips haven't forgotten the temptation to whisper the tune.

'Don't stop,' Lukas says.

I shake my head, embarrassed to have been caught. But to my surprise, another voice soon continues the song. It's Maisy. A moment later, she's joined by Teddy, and then I find myself singing along again.

It's ridiculous, really, to hold a campfire sing-along out here. For a start, we don't have a campfire. Besides, we're all exhausted and starving and grieving. But the song makes me feel like a kid again: safe and warm. The others must feel something similar, because countless Rourton parents choose this song as a lullaby.

Oh mighty yo,
How the star-shine must go
Chasing those distant deserts of green.
We shall meet with the tree-lands
Then bet with the stream's hands
As star-shine's fair pistol shall gleam . . .

Lukas sits up. 'What was that last bit, again?'

'*As star-shine's fair pistol shall gleam,*' I repeat. I don't see why he's looking so excited about a corny folk song, but my words seem to confirm the glint in his eye.

'And before that,' he says, 'the bit about the tree-lands, and the stream . . . Don't you see, Danika? Don't you see what this song is about?'

And suddenly, I do. I see what's been before our eyes the entire time, what I've been too blind to realise. This song started life as a smuggler ditty, and smugglers don't do anything without a reason. This song isn't just a pleasant tune. It's a map.

It's our map to the Valley.

'*The tree-lands*,' I whisper. 'That means the forest, doesn't it? And the line about the stream's hands – that's how Radnor knew to follow the river!'

Teddy's mouth splits into a grin. 'And it doesn't just say "the stream," it says to *bet* with the stream! Remember what I said when we first saw the Marbles? It looks like you could bet on a game of marbles out there . . .'

We all stare at each other, numb with hope and excitement. If we're right, if the whole song started as a smuggler's map to the Valley . . .

'*As star-shine's fair pistol shall gleam*,' says Maisy, pointing upwards. 'Do you think . . . do you think that's our next clue?'

I follow her gaze up to the right, where the Pistol constellation shines. Pointing our way forward through the night. And I know, suddenly, that she's right. This constellation is our map. The Pistol will guide us out of these fields. So long as we can see the stars, we will never be lost.

'There's another verse,' says Teddy. 'Do you reckon it tells where to go next?'

All at once, as though by prior arrangement, we recite the second verse of the song.

> *Oh frozen night,*
> *How the dark swallows light*
> *When the glasses of hours hold on*
> *I shan't waste my good life*
> *I must follow my knife*
> *To those deserts of green and beyond.*

There's a moment's pause as we all digest the words.

'What does that mean?' says Clementine.

I shake my head. 'I don't know. Maybe we've just got to follow the Pistol for now, and worry about the second verse once we've passed Gunning.'

'Hey, we don't need to worry about it,' says Teddy. 'I reckon Hackel knows what it means, doesn't he? He's a smuggler; he'd know the meaning of a smuggler song.'

Relief fills my belly like warm soup. He's right. We won't be lost forever. If we can just follow the Pistol towards Gunning, and meet up with Hackel . . .

'We're going to make it,' says Lukas. He gives me another quiet smile. And this time, I return it.

CHAPTER SEVENTEEN

GUNNING

IN THE MORNING, WE PAY CLOSE ATTENTION TO where the sun rises in relation to the fading Pistol constellation. Maisy stretches her arm to draw a line between the sun and our packs, figuring out the angles.

'Right, I've got it,' she says. 'I think I can find our way.'

I hate stepping back into the grass. I feel like a tiny ant, venturing blindly into an enormous carpet. But at least we're not so lost today. Maisy keeps an eye on the sun, using it to guide us forward. Even as it shifts across the sky, she seems able to adjust the angles in her head. I can't help wishing for a bit of her intelligence myself, since I find the grass completely disorientating. On city streets, I'm confident and savvy. Out here, I'm prey.

The day is cold, but also bright. Around noon, the sun is right above us, so I roll up my sleeves to absorb the warmth. It's one of those quiet winter days when the air seems somehow frozen and alight, all at once. My nose isn't stinging too badly, and even Maisy rips off her improvised gloves.

'Look!' says Lukas, pointing up.

I squint. All I see is the sun, blindingly aligned above our heads. Then I spot the movement: a lone hawk, rising against the sky. It reminds me of Lukas's kite, the way it dips and soars in the wind. 'Can you borrow its eyes?'

He nods. 'Yeah, I can. Is it all right if we stop for a minute?'

The others nod. Teddy seems to have a clear idea of what Lukas intends to do, because he jostles the rest of us out of the way. 'He'll need a clear line of sight. I've done this with rats a few times in Rourton, and it's trickier than it looks.'

'Rats?' says Clementine, looking disgusted. 'Why would you want to look through the eyes of a *rat*?'

Teddy grins. 'Hey, rats see more than you'd think. They're experts on breaking into richies' houses.'

Lukas stands stiff and tall, craning back his neck to survey the sky. He's clearly waiting for something, but I'm not sure what, because the hawk is still visible overhead. He must need a certain angle – perhaps a clear view of the creature's eyes – because he steeples his hands together and points them skyward, then peers along the resultant line.

His body jerks and his green eyes flash. He lets out a horrible cry. For a second I think it must be pain, then I realise it's the screech of a hawk. The entire thing might be comical if everyone didn't look so serious, and if Lukas's eyes weren't as empty as gutters. He opens his hands slowly, like unfolding butterfly wings, and stares into his palms.

'What's he looking at?' I whisper to Teddy.

'Using his palms as a screen, I reckon,' says Teddy. 'He can see what the hawk's seeing, reflected down onto his own skin.'

'You *reckon*? Why, what did you do differently?'

'Well, I use mirrors instead of my hands. They're a lot clearer.'

I glance at Lukas's hands. They look normal to me: just dirty skin and a few scratches from our journey. I certainly can't see what the hawk's seeing, anyway. But Lukas must have noticed something, because his mouth splits into a grin and he lets out another screech.

Teddy rolls his eyes. 'Amateur.'

'What do you mean?' I say.

'Hey, no need to get all defensive,' says Teddy. 'I just mean he should learn to control his noises. I would've been caught in seconds if I'd run around squeaking in the middle of burglaries.'

'I'm not defensive,' I say, irritated. 'Maybe it's harder to control yourself when you're seeing the world from up there . . . I bet it's much more exciting to look through a hawk's eyes than a rat's.'

'Unless the hawk *eats* the rat,' Teddy grins. 'Then you'd get an awesome firsthand look at a hawk's digestive system.'

Lukas's eyes flash again, before returning to their usual green. He looks a little dizzy, like some of the patrons I've seen on the late-night bar circuit, and he sways lightly on his feet.

'Whoa!' I catch his arm. 'Are you all right?'

He gives a woozy nod. 'Yeah, I'm just . . .' He shakes his head, as though trying to clear it. 'Sorry. Yeah, I'm fine.'

'What did you see?'

Lukas lowers his hands, glances between us, then glances back up towards the sky. 'I saw a town.'

'What?'

'I saw a town, Danika. On the side of a hill, less than a day away – if we hurry, we might get there tonight.' He smiles, letting his news sink in. 'We're going the right way.'

BY THE TIME WE APPROACH GUNNING'S HILLSIDE, THE grasslands have thinned out into cultivated fields. It's a relief to escape my claustrophobic response to the grass and to breathe some fresh air. I can even see the horizon now.

Unfortunately, this also makes our journey more dangerous. The fields are dotted with farmhouses, and we often see people in the distance. Once, we're almost spotted by a boy with his sheepdog; we throw ourselves into a muddy ditch to hide. Clementine scowls as we clamber back out, ten minutes after the boy has gone.

'Couldn't we just tell him we were here?' She swipes fistfuls of mud from her clothes. 'I would hardly think we're the first refugee crew he's seen; he might even have helped us!'

'Yeah, helped to turn us in,' says Teddy. 'Or have you forgotten the price on our heads? That kid was skinny as a richie's croquet mallet – do you really reckon he'd say no to a big sack of coins?'

'A price on *her* head,' mutters Clementine, throwing me a dirty look.

'If you still want me to leave the crew,' I say, 'then why don't you just say so?'

210

'I don't.' Clementine looks away. 'I don't want you to leave, all right? Not any more. I just wish . . .'

'Yeah, so do we all,' says Teddy. 'But I reckon we'll feel safer when we find Hackel again, right? I mean, you paid the bloke to get us halfway across Taladia.'

We stop near a dam to clean ourselves, scraping as much muck as possible from our clothing. It's important to look respectable; we won't survive long if we traipse into Gunning looking like a battered refugee crew.

'We can't take the foxary into town,' says Lukas. 'Everyone must know your crew rode foxaries out of Rourton. It'll be a dead giveaway.'

Teddy doesn't look happy. 'What are we supposed to do with him, then? We can't just let him loose – he'll kill someone if he's not restrained.'

'We should sell him,' says Clementine. 'Foxaries are too expensive to just throw away. If we sold him to a farmer, at least I'd get some of my money back.'

'I'll do it,' says Lukas. 'I doubt there's been coverage of my face in the papers, so the farmers wouldn't recognise me.'

Teddy shakes his head. 'How do I know you won't just run off and steal him for yourself?'

'He saved our lives, Teddy,' I say.

'So what? Maybe he just wanted to nick our foxary. That's what I would've done, anyway.'

'Yeah, but not everyone is a thieving pickpocket!'

I can feel myself getting worked up, which is ridiculous, because the most important thing for a crew is to trust one another. But I just want to get this stupid argument over with. The sooner Lukas can dispose of the foxary, the sooner we can get into Gunning and find Hackel.

There is a large farm nearby, with heavily bolted barns and machinery sheds. The walls are stone, not wood, and Teddy lets out a low whistle at the decorative bronze window frames. This is the farm of a richie landowner, not a starving peasant. If anyone around here were in the market for a foxary, it would be the owner of this place.

We position ourselves in a scraggly grove and unload our three remaining packs. Teddy insists he should accompany Lukas to sell the beast, promising to stay out of sight.

'Too dangerous to go without me, I reckon,' Teddy says. 'I'm the one keeping him under control.'

'You just aren't ready to say goodbye,' says Clementine.

Teddy laughs and gives the foxary a rub behind the ears. 'Yeah, maybe.'

I suspect that Teddy's real motive for accompanying Lukas to the sale is that he still doesn't trust him. This idea is oddly irritating, but I remain silent and try to avoid another argument.

'Bye, Borrash.' I give the animal a pat on the back. It emits a low grumble, like an alley cat purring, and I'm unexpectedly sorry to see it go.

Lukas and Teddy are gone for almost an hour. By the time they return, I'm pacing in circles and Maisy looks ready to gnaw a branch off a nearby tree.

'What took so long?' says Clementine.

'Wasn't our fault – that old geezer drove a hard bargain.' Teddy slaps a handful of coins into Clementine's hands. 'Here you go.'

Clementine scowls as she counts the money. 'I paid three times this much!'

'Yeah, but I reckon it's easier to overcharge a spoiled richie than a farmer,' says Teddy. 'Anyway, that bloke knew he could bargain down; there's no one else around here who'd pay more.'

By the time we reach Gunning's outskirts, it's twilight. We are exhausted and filthy, worn ragged from another day of traipsing through the wilderness, but at least there's been no sign of hunters.

Despite the fading light, we have a decent view of the surrounding farmland. A dirt road leads from

Gunning to the west. In the distance, I can just see the point where it meets a larger road: a wide grey snake under the evening sky.

'Is that . . .?'

Teddy nods. 'Must be the main trade route. Blimey, good thing we didn't come that way.'

We all nod, silent. The trade road runs towards the northern horizon, cobbled with enough stone to build a hundred city walls. But despite its size – or perhaps because of it – the route is painfully exposed. I can imagine hunters scouring its surface, or biplanes soaring overhead. Nowhere to run. Nowhere to hide. On a road like that, we'd be as helpless as crickets in a cooking pot.

Clementine lets out a slow breath. 'I suppose Hackel was right. The smugglers' route might be harder, but it's safer.'

We stare at the road for a moment longer, before turning our attention back to Gunning itself. The town spills down the hill's southern slope, pouring its streets like treacle. There's a train station on the southern outskirts of town, with a couple of carriages visible beyond the platform. The line itself looks as if it's coated with silver, gleaming beneath the moon. The train must be partially fuelled by alchemy.

'That looks like the end of the train line,' says

Maisy. 'They've extended the line since my encyclo-pedias were published; I didn't think it came this far north. I thought it was impossible to run a train over the mountains.'

'Apparently not,' Teddy says.

I eye the train line appraisingly. The horizon sinks into dusk behind it, but I can still make out the Central Mountains: an alpine belt across the country, dividing the north from the south.

Unlike the Eastern Boundary Range, it's possible to cross these mountains if you're willing to put your life on the line. Back in Rourton, a shortage of oranges in the market usually meant a snow-storm had buried the mountain road – and in all likelihood, a convoy of fruit traders with it. There was even a jump-rope rhyme about it: *'Frost and ice and traders slow: orange juice beneath the snow.'*

Standing here, the tune seems a lot less witty and a lot more morbid.

I notice that the others aren't watching the moun-tains. Their gazes are locked on the train line, with its station at Gunning's southern gate. It isn't hard to guess what they're thinking: if we could sneak aboard a train somehow . . . maybe even hide inside a cargo carriage . . .

'Maybe that's Hackel's plan,' says Clementine. 'That's probably why he wanted to meet us in

Gunning, of all places. We can hitch a ride south on the train.'

I want to believe that she's right. It makes sense, doesn't it? This must have been the real plan all along. We were to follow the river to Gunning, then bribe our way onto a train. It's the route of a savvy smuggler, if ever there was one, and a far cry from the usual refugee plan of pretending to be honest traders on the road.

And above all, it's a lot less likely to end with us under the snow.

*

GUNNING HAS A CITY WALL, BUT THE GATE ISN'T manned. Actually, there's no sign of guards at all – and that worries me more than if there'd been a fifty-man platoon to greet us. I know how to handle myself with Rourton's guards, but an unguarded city is a foreign experience.

'Looks like security's a bit slack.'

Teddy grins. 'I like this place already.'

'It's a smuggling town, isn't it?' says Clementine, as we pass through the gate. 'That's what Radnor –'

Her voice hitches on the name.

A long moment passes. She takes a quiet breath and tries again. 'That's what Radnor said. People come here to do deals, and make money. Maybe the palace turns a blind eye to this area a bit, since it's not a major security risk.'

'Yeah,' I say. 'Because it's much more important to drop alchemy bombs on Rourton than to keep a lid on a town full of criminals.'

'Well, people here aren't a threat, are they?' says Teddy. 'They're happy making money their own way, and the current system suits them just fine. I reckon it's the normal people, in places like Rourton, that are dangerous to the king.'

'Why?'

'Because they're the ones desperate enough to do something stupid.'

'Like what, run away with a refugee crew?' says Clementine.

'Yeah, exactly,' Teddy says. 'Or start a revolution.'

A revolution? I try to picture my parents or my brother rising up against the palace. I can't see it. They were no threat to King Morrigan – they were just in the wrong place at the wrong time. Collateral damage in the palace's fight to remind us who has control. And suddenly I *hate* the royal family, with loathing stronger than I've felt in years.

When you're struggling for survival, it's easy to forget who put you there. I've focused on filling my belly, not wasting my energy on fury. But just for a moment, I feel like I did in the early days. I think of the bombs falling, my family dying. I think of star-shine blooming above the rubble. Of scruffers starving in the streets, and soldiers dying in distant wars.

Of Radnor's body slipping over that waterfall.

And suddenly I wish someone would drop an alchemy bomb on the royals' palace, and teach the stinking Morrigans what it feels like to lose someone.

'Look!' whispers Maisy. 'Danika, it's you!'

I follow her gaze. Sure enough, a dozen posters hang from a nearby wall: *'Wanted Fugitive.'* There is a picture of me in the centre of the design: a still taken from the wall's picture spell recording. I'm crouched in the turret of a guard tower, lighting the fuse of my stolen flare.

Or, in the eyes of the palace, preparing to take a biplane out of the sky.

I sidle closer and strain to read the smaller text beneath my picture.

On behalf of His Majesty, King Francis Morrigan of Taladia, we announce the offering of a reward of ONE THOUSAND GOLD COINS for the capture or SEVEN HUNDRED GOLD COINS for the killing of this fugitive. Sources upon the

streets of Rourton confirm the fugitive's identity as
DANIKA GLYNN of NO FIXED ADDRESS.

   This fugitive is wanted for the MURDER of a
brave and innocent airman who fought on behalf
of King and Country to make Taladia a safer
place to live.

'Yeah, a safer place to get bombed,' says Teddy.

I smile, but really I feel sick. Just how much
trouble I'm in is hitting home now. Even my old
acquaintances in Rourton have sold me out; no
doubt old Walter from the Alehouse would have
accepted a princely sum for revealing my name.
I have no one to truly trust, and I can never go back
to Rourton. Nowhere in Taladia is safe for me now.
I must reach the Valley, or I will die.

We move along the wall of posters, glancing at
other criminals' names. Soon I find the rest of my
crew: Teddy Nort (*'a dastardly pickpocket and well-
known thief'*), Clementine and Maisy Pembroke
(*'daughters of a prominent businessman, led astray by
the cruel wiles of criminals'*) and finally Radnor. They
haven't dug up much information about Radnor.
He's just *'a boy of No Fixed Address'*. Even so, the
picture of him fleeing Rourton is enough to make
my stomach clench. He looks so young. So alive.
Dark hair, dark eyes. His expression wild, his mouth

open in a cry. What is he saying? Is he calling the others onward, urging them through the gate into the wilderness beyond?

The wilderness that would claim him?

The others' posters are much less prominent than mine, and their rewards are only a hundred gold coins apiece. Teddy looks a little insulted.

'I'm the real criminal here,' he protests. 'I reckon I'm worth eight hundred at least.' He pauses. 'Nine, if they knew about the mayor's diamond ring.'

Clementine gasps. 'That was you?'

'Of course it was,' says Teddy. 'Who else in Rourton could pull off a heist like that?' He brightens. 'But hey, at least they reckon I've got *cruel wiles*, right?'

'I wonder why your rewards aren't more,' I say, glancing between the posters. 'They know we're travelling together.'

'The rest of us are just a refugee crew,' says Maisy. 'There are so many refugees on the run; the palace can't afford to set a precedent by offering huge rewards for us.'

'You're a murderous plane shooter, Danika,' says Clementine, as if I need reminding. 'Of course they have to offer a more serious reward for you.'

A night wind trips along the street, and we all shiver. It ruffles the posters a little, and my own face flutters in the shadows. For a moment I consider hiding: sneaking back out through the city gates, leaving the others to find Hackel. But what if my crewmates don't return? What if they decide I'm a liability and this is their chance to ditch me? Or what if they're caught, or killed, and I'm left crouching in some farmer's field with no idea they're even in danger? The hours ticking away, my fingers turning numb, tension tightening around my spine until –

No. I can't let them out of my sight.

'Now can we find somewhere to sleep?' Clementine says. 'We shouldn't hang around these posters, anyway.'

'Good point,' I say.

There is silence as we all wait for someone else to decide our next move. It still feels strange to travel without Radnor, who always had instructions ready on his lips. I clench my eyes shut for a moment, fighting to clear away the image of his face. This isn't the time to be distracted.

'Where are we supposed to meet Hackel?' says Lukas.

'Radnor said to meet him at the market, didn't he?' Clementine says. 'At twelve, I think.'

'Twelve noon or twelve midnight?' I say.

'Either, I guess.'

'But what about curfew?'

Clementine glances around. 'Maybe they don't have one here. It doesn't seem like people are in a hurry to get home.'

She's right. It doesn't take much ear-straining to hear the thrum of movement around the city: voices in the streets, a distant whirl of music. If there's a curfew here, the locals are in no hurry to obey it.

'Come to think of it,' Teddy says, 'I reckon Rourton's only had its curfew for a couple of decades. My grandpa was always banging on about life in the old days, when the markets ran all night.'

'It was the conscription riots,' Maisy says quietly. 'When King Morrigan inherited the throne and brought in army conscription, people rioted all night in Rourton. That's when they brought in the curfew.'

'But not in Gunning?' Teddy straightens up, a devious glint in his eye. 'I reckon I could get used to this place.'

We head off cautiously through the town, sticking to shadows and alleyways. I feel almost at home as we stalk behind rubbish bins and sneak across people's yards. This is where I belong: urban streets, with solid stone beneath my boots.

It doesn't take long to find the market. My ears pick up its location before my eyes do. There's a clamour of voices, a sizzle of frying oil and the buzz of music through someone's radio. They've turned the volume up too loud – perhaps to attract customers to their stall – and the singer's wails are so distorted that her love song sounds like a goat being slaughtered. There's a smell, too: the whiff of hot food and smoke.

'Onions!' Teddy pats his stomach. 'Fried onions and garlic . . . and mashed potatoes! Can you smell it, Maisy?'

Maisy looks startled to be addressed specifically, but she gives a shy little nod. I'm still not sure what to make of her. When it comes to book smarts, she's happy to share her knowledge, but other forms of social interaction just leave her silent. Maybe she's used to being overshadowed by her twin. It's not as if Clementine is afraid to speak her mind.

We turn a corner and step into the world of Gunning's night market. It seems to writhe with colour and movement – stallholders shout out specials for hot food, drunks stagger around getting sloshed on cheap beer and everything is illuminated by alchemical streetlights.

A clunky old radio sits in the centre of the marketplace, cranking out music for the drunkards to dance to. As they stagger in circles – occasionally tripping over an unconscious friend – I can't help remembering my own family's radio dances. Those cold winter nights, when I dressed in my best clothes and paraded around the apartment like a princess . . .

Teddy looks around, grinning. 'Seriously, this place is brilliant. Imagine how easy it'd be to nick that bloke's wallet.' He points at a nervous-looking richie near one of the stalls, who's trying to buy a potato cake with a whole gold coin.

'What an idiot,' says Teddy, as the man fumbles for smaller change. 'I'll bet you twenty silvers he's been fleeced by midnight.'

'You haven't got twenty silvers,' I remind him.

Teddy flexes his fingers. 'Not yet.'

I grab his arm. 'We're in enough trouble without you nicking people's wallets. We shouldn't draw any more attention to ourselves.'

'All right, all right.' Teddy scowls. 'But it'd be so easy . . .'

'I've got money,' says Clementine. 'So don't you dare steal anything.'

We rummage through the packs until Clementine locates her emergency funds, wrapped up in one of her sparkly blouses.

'I hid some money in all of the packs, just in case we lost one,' she explains, and I actually feel a little impressed. It's more logic than I'd expect from a girl who brings sequinned clothing on a refugee trek.

224

Lukas hurries off to buy us some food. I watch as hawkers swarm to sell him trinkets, shouting and shoving wares into his hands. One hooded man is so insistent that Lukas's thumb is left bleeding from the thrust of an ornamental penknife.

'No, no – I don't want it!' he says.

The merchant lets out a string of curses, and slinks away into the crowd. I throw an anxious look at the twins, but they shake their heads. We can't risk venturing out from the shadows – not with those wanted posters across the city.

Lukas returns with a paper bag of greasy chips, and a carton of baked apples with cinnamon and honey. I examine his wounded thumb in concern, but luckily the cut is shallow.

'It's nothing,' he assures me. 'Just a bit hectic out there.' He turns to face the rest of the crew. 'There's a richie party going on at the town's main hotel. All the stallholders are talking about it.'

'What are a bunch of richies doing in a town like this?'

'Gambling, mostly, I think. It looks like Gunning's become a popular "relaxation" town since they've extended the train line.'

'You mean they're travelling here for *enjoyment*?' I frown. 'Back home, we weren't allowed to travel without a trading licence. Not even richies.'

Lukas shrugs. 'The rules vary between cities, I think. Depends how much trouble you've caused the king.'

Trouble? My frown deepens. I've never thought of Rourton as particularly rebellious. But then I remember the whispers of late: unhappy gossip about King Morrigan's wars. I think of Maisy's revelation about our conscription riots, and the introduction of the curfew . . .

'It would have been nice to have night parties back home,' Clementine says. 'A chance to get out of the house.'

Teddy grins. 'Imagine all those drunk richies wobbling around the streets, coin purses hanging out of their pockets . . .'

Clementine gives him a pointed look.

'What?' Teddy says. 'I reckon I'd be doing them a favour – stop them getting any drunker. I mean, it's practically a public service.'

'Of course. A thief with a heart of gold.'

'And silver,' Teddy says. 'And copper too, if they've got it in their purses.'

My stomach is rumbling at the scent of the food, and it takes all my willpower to keep from scoffing the lot as we move into a nearby alley for our picnic. But we restrain ourselves until we've found a suitable hiding place: a patch of shadows, shielded from view by a pile of broken bricks.

As soon as we're settled, we dig with desperate fingers into the bag. It's been far too long since our last decent meal. The chips are hot and salty on my tongue, and the apples are even better: crunchy skin, gooey flesh, and dripping with honey. I lick my fingers over and over, trying to suck every last skerrick of sweetness from my share.

As we eat, we keep an eye on the square. There's no sign of Hackel: just drunks and merchants and furtive-looking smugglers making trades. At one point, a couple of figures duck into our alleyway to make a deal. We hold our breath and hope they don't smell our food, but they're too busy swapping trinkets to pay attention to the shadows behind them. When I spot a glint of silver in their fingers, I wonder whether it's an alchemy charm that they're trading.

Soon we start to relax a little, placated by the relief of filling our bellies. People in Gunning are too wrapped up in their own dodgy trades to worry about anyone else's business. Teddy starts to joke about burgling the stallholders for another bag of chips, and I actually find myself smiling. We feel safe in this alleyway, in this town of criminals.

There's been no sign of hunters, no sign of guards, and we've avoided raising anyone's suspicions. The only peril we've faced is an enthusiastic merchant.

Then a figure steps out of the darkness. A match flares. And Hackel points his fiery fingers straight towards my head.

CHAPTER EIGHTEEN

CAPTURED

CLEMENTINE SHRIEKS, THEN CLAPS A HAND ACROSS her mouth. Everyone else tenses around me – the air shifts as their muscles freeze. The casual atmosphere of our meal has been blasted away, obliterated by a threat as sudden as an alchemy bomb.

Hackel presses his match to a candlewick. As soon as the candle flares into life, he tosses the match aside and points his finger back at my face.

Lukas makes to move towards me. 'What are you doing?'

'Stay there!' snaps Hackel. 'Stay there or I'll blast her. The reward is for capture or killing; I'll still get seven hundred for her body.'

'You're supposed to be our guide!' says Clementine. 'We paid you all our savings, we did what you told us to do – you can't just sell us to the authorities.'

'Why not? This way I get paid by both sides.' Hackel grins. 'Nothing personal, ladies. Just a business transaction, that's all.'

'You thieving scumbag –'

'You're the one travelling with a thief,' says Hackel, nodding towards Teddy. 'I wouldn't get all high and mighty if I were you, Pembroke. We're all criminals here. If you deal with smugglers, you can't go running to the law.' He gestures for me to stand. 'Come on, Glynn.'

I don't want to obey, but there isn't much choice – not when he's holding a candle. It would only take him a second to redirect that flame into my face, and I'd burn as readily as the hunter he torched in the forest. So I clamber to my feet and silently order my hands to stop shaking. I won't let this traitor see that I'm afraid.

'You're not taking her!' says Lukas, rising beside me. 'You treacherous –'

Hackel laughs. It's a horrible, hacking sound that cuts off Lukas mid-sentence. '*I'm* treacherous? Oh, and I suppose you've told your little friends here who you are, Lukas?'

I freeze, caught between fear and confusion. What is he talking about? And how does he even know Lukas's name?

Lukas stiffens. 'I don't know what –'

Hackel brandishes a fistful of silver. Alchemy charms, pilfered from his victim's corpse in the forest. He flicks his fingers to show one particular charm: a swirl in the shape of a blood drop.

'Bloodline charm,' he says. 'Very rare, this one.'

His fingers close back around the charm. With a jolt, I remember the hooded merchant in the market, and his thrust of the penknife into Lukas's hand. Not to *sell* it to Lukas, but to harvest a drop of his blood.

The candle flickers.

'When I spotted a stranger with my runaways, I decided to satisfy my curiosity. But I must say, I wasn't expecting *this*.' Hackel's lips curl into a smile. 'I've got no quarrel with you, Lukas. If you want to buy my silence, you know the price. Just give me Danika Glynn, and I'll –'

Maisy emits a sudden hiss and Hackel's candle goes out.

The alley plunges into darkness. At first, I don't know what's happened. There's a mad jumble, confusion, bodies colliding in the shadows and a couple of muffled shrieks. My foot comes down on

231

the greasy chip packet and I slip, falling sideways into the group. Why did the candle go out? What happened? How did Maisy –

Then it hits me. Maisy knows her proclivity. She must have known it for some time: long enough to gain control, to figure out how to use it. And it isn't a little mouse, or a flower, or rain. It's Flame. Maisy's proclivity is *Flame*. Of all the people to have such a ferocious power . . .

My eyes adjust and suddenly there's no more time to worry about Maisy. Hackel's arms are gripping Clementine's throat, and she squeaks as her air supply is cut off. Hackel might not have a flame at his disposal any more, but he doesn't need it. Not when a single crank of his arms could snap our crewmate's neck.

'Let her go!' I start forward, but Hackel tightens his grip. Clementine releases a little choke and I freeze. If I take another step, she will die. I can see that much in Hackel's eyes. And there isn't much I can do – not without a weapon. I've got my climbing picks from the Rourton city wall, but they're wrapped up securely in my jacket's inner lining. If I even try to reach for them . . .

Hackel keeps one hand wrapped around Clementine's throat, but raises the other above her shoulder. Then he swivels towards the marketplace, and that horrible smile cracks back across his face.

He snaps his fingers.

There's a shout from the market, and we all spin around. Fire leaps up between the stalls, and I know instantly that something is very wrong. This is not the spark of a cooking fire – it's the roar of bursting flame. People are screaming, the music of the radio cuts off, and fragments of stalls burst sideways as though a bomb has exploded.

'What's going on?' I gasp.

Hackel laughs. 'People shouldn't store so much alcohol near their cooking fires.'

'*You* did this? Why?'

He shrugs. 'I like a bit of chaos. Gives me a better chance to smuggle you out of here, Glynn, without anyone trying to steal my prize.'

Maisy is clenching her fists, clearly trying to snuff out the fire, but nothing much happens. A cry of frustration escapes her lips, and Hackel laughs.

'You haven't had your proclivity long, have you, Pembroke?' he says. 'Well, I have. I'm a much more experienced friend of the flames than you are, and they'll listen to me before a little pipsqueak like you.'

He tightens his grip around Clementine's neck and she makes a horrible noise. I don't know if she can't breathe or if it's just the sound of terror.

'Let her go!' I say. 'I'll come with you, all right, just . . .'

233

'You swear?' Hackel tightens his grip again.

'Yes, all right! I swear.'

'Good,' says Hackel, glancing around the rest of my crew. 'Because that fire is under my control, and right now it's contained to the market. But if anyone tries to stop us, the fire is going to explode and a lot of people are going to burn. Got it?'

The others nod, looking pale.

Hackel slams Clementine back into the wall and grabs me, dragging me out towards the end of the alley. I twist back to see a couple of the others about to follow, but I shake my head. 'No, don't!'

A small, selfish part of me wishes that they won't listen – that they'll intervene and save me. But what would that achieve? Hackel could burn them all. No, it's better that they let him take me. Perhaps I can break away later, before he hands me over to the hunters . . .

Lukas runs towards us, raising a fistful of silver charms. 'Let her go, you smuggler scum, or I'll –'

'You'll what? Set your father's army on me?'

I twist aside, trying to catch Lukas's eyes. But he looks away from me and flinches when I ask, 'Lukas, what's he talking about?'

'Nothing, Danika. He's a liar. Don't listen to him!'

'Interesting you should say that,' says Hackel. 'I was always taught it takes a liar to know one.'

'You can't –'

'Oh yes,' Hackel grins. 'I can.' He turns back to me with a glint in his eyes. 'I'd like to introduce you to Prince Lukas Morrigan, son of the king.'

My heart stops.

Hackel pauses, letting this sink in, before he adds, 'And he was the pride of the royal air force, I believe, until your flare shot his biplane out of the sky.'

CHAPTER NINETEEN

AFLAME

SHOCK. THERE'S NO OTHER WORD FOR IT. I CAN'T think, can't feel. Everything is numb and cold, even among the smoke from Hackel's fire. Lukas is a prince. Lukas is a *prince*. Everything he has told me is a lie. He is a Morrigan, a member of the family who killed my parents. Who killed my brother.

And he is the pilot of a bombing plane.

'You –' I choke out, but there's suddenly a crash of heat and fire from the square.

I fall to the ground, knocked down by a *whump!* of energy. It's like being whacked by a sledge-hammer; everything throbs as my body crashes onto the stone below. Hackel has clearly lost control of the market fire. It erupts in a tumult of alcohol and cooking fuel, too wild and engorged for his proclivity to govern.

Hackel grabs for me, but a figure looms out of the shadows and smashes a chunk of broken brick into his head. Hackel falls, spurting blood from his forehead, and his skull makes a nasty cracking sound upon the street. His eyes do not reopen.

'Come on!' says Teddy, throwing aside his brick, and I barely register what's happening before he drags me to my feet. Clementine and Maisy join us and we run. We pelt towards the square, towards the fire, leaving Hackel's body behind. The fire is spreading now – leaping between barrels of alcohol, shooting up like firecrackers – and I whip my head around, frantic. 'Where's Lukas?'

Teddy shakes his head. 'Who cares? He's a *royal*, Danika!'

And I know it's true, but I can't help taking one last glance around for the boy with the bright green eyes. He's gone. He has fled into the smoke, disappeared forever. Now that his lie has been exposed, Lukas can't face us. He must be too afraid, too cowardly to face up to our fury. My fury.

A horrible snarl escapes my throat. I've never felt so furious, so betrayed. If I got my hands on Lukas Morrigan right now I might attack him. But there's no chance of that, in the smoke and flames of Gunning's burning marketplace. So I flee with the others and join the throng that heads downhill towards the outskirts of town.

People pour out of buildings, screaming and hauling their children. One old man drags a keg of wine behind him, and I want to stop and shout at him that alcohol is flammable. But he's lost in the crowd, just another panicked face in the night.

Some people run towards the market, thrusting out their hands. They must be people with Flame proclivities, running off to control the fire. I feel a moment of admiration for their courage, but there isn't much I can do to help. I don't even know what my proclivity is yet, so I'm about as useful as the knee-high children that scurry through the crowd.

'What do we do?' says Clementine, her face concealed by a mass of sweaty blonde hair.

Teddy hesitates. 'We blend in. We pretend we're just normal travellers, caught up in this mess. No one will pay us much attention now, not with this going on.'

Soon our faces are covered with soot. The crowd surges down the major streets of Gunning until we reach the southern wall. But people don't pass through the gate; instead, they simply mill around in terror. I notice a group of richies about twenty metres away, dressed in shining party clothes.

Some look furious, others terrified, but they don't seem to be talking to each other much. It's like they're strangers, brought together for the sake of a party . . . They must be the richies that Lukas mentioned, the tourists holding a gambling event in the Gunning hotel.

Then I see the reason for the holdup. Guards.

This is the first time I've seen guards in Gunning; they must have spent their evening in the bar or something, because they sure weren't guarding the town earlier. Now they're checking people as they pass through the gates. They seem to be letting the rich partygoers through, and occasionally a family of locals that they obviously recognise, but no one else. Anyone suspicious is pushed back into the crowd and imprisoned within Gunning's walls.

The guards are weeding out suspects, I realise. That fire was too strong for a mere accident. By the time it's extinguished, the locals will want someone to blame. If we're trapped inside this town, looking like strange travellers, we will be questioned. No doubt about it. And when the guards see my face . . .

'The clothes!' I say. 'Come on, I've got an idea.'

We hurry down a nearby alleyway, beyond the view of the panicking masses. I rifle through our packs, searching for the bag of Clementine's sparkly evening clothes.

'What are you after?' says Teddy.

'Remember what Lukas said? There were a bunch of richies having a party in the hotel tonight – I think that's them over there! If we dress in some nicer clothes, maybe we can pretend we're in their group.'

'What's the point in that?'

I pull out a glittery purple headpiece. 'Well, for a start, they won't expect a biplane shooter to show up wearing this.'

'Or a refugee crew to be dressed in silk blouses,' adds Clementine, plunging into the bag with sudden enthusiasm.

'Hate to break it to you,' Teddy says, 'but I don't reckon I could pull off a ball gown.'

'Here,' says Clementine. She thrusts a bundle of fabric into Teddy's arms. 'This should be all right for a boy.'

It's a light trench coat, and the only sign of glitter is a turtle-shaped brooch on the collar. Teddy unpins it, buttons the coat over his chest and offers a cocky grin. He could do with a tie and a neater haircut, but in the middle of this chaos he *might* just pass for a flustered richie.

I slip into a long satin skirt covered with ruffles and bows. Its only saving grace is that it puffs over my trousers, saving me from the need to undress entirely. Clementine selects a silky violet dress and Maisy locates a jade-coloured blazer. The green shine reminds me suddenly of Lukas's eyes, and betrayal hits me again like a slap.

'I'll go in front,' says Teddy.

'Why?'

He grins. 'I'm pretty good at bluffing.'

There's no use arguing with that. We follow him closely, clutching each other's sleeves to keep from being separated in the crowd. I'm worried that our packs might give us away – why would a bunch of richies carry travellers' packs away from a party? But other people have saved stranger possessions from the flames – patchwork quilts, a child's rocking horse and even a double bass – so our packs seem relatively normal in the throng.

The crowd surges and we're shoved forward, crushed in a sea of bodies and shrieks. Everything tastes of smoke and sweat, and soon my face is squashed into a local woman's massive head of curls. I spit a few strands of hair from my lips and try not to inhale the stink of urine as I trip against a little boy. He's trying to cover a wet patch on his pyjamas and I can't help feeling sorry for him; he must have been startled out of bed by the fire. Children are screaming in all directions, their wails distorted eerily through the smoke.

The air gets hotter and thicker as we approach the gate. Guards bearing rifles block most of the gate and the crowd is being squeezed through like toothpaste from a tube. We're only a few metres away from freedom, then even closer, and finally we're face to face with the guards themselves.

'Hey, fellas,' says Teddy, with an artfully performed drunken grin. 'Talk about a party, eh?'

The guards exchange glances.

'We're together,' Teddy adds, gesturing at me and the twins. 'We were at the hotel – this town has really good beer, you know . . .'

The nearest guard raises an eyebrow at my sparkly headpiece. I duck my head a little, pretending to be in tears from shock – or maybe just intoxication – when really I'm hoping he won't recognise my face.

'All right, hurry up,' he says, and waves us on.

As we pass through the gates, the crowd surges again and a funnel of bodies spits us out into the night. The hillside is covered with people – richies, locals, crying children – but I keep a firm grip on Maisy's shoulder. The last thing we need is to lose each other.

'What now?' whispers Clementine.

I shake my head. There's no hope of running off into the fields – not yet, anyway. There are guards on a turret above the wall now; they're keeping their rifles trained on the crowd. The situation grows more chaotic by the minute. The real richies remind me of rats in an alleyway, squeaking their heads off as they scurry through the dark. Then I feel guilty for making the comparison, because rats are actually quite smart. They'd be better at surviving than this lot, anyway.

'They can't keep us here forever,' Teddy points out. 'Once the fire's out, I reckon they'll let us go.'

'Go where, though?' Clementine says. 'We were relying on Hackel to guide us . . . what are we supposed to do now?'

She's right. Even if we escape this crowd, we're in serious trouble. We've got no food, no plan, no guide. We don't even have a map, apart from the cryptic second verse of the star-shine song.

There's a blast of steam from the hillside below. It's followed by a sharp whistle, so loud that several nearby richies scream.

'The train!' I say.

The others' eyes widen, but Clementine shakes her head. 'The guards won't let anyone leave Gunning, will they?'

But as we watch, richie partygoers push towards the train. They brandish fistfuls of coins, shouting over each other to purchase tickets. The guards don't move to stop them; clearly, these people aren't suspects in the fire. They're just stupid drunks, here for the booze and the gambling, and the guards won't bother to stop them from fleeing town. If anything, getting rid of these richies will make their investigation easier. Tomorrow morning they can rough up the town's scruffers – and probably shoot a few scapegoats – without any hungover tourists getting in the way.

'Come on!' Clementine says, but the rest of us don't need telling. We're already pushing into the surge, baying for tickets like the rest of the crowd. From here, I can make out the train's name, painted in gleaming gold upon her side: *Bird of the North*.

A railway employee is selling tickets from a basket, grinning like he's won the lottery. No wonder he's happy; in all this confusion, he'll probably pocket half the proceeds. His bosses won't have a clue how many richies piled aboard their train.

Clementine squeezes through the shouting masses just long enough to purchase four tickets. Then she's back by our sides, clutching the tickets in sweaty palms as though they're made of gold. To us, of course, they're worth even more. Those little scraps of paper might save our lives.

We make it to the platform and stumble inside a carriage. The walls are lined with dark velvet, ready to appeal to richie passengers. There are

244

small compartments along the corridor, obviously designed for couples, but we all squeeze into one of them and slam the door. There are so many passengers crammed onto this train that our choice to share a compartment should look reasonable rather than suspicious.

It's lucky we're all so thin after our days of hunger, because otherwise we'd have trouble fitting inside. Teddy takes one seat, Clementine and Maisy squish onto the other, and I'm left to perch atop our packs in the middle. Soon there's another whistle and the thud of slamming doors.

Then we're off, blasting with a jolt into the night.

CHAPTER TWENTY

BIRD OF THE NORTH

'LUCKY THEY EXTENDED THE TRAIN LINE TO GUNNING,' I say.

None of the others respond. The shock is wearing off now, fading into sheer exhaustion. But if I let myself succumb, if I give into the silence, there will be no distraction from what happened tonight. I will have to face up to it – all of it. The wanted posters, Hackel's betrayal, the fire . . . and Lukas Morrigan, son of the king.

For all I know, Lukas could be dead by now. Maybe he burned in the fire. Wasn't that what I wanted, for all the Morrigans to burn like my family? But all I can see is his green eyes, his smile, the calculated betrayal as he pulls his kite down from the stars.

It makes an awful kind of sense now. Why Lukas appeared in the forest, only a day's travel from the crashed biplane. Why the plane's captain was missing from the wreck. Why he carried so many priceless alchemic objects, why he knew so much about Sharr Morrigan, who must be his *cousin* . . . The thought makes me feel nauseated, so I pummel my forehead with my knuckles and try to restart the conversation.

'I wonder why they extended the train line,' I say. 'Maisy, didn't you say this part of the line didn't exist when your encyclopedia was printed?'

Maisy nods. 'And the book's only a few years old. They must have extended the line very recently.'

'I thought most of the tax funds were being spent on the war effort . . . you wouldn't have thought they'd waste all that cash on a train line to Gunning, of all places.'

'I reckon the bureaucrats were just keen for a party at the Gunning Hotel,' says Teddy. 'Wouldn't put it past 'em.'

'It's strange,' says Maisy. 'The railway never came this far north because it was too hard to cross the mountains. They tried tunnelling through, decades ago, but the earth was too unstable. And they can't just run a track over the mountaintops – not with the height of those peaks, and the risk of snowfall and falling trees . . .' She frowns. 'I wonder how they've done it.'

'And *why* they've done it,' I add.

We fall into silence, staring out the compartment window. It's dark outside, so mostly we just see our own reflections, but occasionally a farmhouse or village will provide enough light to pierce the glass.

Maisy's question is answered after several hours of travel, when we reach the top of a craggy hill. The country around here is ridiculously uneven – it's obvious from the train's movements that we're heading towards the mountains. Just as we're cresting the top of the hill, there's a violent jolt in our carriage.

I jerk upright, startled out of my misery. The others are suddenly alert and wide-eyed. Their knuckles whiten on the edges of their seats. There's another jerk, then a whistle. Something yanks from above, as though the train is a fish on a hook.

'What's going on?'

'I don't know!'

The carriage *lifts*. Machinery grinds, the whistle blasts, and then our carriage clunks up to meet the sky. I stagger upright and heave our window open. A blast of freezing air floods the compartment, but I stick my head outside.

A vast concrete pylon sprouts from the top of the hill, illuminated by the train's headlight. Dozens more punctuate the route ahead, painting a line of pylons up into the encroaching mountains. They are joined by a thick network of stone and cables, arranged like an upside-down lacework. The cables spark with silver and alchemy. Our train has been jerked up away from the ground and now we dangle from the cables, ready to be winched towards the mountains.

It's ingenious, really: a perfect shortcut across the mountains that divide Northern Taladia from the south. King Morrigan couldn't drill through the mountains, or run a normal train line over its peaks. But this solution – a suspended train, winched between pylons – is enough to take my breath away. I can't begin to grasp the amount of silver, or alchemic enchantments, that went into crafting this sky-bound railroad. The train's name makes sense now: *Bird of the North*. A train that almost seems to fly between our nation's divided halves.

I duck back inside and slam the window. It's too late to keep the cold out, though. The others rub their hands together and shiver as I report my findings.

'It's like a chairlift,' Maisy breathes. 'I read about them in a history book – they used to build them in the ancient western cities. But a chairlift large enough to carry a whole train . . .' She shakes her head. 'Imagine the level of alchemy involved.'

'Imagine how much it must have cost,' says Clementine, looking impressed.

'Yeah,' mutters Teddy. 'Bet you could feed Rourton's scruffer kids for years with that much cash.'

I stare at the black window, and my reflection stares back. The train is tilting upward now, into the mountains. Outside we must be passing pylons, climbing that network of cables through the dark. If I ever needed proof of King Morrigan's resources . . .

But why? The king doesn't need to impress anyone – let alone a pack of richie partygoers. There must have been some urgent need, some hidden reason to build this route across the mountains.

'Why?' I say aloud. 'Why bother to build it now, and why to a useless town like Gunning?'

There is no response. We settle back into our spots and wait for the night to pass.

✱

WHEN MORNING COMES, I AWAKE TO SUNLIGHT through the compartment window. I must have dozed off because my eyes are bleary, and I can't remember the last few hours passing.

Teddy and Clementine are still ~~asleep, b~~ the
smiles at me when I open my eyes.

'Are you all right, Danika?' she wh~~is~~

I nod. 'You?'

'Yes, I'm okay. I was just looking ~~out at the~~
mountains.'

I twist around to stare out the window. N~~ow that~~
it's light outside, I can actually see the land~~scape~~
passing by. We are high above a valley, in the m~~iddle~~
of the Central Mountains. Below our carriag~~e,~~
everything falls away into a white fog. I don't want
to imagine how cold it must be outside. I can see
the very top of each pylon as it passes – but below,
all is mist.

'I wonder if this is how birds feel,' I say, pressing
my fingers against the glass.

I find myself wanting to turn to Lukas, to ask
him if this is what he sees when he borrows the eyes
of an eagle. Then I remember, with a surge of fresh
pain, why he is not here. He doesn't need to borrow
a bird's eyes to fly through clouds. He's done it
himself, in a palace biplane full of bombs.

'Are you . . .?' Maisy begins, a little hesitant. She
wrings her fingers together nervously, then starts
again. 'Are you worried about Lukas?'

'Why would I worry about *him*?' I realise
from Maisy's expression that I'm at risk of waking

others, so I force myself to lower my voice
ore I continue. 'I mean, he's a traitor. He's a
yal. He dropped bombs on Rourton, just like the
est of those filthy pilots.'

'No, he didn't,' Maisy says.

'Of course he did!'

Maisy shakes her head. 'When we found his
plane in the forest, all of the bombs were still intact.
Remember? I thought it was strange that a biplane
pilot would wait around after the attack without
having dropped any bombs.'

I turn back to the window. 'Who cares? He was
still part of the bombing raid. Maybe something just
went wrong with his mechanism and he couldn't
drop the bombs.'

'I don't think the royals have much choice,
Danika,' says Maisy. 'They *have* to become soldiers
or hunters or pilots when they're young. It's a
tradition. And he's King Morrigan's own son – for
all we know, the king might even have chosen his
skill for him.'

'Lukas should have run away, then! He shouldn't
have joined a mission to bomb innocent people's
houses.'

Maisy doesn't have an answer for that. Maybe
I've snapped too angrily, scared her into silence
again. She's been speaking up more often in the last

few days, and I'm starting to forget how timid she can be.

The train jerks to a stop regularly, every fifteen minutes or so. It only lasts twenty seconds – just long enough for power to sizzle across the cables, recharging the train's energy. There's nothing new to see, though, just fog. I press my fingers against the glass and stare into a sea of white.

When the others wake up, we try to figure out a plan. Clementine wants to stay on the train as long as possible.

'But we don't even know where the train line heads next,' Teddy says. 'I don't reckon it's gonna veer off east towards the Magnetic Valley, do you?'

Clementine scowls. 'Of course not, but it's better than nothing. If we cover enough distance by train, we'll save ourselves weeks of walking.'

'Yeah, great plan,' says Teddy sarcastically. 'And if anyone recognises our faces, we'll save ourselves decades of breathing.'

I clear my throat. 'Um, aren't you forgetting something?'

'What?'

'This carriage is hanging in the air. We could be hundreds of metres high, for all we know. Unless you've got a way to sprout wings, we're stuck on this train whether we like it or not.'

'There!' says Clementine, looking satisfied. 'Good. I don't want to waste weeks of my life trekking through those mountains.' She shudders. 'Imagine how cold it must be in the snow.'

As much as I hate feeling trapped, I find myself silently agreeing. I know all about the cruelty of winter. If we tried to hike through these mountains ourselves, with no food supplies and not even a foxary to carry our remaining packs, we'd be frozen dead in days.

Teddy doesn't look happy but after a few minutes' silence, he seems to accept the situation and brightens a little. 'Hey, I wouldn't say no to a gourmet breakfast. Reckon I could bluff my way into the dining cart?'

'I thought you were scared of being recognised,' says Clementine.

'Yeah, but it'd be worth it. I bet they've got those fancy caviar rolls.'

I can't help smiling. If there's one thing I can rely on with Teddy Nort, it's his ability to find the best in a bad situation. Maybe it comes from too many years of getting stuck up richies' chimneys.

Unfortunately, this talk of breakfast has set my stomach grumbling. It reminds me of the days we were lost without food in the wilderness. In a way, this hunger feels even worse, because I *know* there's wonderful food nearby but I can't go near it. I close my eyes and lean into the packs, imagining the train's dining cart. There could be spicy potato wedges, perhaps, or bowls of steaming pumpkin soup . . . massive platters of deep-fried pastries and sugar puddings with syrup and cream . . .

Maisy's stomach grumbles. She looks embarrassed, but I offer her a smile. 'I know how you feel.'

To take our minds off the hunger, we decide to improve our richie disguises. Clementine digs through the packs to offer more stylish outfits, better coordinated than the rushed ensembles we threw ourselves into last night. Teddy selects a peacock waistcoat and I choose a gauzy veil to cover my face. Clementine tells me it's supposed to look 'alluring', but I'm just happy to find a way to conceal my features. Since my face was plastered all over Gunning, the irritation of draping mesh across my eyes seems worthwhile.

Teddy holds up a pink satin sash with obvious distaste. 'Why did you even *bring* all this junk?'

Clementine shakes her head, refusing to answer.

'Our mother created all these clothes,' says Maisy. 'She was a fashion designer.'

My breath catches in my throat. This is the first time I've heard the twins mention any family. Their wanted poster called them *'daughters of a prominent businessman'* but that applies to almost every rich girl in Rourton.

'Oh,' says Teddy. *'Was?'*

Maisy glances away. 'She died a long time ago.'

Teddy looks a little guilty, and I feel the same. All this time I've assumed that Clementine brought the clothes because she was vain and stupid – not because they might have sentimental value. I finger my own mother's bracelet, which is looped around my wrist. I'm slightly shocked when my fingers touch Lukas's silver rose charm. I had forgotten about it. Part of me wants to throw it away, but not in front of the others. I don't want to get them talking about Lukas.

I glance out the window to distract myself. The world is pure cloud, white and tumbling. And with a sudden stab, I'm reminded of Radnor's waterfall. White water, churning. His body, falling. I squeeze my eyes shut. There is too much to remember.

Radnor is gone. Hackel is a traitor. Lukas is the king's own son.

And for a moment, I wish I could go back. I wish I could turn back time and reverse this whole insane trip. Climb back over Rourton's wall, and call that flare back down from the sky. Slip into the dark of the alleyways, and the wine-scented air of the Alehouse. Back to a time when I didn't need anybody. When I was better off alone.

When there was no risk of losing someone.

But it's too late. There are hunters on my trail, and a price on my head. My face bedecks a hundred wanted posters, and the scruffers of Rourton would sell me out in a second. And even if I *could* go back, what then? Would I go back to living alone? Trusting no one?

I open my eyes and glance around the compartment. I see Teddy, in his peacock waistcoat. Clementine, blonde curls splayed against her seat. Maisy, fingers knotted in her lap. Their mouths are hard, and their eyes are tired. But there's a silent resolve beneath those stares. Solidarity. Unity. And it strikes me, suddenly, that we're in this together.

To go back to my old ways . . . it would still mean losing something. Not through death, or treachery. But a loss, nonetheless.

The train jolts into one of its regular stops. Out the window, the cables sizzle with a recharge of alchemy power. The pause only lasts twenty seconds, then we're off again, flying into the mist.

Clementine takes a deep breath. 'I need some air. If I stay in this compartment, I'm going to go insane.'

No one answers. It's risky, of course, but we can't stay crammed in here forever. The train trip might last days, for all I know, and we won't survive long without food or water. And I have to admit, the idea of escaping this cabin is tempting.

'I'll suss out the other carriages,' Clementine adds. 'There might be a way to get food.'

'I'll come too,' says Maisy.

'And me.' I gesture at the gauze across my face. 'No one's gonna recognise me behind this thing.'

We turn to look at Teddy, who frowns. 'Try not to let anyone see your faces,' he says. Then he slaps a flowery hat over Clementine's head, concealing her blonde curls. It helps disguise the fact that she and Maisy are twins, so I give an approving nod.

'What are *you* going to do?'

Teddy shrugs. 'I'm going to find a way off this train. If anyone's gonna find an escape route, it's the professional burglar, right?'

We leave Teddy in the compartment and head off down the corridor. There aren't many people about – perhaps they're sleeping in, too exhausted by their ordeal in Gunning to bother with a gourmet breakfast. The compartment doors are closed, with 'Do Not Disturb' tags hanging from the handles. Whenever the train bumps past one of the line's support pylons, the carriage jerks and the tags all flap against the doors.

At the end of the corridor, there is a thick metal

door with a window. I peer through the glass and flinch at the sight beyond. To go any further, we have to cross a buckled metal platform between the carriages.

'That doesn't look too safe,' Clementine says doubtfully.

'Do you still want to go?' I say.

The twins nod, so I open the door. There's a blast of freezing air, and the world seems to fall away below us. White fog coats my hands and face with the sting of frost. I step onto the platform and try not to look down. There's a valley somewhere below, or a mountain slope, but it's too foggy to see. If not for the safety rail, I might fall fifty metres – or five hundred.

I push open the next carriage's door and slip inside. The others stumble in after me, and we slam the door behind us. Maisy looks as white as the fog; too late, I remember how sensitive she is to the cold. She doesn't have any coverings for her hands, so she rubs them together and blows on them to soothe the redness.

This carriage is the same as our own. We hurry down the corridor, take a deep breath, then brave another few seconds outside to cross into the next carriage. We repeat this trauma four times before we open the door onto anything different, and by this point I'm just about ready to quit. But then

Clementine shoves open the final door and we stumble into a carriage full of people.

This is not a sleeping cart. It must be the dining carriage. There are no compartments, no narrow corridors. It's a wide, open space, with wooden tables and metal cutlery that winks in the light. There are massive windows, much larger than the one in our compartment, and for a confused second I think I'm still outside between the carriages.

Then I spot the dozens of figures. Richies, the lot of them, clustered around the tables. I'm relieved to see a few other teenagers – the last thing we need is to stand out from the crowd – but the majority are middle-aged gentry. The closest is only metres away: a hungover man who repeatedly stabs his tablecloth with a fork. He is dining upon some kind of break-fast pudding, made with peaches and custard, and the scent of hot cinnamon makes my mouth ache with hunger.

'There are guards!' whispers Maisy.

I follow her gaze to the far side of the carriage. A group of men and women stand munching on toast, with pistols sheathed in their belts. I don't recognise their uniform, but the letters 'B.O.N.' upon their sleeves suggest they're special guards for the *Bird of the North*. I raise a panicked hand to check that my veil is in place.

'Where are they going?' says Clementine, as the guards open the door and cross into the far carriage.

'Maybe they're checking the carriages one by one?' I say quietly. 'We should get back and warn Teddy – if they start questioning people about the fire . . .'

I hurry forward for a closer look. If I can glance through the windows, perhaps I can glimpse what lies in the carriage ahead. It might be another dining cart, or perhaps more sleeping carriages. Maybe it's even the front of the train, and the guards are going to consult the driver. But I'm too late; heat has already returned to the carriage, fogging up the window and blocking my view.

When I turn back to the others, I see that a stranger has joined the twins on the far side of the carriage. It's the hungover man with the fork. He's given up on stabbing his tablecloth, and instead he's lurching at Clementine and Maisy with a hungry expression. He leans towards Maisy, lips parted, and huffs stale breath across her face.

'Hey, sweetheart.' He grabs her hair and yanks her head towards him. 'You're really pretty. Fancy a kiss?'

Maisy has frozen. She doesn't speak, or cry, or slap him. She just closes her eyes. I shove through the carriage, fighting to reach them. A richie woman snarls at me when I trip over her handbag, spilling coins and fancy lip stains across the floor.

Then Clementine is there. She grabs a knife from the nearest table and thrusts it towards the man's eyes. Now *he's* the one who's frozen, the one who wants to break away.

'Whoa!' he says, and releases Maisy. 'What're you doing? We were just having a bit of fun, weren't we, sweetheart?'

Maisy scrambles backwards, paler than I've ever seen her. She's faced hunters and waterfalls and traitors and fire. But I've never seen her lose control like this. She shrinks into the corner, trembling against the carriage's velvet wall.

'If you go near my sister again,' says Clementine, 'I will cut out your eyes. Do I make myself clear?'

The man looks like he wants to nod, but the blade is too close to risk any movement. 'Yeah, all right.'

'We gave up everything to get away from old creeps like you!' Clementine presses the blade against his eyebrow. 'Stop *looking* at her!'

'All right, I get it! I'm sorry!'

She digs the knife into his skin, enough for a thin droplet of blood to run across the metal. Then she yanks it away. The man sinks to his knees, clutching a hand to his face, just as I reach them.

The rest of the carriage has fallen silent. Dozens

of richies are staring at us, eyes wide and horrified, their hands across their mouths.

'Come on,' I say quickly. 'We've got to get out of here.'

We pull Maisy to her feet and hurry back towards the carriage door. So much for an easy ride over the mountains. We need a way to escape the train – and we need it now. As soon as the man finds a guard, as soon as he reports that he's been attacked . . .

'Hurry,' I say. 'We've got to find Teddy and get out of here. That man's going to find a guard, and –'

'He was asking for it!' snaps Clementine, as though I'm questioning her judgement.

'I know,' I say. 'You did the right thing, but we've got to *move*.'

We wrestle with the door between carriages, then step out onto the platform. It's as terrifying as ever – the feeble handrails, the hidden drop below, the blast of snowy wind – but there's no time to worry about the height.

We've got more pressing dangers to deal with.

CHAPTER TWENTY-ONE

FLIGHT

WE COLLIDE WITH TEDDY IN THE CORRIDOR OF THE third carriage. He takes one look at our faces and stiffens. 'What's wrong?'

'Some creep grabbed Maisy, so Clementine grabbed him back,' I say. 'And if we don't hurry, we'll be neck-deep in guards.'

Teddy just nods, grabs my arm and says, 'This way.'

'Did you find a way off the train?'

'Sort of.'

There's no time for further questioning. We squeeze down the corridors of six more carriages, stopping only to grab our packs from our compartment. Every time I cross a swinging metal platform,

264

the wind slaps my face with a reminder of the weather we'll face down below. Staying on this train now means certain death, but escaping it – here, in the middle of the mountains – will probably mean the same.

'There's one good thing, at least,' Teddy mutters, pressing a hand against the wall to steady himself. 'Feel that angle?'

I frown, confused for a moment. Then I feel it. The train is tilting slightly downwards now, angling its weight towards the front carriages. It's as though the train has stopped its upward climb into the mountains, and is now winching its way down the other side . . .

'We're over the peaks?' I say.

'That's what I'm hoping,' Teddy says. 'If we've gotta get off this train in the mountains, better to do it on the downhill slope.'

The last carriage is larger than the others, and there's no safety rail to help us clamber inside. For a second, terror seizes my throat and I think I'm going to fall. But I can't afford to be weak now; not when Maisy is shaking and Clementine is still clenching her fists with rage. This crew needs every level-headed member it can get.

The carriage, as it turns out, is not designed for passengers. Half the floor is filled with cargo: leather trundle cases and barrels of supplies. The other half is caged off, separated by a mesh of metal that sparks whenever the carriage jolts.

'What's back there?' I ask.

Teddy shakes his head. 'Dunno, but I'd bet ten silvers it's nothing good.'

I remember our conversation about the recently extended train line, about why King Morrigan would waste so much tax revenue to give richies a holiday in Gunning. Maybe this is the real reason for the sky rail: this unknown cargo in the back of the train.

I step closer, keen to peer through the mesh, but a gasp from Clementine brings me to reality. She points back through the tiny window on the carriage door. The glass is blurry, obscured by fog, but a faint shadow moves outside. Did someone see us slip into this cargo carriage?

'Hide!'

If we had time, we could burrow into a pile of cargo, then rearrange the racks to hide ourselves. But our pursuer will be here in seconds, and there is no time to move a thing. We throw ourselves into the darkest corner we can find, behind a well-balanced stack of kitchen supplies. My face is crushed against a sack of flour, and I strain my muscles to pull back my weight. If I lean too heavily against this bag, it might tip forward and . . .

The carriage door flies open.

A pair of guards burst inside on a flurry of icy wind: one man, one woman. They hold pistols ahead of them, aiming nervously into the dark recesses of the carriage. At first I think it's ridiculous for professional guards to seem so afraid of us. We're just a bunch of half-starved teenagers. But they're looking for a girl who held a knife to someone's eye and threatened to slice it out, aren't they? And they're probably on edge already, considering the crazed influx of passengers after the fire. They might even be afraid the Gunning arsonist snuck aboard this train . . .

'Show yourself!' says the nearest guard. He's a middle-aged man with a bit of a belly, but still fit enough for the muscles to shift visibly when he adjusts his grip on his gun. 'Come out now, or we'll shoot.'

I try to control the sound of my breathing. I don't need to hold my breath completely, luckily, because the sway and rattle of the train is enough to conceal it. If he comes any closer, though, we'll be in trouble.

I sense a movement behind me, as though someone is sliding a hand into fabric. It's Maisy, reaching into the side pocket of our largest pack. She keeps her gaze upon the guards and feels around with her fingertips, wide-eyed and trembling against my shoulder. Then she withdraws her hand and holds out a pair of magnetic plates.

The guards are searching the cargo now, shining lights into every nook and cranny they spot. In twenty seconds they'll be upon us, shining that beam into our startled faces. I don't think two magnets will be enough, but the others must be too hard to reach because Maisy doesn't reach into the pocket again. She slides the first magnet onto the floor, pinning it beneath the edge of a sack of potatoes. Then she thrusts the other into a crack between two biscuit tins, and turns to look at me.

I try to build my illusion. I picture our corner, dark and empty, with nothing but dust and potato sacks. I struggle to push the illusion outward, to paint the image between those magnets like strands of spider web. There's a yank behind my gut and then it's done: an unnatural shimmer upon the air.

A second later, the guard is here. He shines his light towards our corner, then gives a snarl of frustration. This is the last corner for them to check in the carriage; if we're not here, they'll have to go back and search the rest of the train.

The train crosses a pylon hook, and the carriage lurches. The shelf holding the biscuit tins jerks sideways. Only a centimetre at most, but it's enough to disrupt the flow between the magnets and cause a momentary hitch in the sheen of my illusion. The flaw only lasts a second – a jerk, a shimmer in the air. But the guard's eyes widen and he leans in closer, fingers on the trigger.

I hold my breath. I can feel the others do the same; Maisy digs painfully into my shoulder, and one of Teddy's knees is pushing against my gut. I'm still tensing my muscles, straining to hold back my own weight – and the others' now, too – from tipping aside the sack of flour.

'Hey!' The female guard gestures at the wire mesh partitioning the carriage. 'Reckon someone could hide back there?'

The guard above us pauses, then pulls away to follow his companion's gaze. 'Don't think so. What's back there, anyway?'

'No idea. Boss said it was above my pay grade. Hers too, matter of fact.'

The man laughs. 'That'd be right. Anyway, how the hell could someone get through that? It's all lit up with alchemy juice.'

As he speaks, silver sparks across the mesh.

'Let's get out of here. I reckon the girl's nicked off to a compartment.'

They yank open the carriage door and barrel into the cold outside. The door slams and we wait several seconds before daring to move. Then I release my breath in a low gush. It sets off a domino chain of relieved exhalations from the others.

'I reckoned we were goners,' says Teddy, cracking a shaky grin. 'Good job on the illusion, Danika.'

'It was Maisy's idea,' I say.

I turn to Maisy, suddenly remembering her terror when the man grabbed her. She is no longer trembling, but she looks at the floor to avoid my gaze. I open my mouth to ask if she's all right, but Clementine cuts me off. 'What's the plan, Teddy?'

'Huh?'

'I thought you had an idea for getting off this train. And it had better not involve jumping, because from this height –'

'Nah, not jumping,' says Teddy. 'I was looking out the window at those pylons, right? They've put it where it's hard for passengers to see, but I stuck my neck out and I reckon they've got something buckled down the other side of the poles.'

'You don't mean –'

Teddy nods. 'Ladders. They must have 'em, right? They need a way for maintenance crews to get up and down, to fix the cables . . . or if they need alchemists to update the spells on the cables . . .'

'Wouldn't they just choose workers with Air proclivities, so they could ride the wind?'

'They wouldn't be able to carry much up with them, though. All their tools'd be too heavy, I reckon. They need ladders.'

'We'd better hurry,' I say, gathering up the magnets. 'Those aren't the only guards on this train – there could be another pair along any minute now.'

We stuff our packs with food: a sack of flour, potatoes, a tin of cocoa powder and even fresh oranges. Maisy finds a leather knapsack and empties it out, spilling fancy stationery and bringing our tally of packs back up to four. She adds a box of mixed spice and herbs, then we pile in oats and dried fruits. I grab a few wineskins we can use to carry water. The last addition is a hefty bag of candied nuts.

'We'll need the energy,' says Teddy. 'Anyway, I reckon my tastebuds have earned a reward after all that cold porridge.'

When I think of the snow, and how freezing nights will increase our hunger, I crack open a biscuit tin and cram its contents into my pockets. I hack open the nearest few cases and rifle through their contents until I find warmer clothing. The others realise what I'm doing and mimic my actions, until we're all dressed in thick winter travelling coats and gloves.

'Ready?' says Clementine.

I nod. If we had time, I would rummage through the other containers for supplies – blankets, perhaps, or a medical kit. But we don't have time to waste searching, and can't afford to carry baggage that might not contain anything useful. 'Let's go.'

'The train stops to recharge every fifteen minutes,' reminds Teddy. 'As soon as it stops, we'd better move quick – we'll only get twenty seconds to get out of its way.'

We strap the packs on securely before we open the door, and a lash of winter wind hits us. The cold is so sharp that it hurts my face, but it's remarkable how the travelling clothes protect the rest of my body. I'm glad that richies are so intent on buying high quality garments.

Clementine slams the door shut. 'Let's wait until the train slows down.'

We all nod in agreement. Better to wait here than brave the cold. But still, I don't want to imagine what will happen if we move too slowly. If the train begins to move again before we're safely away, we'll be crushed: smeared like insects against the pylon, or knocked aside to fall through the fog below. Either way, our deaths will not be pretty.

As soon as the train hints at slowing, we fling open the door. There isn't room for all of us on the platform. I let the twins sidle out first, while Teddy and I wait in the carriage doorway. The train takes a century to stop. Theoretically, I know it's only a minute, but the freezing wind and my fear of the guards is enough to make each second drag.

Then it happens. We jerk to a halt and I stumble and almost fall backwards into the baggage cart. But there's no time to readjust, because our twenty seconds are already ticking away.

'Go!' says Teddy.

Clementine reaches for the pylon. She lurches out into the fog and for a terrible instant I think she is falling. But then she steadies herself and clambers around and out of sight. I let out a shaky breath; she's found the ladder.

Maisy follows. She's fast and light, but in my head I'm already counting down the seconds. The wind soaks my gloves with an icy damp, and I don't know if I'll even be able to grip the ladder when my turn comes. Fourteen, thirteen, twelve seconds to go . . .

Teddy waits for a precious three seconds until he leaps. I know it's not his fault; he can't move until the others are out of the way. But I'm still shouting at him to 'Go, go, go!' by the time he hurls his body at the pylon.

And suddenly it's my turn. I throw myself off the platform. My gloves slip, but I manage to grab a handhold on the side of the pylon. I take a terrified huff of air and stiffen my muscles. Teddy hasn't moved far enough down the ladder yet; if I swing around now, we're going to collide.

There are five seconds left, then four, three, two . . .

I swing around to the back of the pole, into the space Teddy has vacated, with a second to spare. The top of the pylon jerks above us, spitting light along the silver cables. And then the train is gone, shooting off with a blast of fuel and alchemy.

'Is everyone all right?' shouts Clementine, somewhere down in the fog. I can't see her – in fact, I can't even see my own feet, let alone anyone further down the ladder.

'Yes! We all made it,' I say.

'All right,' Clementine says, 'I'm going down.'

I count to ten before I begin my own descent. Hopefully that's enough time for the others to cover some ground. I'm afraid I might step on Teddy's fingers, or kick him in the head. That could be enough to make him fall. The back of my neck is itching again, worse than ever, and I find myself pondering the odds of spontaneously developing an Air proclivity if I slip off the ladder. It doesn't help that I'm favouring one arm, keeping weight off the shoulder that I dislocated in Rourton. The injury is largely healed but I'm afraid of jerking it out of place again.

Our descent is slow. This mountain wind seems harsher than even the rapids in the river, and doubly cold. Everything is white, as though I'm climbing through a cloud. In a way, I suppose I am. It's a risky thing to imagine, because the whole world begins to feel like a dream. My only link to reality is the cold rungs of the ladder right in front of my eyes. There is nothing up, nothing down, nothing to my sides. Just white.

Maybe it's disorientation, or maybe the air up here is too thin, but – for whatever reason – I want to let go. I want to float away into the clouds like a bird. I have to shake my head, grit my teeth and remind myself that this is real. This is not a dream. If I let go of this ladder, I will die.

My toes turn numb with cold after several minutes of climbing. After a while, I can't even feel the itch in the back of my neck. If I didn't know better, I might welcome the numbness as a relief from the pain. But I've survived enough winters to know the perils of frostbite. I don't want to end up like the girl I shared a doorway with once, who peeled off her boots and left her toes inside.

As we descend, the fog begins to clear. The morning sun grows strong enough to burn the mist, and I start to see Teddy's figure below. Then I make out Maisy, and finally Clementine. I'm no longer lost in a sea of white. We clamber down one leg of the pylon, which props up the main pole, forcing us to climb at a diagonal. The ladder falls into a brownish mess of trees below.

Finally, we reach the bottom. I collapse into half-frozen sludge and undergrowth. The others already lie nearby. Their chests rise and fall in steady huffs, gasping clouds into the frost. And I just lie there, relishing the cold of mud beneath my spine. It's solid. The world is solid again. I'm no longer in danger of floating away.

CHAPTER TWENTY-TWO

FROZEN NIGHT

AS MY SENSES RETURN TO NORMAL, I REALISE THE undergrowth is coated with mucky snow. We are up in the mountains, not down in the fields, and the cold here could kill us on a whim. If we hope to survive this trek, we must always be prepared to defend ourselves – not just against hunters, but against the climate.

There is no real shelter here: just the railway cables, swallowed by cloud above our heads. And once the guards figure out how we escaped, the first place searched will be the base of these pylons.

I force myself onto my knees. 'Come on. We've got to move.'

Clementine moans and the others just ignore me. I want desperately to join them, to close my eyes and pretend that none of this is happening. But one of us has to get the crew moving. Radnor is dead. Hackel tried to sell us to the hunters. So if no one else wants the job, it looks like I'm stuck taking charge.

'Come on,' I say again. 'You can rest soon, I promise.'

No response.

'We've just got to find a safe spot, that's all, and then we'll set up camp and –'

Teddy runs a hand through his hair. 'Yeah, all right, Danika. No need to ramble on about it. We're coming.'

I help pull the others to their feet. We sling the packs back on and stagger forward into the snow. Our only luck is the bristly undergrowth, which stops us leaving any obvious footprints.

Hours fade together in an endless haze of white and brown. Snow and trees. The only variety is occasional wildlife: birds above the canopy, and a startled rabbit in the undergrowth. Clementine mutters that we should have caught it for supper, but none of us has the slightest clue how to hunt. We're city born and bred, and the only food I've hunted for was found in a restaurant rubbish bin. Besides, I don't think I could bring myself to kill the rabbit. Not when it's out here, like us, just fighting to survive. I know how it feels to be hunted.

The sun treks across the sky, melting away the rest of the fog. As the horizon clears, I'm relieved to see that Teddy's earlier guess was correct. We've already passed over the highest peaks, and we're heading down through the southern slopes. Even so, the air is cold enough to sting. I don't want to imagine what would have happened if we'd ditched the train an hour earlier. Up in the bite of the highest peaks, lashed by wind and frostbite, we would already be dead.

In early afternoon, Maisy points out one of the mountaintops. When she speaks, her voice is oddly tight. 'I think that's Midnight Crest.'

At first I think the peak's completely bare: just rock and snow, silhouetted against the sky. Then I squint, and realise what I'm really staring at. Ruins. The ruins of a fortress, perhaps – perched like a broken bird on the summit.

'I didn't realise we were so close,' Maisy says quietly. 'It's from the time of the earliest Morrigan kings, hundreds of years ago.'

'Why would anyone want to live up *there*?' Clementine says.

'It wasn't for living. It was death row for traitors. They were bound inside magnetic cells, and left to slowly die in the cold.'

I stare up at the ruins. There isn't much left now: just broken stone and blackened wood, half-buried in snow. But my imagination fills in the details. I picture walls of oak arching high over stone. Metal bars. Frostbitten fingers. Frozen breath and faltering heartbeats.

'Why'd they shut it down?' Teddy says.

'Some of the prisoners escaped,' Maisy says, 'and burned it to the ground. That was when they trained the first official platoon of hunters – to hunt down those prisoners in the mountains.'

I blink. I've never thought about the start of the hunters. It seems like they've always been there – like wind or rain or fire. It's unsettling to think that this is the place it all started: right here, in the Central Mountains. I think of prisoners running, screaming, their blood on the snow.

Then an even worse thought hits me. This place . . . this is what the hunters exist for. This is what Sharr's predecessors were first trained for. Do we really think we can outrun her *here*? Here, where it all began?

'Come on,' Teddy says. 'Better keep moving, I reckon.'

No one argues.

*

THE DAY WEARS DOWN, AND SO DO OUR BODIES. OUR muscles ache and our faces sting. We put one foot in front of the other, again and again, and struggle until we can't go any further.

Finally, I choose a ledge beneath an overhanging section of rock. It's not a perfect shelter, but it's the best place I've seen so far; at least there are trees nearby to muffle the wind.

I use the remainder of my strength to scoop away the snow, clearing a patch of dirt for us to sleep upon, and lay out our magnets to cast my illusion. The back of my neck is itching again, to the point where I suspect my proclivity might be Mosquito. But I've got no energy to worry about that now. The twins gather twigs for a fire while Teddy rolls out the sleeping sacks. Starting a fire is dangerous; the smoke will be a beacon to any nearby hunters, and I doubt my illusion reaches high enough to erase all traces from the sky. But if we don't light one, we'll never survive the night. I'd rather take a chance of capture than a guarantee of hypothermia.

'We haven't got any matches,' says Maisy.

I'm too tired to think straight now. She's looking at me for answers, and for some reason it irritates me. Haven't I done my share today?

'Your proclivity's Flame,' I snap at her. 'Don't try to deny it – I saw you snuff out Hackel's candle back in Gunning. Can't you just make a spark or something?'

Clementine glares. 'You know she can't, Danika. There has to be a flame already present for Maisy to work with. She can't just build a fire out of thin air, any more than Teddy can conjure up a pig for us to roast.' She gives a haughty sniff. 'If you haven't figured out how proclivities work by now, I'm a little worried about your mental faculties.'

'At least I'm not –' I start.

'Whoa, calm down!' interrupts Teddy, throwing up his hands. 'I reckon we're a bit too tired to waste energy on arguing, aren't we?'

I want to snap back at him, at Clementine, at the whole world. It would feel good to rage and storm and act like a sullen child. But I know he's right. It's my exhaustion talking, and the argument is my fault. I shouldn't have snapped at Maisy, not when she's already been upset today.

'Sorry,' I mutter.

'Yeah, me too,' says Clementine.

I look up at her in surprise, but she's turned to busy herself with the fire. No one meets my gaze, so I slouch across to help with the twigs. Maisy tries to rub a few sticks together, but all she manages to do is peel off a bit of soggy bark.

'If we had a match, I could build up this fire in

no time,' she says, looking frustrated. 'I just need a spark to work with.'

'Shame you can't just light another flare, Danika,' says Teddy. 'I reckon that'd start a fire going all right, even with this lot.'

He gestures at the snow-sodden twigs, and his words spark a memory in the corner of my mind. A flare. I remember crouching atop the wall in Rourton, pocketing the guards' supplies. After the trauma of the last few days – and in the haze of my exhaustion – I'd almost forgotten those supplies. An extra flare, a pair of climbing picks, and *a box of matches*.

'Matches!' I say.

'Yeah, Maisy already said that,' says Teddy. 'We haven't got any.'

I unbutton my stolen coat and fish through the pockets of my own clothes underneath. I know I stashed the matches somewhere, in one of the pockets that line my shirt. Did I ever take them out, or put them into one of the foxaries' packs? I know I shoved the second flare into a pack, but I don't remember taking out the matchbox . . .

And suddenly my fingers find it. A tiny wooden box, half-crushed by the weight of our adventures, in a pocket on my hip.

'They might be wrecked,' I say, as I hold them out to the others. 'They've been soaked so many times.'

Maisy takes the box. She bites her lip, as though trying not to get her hopes up. There are only three matches inside. One has a crumpled head, as though mildew has dissolved it. Maisy tosses it aside, leaving two options. She selects the healthiest remaining match and glances up at Clementine.

'Can you make a shield?' she says.

Her sister cups her hands around the match, protecting it from the outside air. Maisy bends down to light the match. My view is obscured by Clementine's palms, but I hear the strike of the match-head against the side of the box. Nothing. Maisy takes a quavering breath and tries again.

There is a strike. There is a sizzle. Faint light shines between Clementine's fingers.

I want to shout out in triumph, but I clap a hand across my mouth just in time. A stray gust of breath could be enough to extinguish the flame, so tiny and fragile on the head of the match. It's barely alight as it is.

'I need a stick,' whispers Maisy, not taking her eyes away from the match.

Teddy wordlessly offers a twig from the pile. He prods it closer towards the match, clearly holding his breath. His face is empty of its usual bravado. I suddenly notice his fingers are trembling. Teddy Nort is out of his depth. This isn't a richie for him

284

to steal from, or a city guard to bluff. This enemy will not be impressed by a confident grin. Either the match will stay alight or it won't.

Maisy stares at the flame.

There is a flash of brighter light, and then fire *spits* itself up to meet the end of the twig. With a rush, the twig is alight. Clementine shrieks and the match is knocked into the dirt, but it doesn't matter any more. We have fire. And best of all, we still have one match left, ready for future emergencies.

Teddy places the twig in the pile, setting our campfire aflame. Maisy coaxes it up into a crackling little blaze and soon we're munching biscuits in the warmth. I melt some snow to make water and we fill our pot with dried fruits and spices. The fruits plump up and turn into mush as the water heats; we scoop it up with our fingers and smear the warmth inside our cheeks. It's amazing how much better I feel, now that my belly is filling again.

Maisy is the first to go to bed, followed by Teddy. When about twenty minutes have passed, and Teddy has started to snore, Clementine looks at me. 'You go to sleep, Danika. I'll keep watch tonight.'

'But you need rest too.'

Clementine shakes her head. 'I'm not going to sleep tonight anyway.'

She stares into the fire. I've never seen her look so miserable. It's not the sort of misery I'd expected from a richie; she's not whining about life's unfairness or anything. It's more a quiet sort of reflection, coupled with slow breaths and clenched fists. Something has shaken Clementine Pembroke to the core.

'What's wrong?' I say quietly.

She blinks. 'Nothing.'

I poke a few more sticks into the fire. They take a while to defrost, but soon the bark starts curling into black. Maisy has done a good job for someone who isn't too experienced at using her proclivity.

'Today on the train,' I say, 'when that man grabbed Maisy, you said you ran away to escape from creeps like that.'

It's not really a question, of course, but Clementine knows I'm angling for information. She twists her fingers together, then looks at me. 'You know our mother's dead.'

I nod.

'She died in a bombing, years ago,' says Clementine. 'She was working late at her studio, breaking curfew, but then the biplanes struck . . .'

I feel a sudden surge of camaraderie with the Pembroke twins. 'My family died in the bombings too.'

Clementine fishes a burning twig from the fire

and turns it between her fingers. As we watch, the end smoulders and flakes into dust.

'Our father runs a finance business,' she says. 'He has friends in government, people who worked for King Morrigan. When the king's planes killed our mother, I thought he would quit – that he'd stop doing business with those murderers.

'But he didn't. He just got more and more wrapped up in his business, started bringing home his "colleagues" for dinner. They were middle-aged men, and most of them didn't pay much attention to us. We were just children. We couldn't earn them any money, so we weren't worth their time.'

Clementine hurls her stick back into the fire. On impact, its charred end disintegrates completely. 'But there was one man, one of our father's closest colleagues, who came around more often. He . . .'

There is a pause. Clementine is clenching her fists so hard that her knuckles look white.

'He what?'

'He took a shine to Maisy. He was always watching her, following her. Leering at her. Slobbering at her for kisses. Maisy has always been shy, but this man . . . he just *scared* her. Maisy started jumping at shadows, looking over her shoulder. Every moment, she thought he might be lurking nearby. Stalking her.

'He asked our father if he could marry her, even though Maisy was terrified. He wanted to *buy* her hand in marriage, Danika, like buying a pig from the market. And our father . . .' Clementine releases an angry breath. 'Our father was going to say "yes".'

My stomach twists. I have misjudged these girls so badly – misjudged them with my scorn and my jealousy of their privileged lives. 'And that's why you ran away?'

Clementine nods. 'I've tried so hard to protect her. I tried for years. Our father didn't care – he just wanted the money.' She pauses. 'One of our servants knew what was happening. She told me she had a friend called Radnor, a scruffer boy who was going to put a crew together.

'I didn't want to consort with scruffers – I didn't want *Maisy* to consort with scruffers – but it seemed like our only chance of escape. So I raided our bank accounts, I hired Hackel to guide us, and I bought those foxaries. I thought it would all go to plan! We had so much more money than normal refugees. I never thought . . .'

She gestures at the snowy darkness, at the trembling form of Maisy beneath her sleeping sack. 'I never thought *this* would happen.'

I wait a moment, then place a hand on Clementine's shoulder. She doesn't pull away. 'We're going to get through this, you know. We're going to cross into the Magnetic Valley, and go to the lands beyond, where the king can't touch us. We'll be safe then. All of us.'

Clementine nods. 'I know.'

I fish some extra biscuits from my pockets. 'Here.'

'We already ate.'

'I know. But it will help.'

And it does. We sit in the glow of the fire, warming our hands and nibbling biscuits long into the night. We talk about little things: the noise of the market in Rourton, the feel of the cobblestones, the sight of a full moon above guard towers.

I tell Clementine the story of a drunkard who mistook a rubbish bin for a donkey and tried to ride it home, and she actually laughs. And when she tells me about her mother – and about the terrible nights that followed the bombing – I think perhaps we're not so different after all.

*

IN THE MORNING, THE FIRE IS STILL SMOULDERING. Maisy ties up a bundle of the glowing sticks. 'I can keep these burning,' she says. 'It will be good tonight, when we set up another camp. That way, we can save our last match for emergencies.'

Breakfast is porridge, made hot and steaming from the stolen oats. We mix candied nuts and dried fruit into the pot, and I decide this is the most delicious meal I can remember. In the cold, nothing can rival the heat of oats upon my tongue.

The mountainside is thick with fog, so it's hard to see where we're going.

'Let's just head uphill,' I suggest. 'If we reach that peak over there, we can get a better look at the rest of our route.'

We haul on our packs, disguise our campsite with broken twigs, and start our day of trekking through the snow. It's a quiet morning, and the only sound is our boots in the undergrowth. My legs are aching from yesterday's hike. One foot, then another. One foot, then another . . .

The first break in the monotony comes when Teddy spots a deer through the trees. I stop to stare, awed by the arch of its antlers. It resembles a tree come to life, branches sprouting above long-lashed eyes. I've never seen a wild deer before; just pictures in storybooks, in the oldest of my memories. My chest feels tight. I think suddenly of lantern light, and my father's voice murmuring. The crackle of pages, and blankets tight around my shoulders.

The deer slips away into shadow. We continue up the slope.

Despite my confident demeanour, I'm not really sure that we're going in the right direction. In the exhaustion of last night, I didn't think to check for the direction of the Pistol constellation. I don't even know if that line of the song is still valid, or whether we've travelled too far south for it to apply.

To distract myself from the cold, I run through the second verse in my mind.

Oh frozen night,
How the dark swallows light
When the glasses of hours hold on
I shan't waste my good life
I must follow my knife
To those deserts of green and beyond.

'I think we're still following the folk song,' I say aloud, as we stumble through a patch of snowy bracken. 'You know, that bit about a frozen night.'

'You think that means to cross the mountains?'

'I don't know. Maybe.'

'It could mean Midnight Crest,' Clementine says. 'A frozen peak, named after the night? That can't be a coincidence.'

'Bit of a useless instruction, really,' says Teddy. 'I mean, everyone knows you've got to cross the mountains to get out of the north.'

I shake my head. 'Yeah, but most people cross further to the west, don't they? Along the traditional trading route? If the song's about the smugglers' secret route, I bet it's telling us to cross further east: near Midnight Crest.'

'But why?' Clementine says. 'I know the Valley's to the east, but . . .' She trails off.

'Maybe the other lines are more helpful,' I say. '*When the glasses of hours hold on* – what's that about?'

Teddy shrugs. 'Hourglasses? I reckon it's just warning us not to slow down. You know, don't waste time or the hunters will catch you. And that's what the next line's about too: if you waste time, you waste your life.'

'Maybe,' I say, but I'm not entirely convinced. The rest of the song has concerned physical land-marks. Its clues involve things you can see: the forest, the river, the Marbles, the Pistol constellation . . .

'Do you think the hunters know where we are?' says Clementine. 'That we're in the mountains already, I mean? Maybe Sharr Morrigan is still searching those fields outside Gunning.'

'She must know we were in Gunning.' I pause, then add, 'Lukas probably told her. I bet that's why he ran off during the fire, so he could tell his precious cousin where we were.'

'Sharr probably figured it out on her own,' says

Maisy. 'We were heading for Gunning, and suddenly there was a huge fire and evacuation there. Surely a professional hunter could put two and two together.'

'Yeah, she must know we got on that train,' says Teddy. 'But does she know we got *off* it again?'

I bite my lip. 'She'll know. The guards will send word to the hunters that we've vanished from the train. I bet that creepy man could give a good description of Maisy and Clementine, and Sharr will put two and two together . . .'

'Great,' says Clementine. 'So Sharr Morrigan's hunting crew will be en route to the mountains now, if she's not here already.'

'Wish Radnor was here,' Teddy says, a strange tightness in his voice. 'He'd know what to do, I reckon.'

We all fall silent, staring at our feet.

The morning passes slowly, in a haze of snow and exhaustion. Despite our growing concerns about hunters, there's no sign of pursuit. There is occasionally a flash of wings overhead, and I almost turn to tell Lukas there's a bird nearby. Then I remember and silently berate myself for being so stupid.

Now that we're free of immediate dangers – apart from the cold, of course – I find myself free to worry about other concerns. The most pressing issue is the itch down the back of my neck. My proclivity is developing, but there's no way to check whether a tattoo has started to form. The itch runs right down the top of my spine; I can tell from the speed of its spread that mine will be a speedy maturation.

I'm tempted to yank down my scarf and ask the others to check for me, to tell me if an emblem has printed itself across my skin. But even out here, the shame of the taboo hangs over me. Part of me feels stupid for worrying about it. After all we've been through, and all the laws we've already broken . . .

But the taboo is more than law. It's like wearing clothes, or refusing to go to the toilet in public. I wouldn't dance naked in front of my crewmates, would I? That's what it would feel like to reveal my bare neck.

'Stop scratching your neck,' says Teddy.

I lower my hand, embarrassed. I hadn't even realised I was doing it.

'I know it's itchy,' says Teddy, 'but trust me – scratching doesn't help.' He gives a cheeky grin. 'Know what it is yet?'

I open my mouth, slightly outraged. What gives him the right to ask?

Of course, the taboo has been broken in our crew already. I know that Teddy is Beast and Maisy is Flame. But that's different – I haven't actually seen their neck markings. And besides, it doesn't stop my squeamishness about revealing my own proclivity. What if it's something useless, like Butterfly? Or something shameful, like Darkness?

I knew a few people in Rourton whose proclivity was Darkness, and they always lived on the outskirts of society. Proclivities like Darkness or Night don't seem trustworthy. They make you seem sneaky, like a thief or a liar. Someone who can skulk in the shadows, or prowl through the dark.

'No idea,' I say. 'Hard to see my own spine without any mirrors.'

For a second I think Teddy might offer to check, but he closes his mouth and shrugs. Good.

'I think your proclivity will be Flame,' says Clementine. 'It's the most common proclivity, isn't it? You took down that biplane pretty spectacularly with the flare. And it would look sort of . . . right.' She gestures at my auburn hair.

I shrug. 'Well, it's not finished developing yet, so it doesn't matter. Whatever it is, I can't use it.'

'It'll be ready soon, Danika,' says Maisy quietly. 'When it's really itchy, that's when you know you're close.'

'Oh.'

For the next few kilometres, I can't think about anything except my proclivity. I wonder when Maisy found out her talent was Flame. Did she check her spine in a bathroom mirror, locked away in her father's mansion on High Street? Did she tell Clementine right away, in a bubble of excited whispers? It must be nice to grow up with a constant companion. Someone to protect you, someone to share your secrets . . .

'Get down!'

Someone pushes me to the ground. I swallow a mouthful of snow and dead leaves. There is barely a second to register what's happening – the rattle of engines, the shriek of falling metal – before the first bomb explodes.

CHAPTER TWENTY-THREE

FIRE IN THE SNOW

THREE BIPLANES SCAR THE SKY HIGH ABOVE THE wintry trees. The first bomb blasts a crater about forty metres from us; snow and broken foliage spin out like shrapnel. A flock of birds explodes from the undergrowth, squawking and flapping in panic.

'What –?' starts Clementine.

'They know we're around here somewhere!' Teddy says, pulling her upright. 'They're going to blast this mountainside to bits.'

'Move!'

Maisy plunges her burning twigs into a nearby pile of snow, extinguishing the flames. We can't carry a smoking beacon through this attack or they'll spot us in seconds.

There's another explosion, further down the slope. This time, the effects of the alchemy bomb are obvious: a sea of crimson flowers explodes from the impact point. The sight is utterly perverse. In a deadened world, in the middle of winter, their petals spatter like blood. But the pilots haven't spotted us yet – they're simply blasting the slope at random. If they knew where we were, we would have been hit already. This means we have a tiny chance, if we can find cover before they spot us . . .

'Come on!'

Every inch of me wants to run, to sprint. To escape this horror as fast as my muscles can manage. But that would draw the attention of the pilots overhead. The branches of the canopy are too thin, too bare, to give us adequate protection. So we throw ourselves into the undergrowth and crawl.

I take the lead, scanning the wilderness for signs of shelter. The leafless twigs are sharp; every movement scrapes my face, and I have to close my eyes to protect them. I'm crawling blindly now. If we pass by any handy caves or ditches, I won't even see them.

Crash!

Another bomb hits, too far away for us to spot its effects. Within seconds there is another explosion up ahead, only twenty metres from our position. The aftershock crumples my body. I'm flung backwards, a rag doll in the snow.

I lie, stunned, unknowing and uncaring. My ears are ringing with the agony of the sound. There's nothing but the clamour of more falling bombs: crashes and thumps and the howls of dying animals in the distance. Are some of those howls my friends? I don't know. We are all going to die anyway. Maybe I'm already dead.

A face swims into focus above me. 'Danika!' it mouths. The sound comes from a great distance, as though the speaker is shouting across an abyss. I blink and try to focus. It's Clementine. Her curls fall above my face like a golden scarf, tickling my skin. I want to brush them aside. I want her to leave me alone.

'Danika, move!' she tries again.

This time her words register. My ears still throb, but I'm starting to get a grip upon myself. I force my body up onto its knees. I tell myself that this is not real, this is just a dream. None of this is real. The pain is not real, nor the fear nor the shock. And so, if it isn't real, I can force myself to keep going. It will be just like my father is reading a storybook to me. This is happening to someone else, because it cannot be happening to me.

Clementine offers me her hand. I accept it. The others are clustered around, waiting for me to come to my senses. Later I might feel ashamed, embarrassed that I wasted precious seconds like this, but for now I'm only grateful that they stayed.

We push upwards. Maisy takes the lead now, and she takes us slightly to the side. At first I wonder why she would make our trek harder. Then I remember the explosion ahead of us. We have to avoid the sites of previous explosions; if we crawl across a smoking crater, we will be easily visible from the air. Besides, the alchemy bombs could have left any number of perils behind – a pit of spiders, perhaps, or poison that burns like acid through our skin.

'Over there!' Clementine points through the snow.

My eyes and ears are still slightly distorted by the explosion, so it takes a second to figure out what I'm seeing. It's a ledge of rock, like a miniature cliff face on the side of the mountain. There are dark shadows around its base. Caves. If we can reach them . . .

There is something sticky running down my face – probably blood, although it's hard to tell. I might just be imagining it. But it doesn't matter because now I've got *hope*, and that's a lot more effective than a bandage would be. I refuse to die of blood loss when we're so close to safety.

Another bomb explodes to our left. It's not close

enough to throw us aside, but I still feel the whoosh smack my face.

'Watch out!'

The bomb shoots fireworks into the sky. A few sparks collide with overhanging tree branches, and suddenly there is fire in the canopy. I don't understand how it's happened, since everything is so wet and cold. Surely these trees can't burn in the middle of winter. But alchemy wins out over nature, and burn they do. Flames leap from tree to tree, sparking odd colours. Branches shrivel and fall. They hiss as they hit the ground, extinguished by snow . . . but some fall into thicker patches of undergrowth, and fire is everywhere.

The fog of the morning is gone. Instead there is smoke. Thick, grey smoke that fills my lungs and pushes me away from my goal. I struggle to keep up with the feet in front of me. I don't even know who I'm following now – I just trust that they're heading in the right direction. Branches thwack into my face. I cough and splutter. I fall. I push myself up again and keep going, because the others have already waited for me once and I don't think they'll do it again.

Suddenly, we're below the shadows of the rocks. There's a clatter of shoes and palms upon stone. I'm vaguely aware of my knees hurting, so I pull into a crouch and scuttle forward. There's another explosion behind us; it spews something wonderful into the air. The scent of baked apples, I think. Apples and cinnamon. Or maybe I'm just imagining it and I've been blasted into insanity.

The cave is cool. The cave is dark. And so I drag my body over the threshold, cough out a lungful of smoke, and slip into unconsciousness.

✳

WHEN I WAKE, IT'S DARK. EVERYTHING SEEMS A BLUR of light and shadow. I think I'm in my parents' old apartment, spinning around beneath the lanterns as my father's radio plays. Or perhaps that sound is my mother singing. *'Oh mighty yo, how the star-shine must go . . .'*

I blink and suck down a deep breath. The world crawls back into focus. I'm lying on stone, inside a cave. There is cold rock all around me. I can see white and shadow outside – snow in the night, perhaps. Someone has draped a blanket across me. No, it's a sleeping sack. I can smell the dirt and sweat.

'Danika?' says a voice.

I crane my neck around. The others are already awake. They're sitting by a campfire near the back

302

of the cave, sipping some kind of liquid that smells of spices.

Clementine puts down her drink. 'Are you all right?'

I suddenly remember collapsing after the explosion, staggering around like a drunkard in the snow. Shame flushes into my system. I almost got the entire crew killed. 'What happened?'

Maisy frowns. 'Do you remember the bombing?'

I nod. The movement hurts my head, but I try not to show it. I've already revealed my weaknesses to my crew today; I'm not about to make it worse. 'Is it over?'

'Yeah, it's over,' says Teddy. 'They used up all their bombs, then they just flew off like nothing had happened. Left half the mountain burning, mind you, but Maisy put out all the fires near our cave.' He pauses. 'Well, she nicked a few sparks for our campfire first, so at least we've managed to save our last match.'

'Are you sure you're all right, Danika?' says Clementine.

I force myself up onto my elbows, ignoring a wave of nausea. 'Yeah, why wouldn't I be?'

'You were in front when that explosion hit – you got it worse than us,' she says.

I feel a ripple of gratitude. It would be so easy to blame me, to tell me off for risking all their lives.

I had no right to have a breakdown out there on the slopes, not when all our survival was at stake. But Clementine is blaming it on my proximity to the blast rather than my stupidity.

'Do you want something to eat?' she adds.

I move to shake my head, but it hurts too much. I stop abruptly and say, 'No, thanks. I think I just need to rest.'

'All right,' says Teddy. 'Sounds like a good idea – I might turn in soon, too.'

I nestle back down beneath the sleeping sack. On my side, I have a clear view of the world outside the cave. The sky is black, and wind blusters against the rocks. Before I close my eyes, I just make out a swirl of white dust falling from the night. I don't know whether it's snow or cinders.

*

FOR ALMOST A DAY, I SLIP IN AND OUT OF CONSCIOUS-ness. I know that we have to keep moving. It isn't safe to stay in this cave, so close to the scene of the bombing. The hunters will be here soon. They will scour the landscape for survivors – or for our corpses. But I feel as though I've been drugged.

'It's all right,' says Teddy, when I try to apologise. It's the third time I've woken – or is it the fourth? –

and he's keeping guard while the others doze. 'You got whacked pretty hard by that blast, I reckon. Anyway, we could all use a rest.'

The only positive is that I'm starting to feel better. Each time I wake, I feel stronger. The world is clearer and my head throbs a little less. Around midday, I feel well enough to sit up against the cave wall and eat an orange. The juice is sweet and refreshing on my tongue.

By the time we hit late afternoon, the others are restless. The twins keep offering me food: leftover porridge, mostly, and mugs of spicy cocoa. They're obviously anxious to get moving, but no one has the heart to force me.

It's up to me now. I have to make up for the weakness I showed during the bombing. I have to force myself to move.

'What's the plan from here?' I say.

The others exchange glances.

'Well,' says Teddy, 'if you're feeling up to it, there's a smallish peak not far from here. More of a crag, really, but it'll give us a better view of our options.'

I frown. 'Options? Don't we just want to get out of the mountains?'

Teddy hesitates. 'Well, maybe. But Maisy reckons there's a passageway somewhere in the mountains

– a sort of shortcut east, that'll take us towards the Valley.'

'A passageway?'

Maisy nods. 'A narrow gorge, heading west to east. The smugglers use it a lot, apparently. And it must be nearby, because it starts just below Midnight Crest.'

'How do you know about it?' I say.

'It's mentioned in a lot of geology books, as an example of fissures in sedimentary rock. They call it the Knife, actually, since it slices into –'

I sit up straighter. 'The Knife?'

'Yes, that's right.'

For the first time in over a day, I let my mouth stretch into a smile. 'Well, then, we're going the right way. It's just like the song: *I shan't waste my good life, I must follow my knife . . .*'

'Follow my knife,' repeats Maisy. 'Yes, that could be a reference to the Knife as a passage east.'

'It'd explain the *frozen night* line too,' Teddy says. 'That's why the song reckons you should cross the mountains near Midnight Crest – it's what you use to find the Knife.'

I force myself to rise. It's not as painful as I was expecting; a day of rest and decent food has done my body good. There's still a slight throbbing in the back of my skull, but I think I can cope with that. At least I'm not likely to collapse as soon as we step outside.

Maisy collects a fistful of smouldering twigs to transport our fire, then stamps out the remaining embers. We scatter the burnt twigs and cover them with snow.

'Don't want to leave an obvious trail,' says Teddy. 'Not if we can help it, anyway.'

Outside, the mountainside is almost unrecognisable. Half the trees have burned away, and the undergrowth is ash. Maisy has to extinguish her fire twigs because the spiral of smoke is too obvious in this barren landscape.

Burnt sticks crunch beneath our boots as we struggle through the snow and ruined forest towards the crag. The air still stinks of smoke, which meshes oddly with the cold tang of the winter wind. I suck on another orange as I walk.

By the time we reach the crag's peak, the light is just beginning to fade. It's a decent observation point: a rocky chunk that juts out from the mountain like a wart. We stumble towards its edge, then drop to our knees. This is nothing compared to the mountains' major peaks, but it still feels dizzyingly high. I almost don't trust myself to get any closer – in my current state, I'll probably topple over the edge.

'Look,' whispers Maisy.

I follow her finger. Down below, to our left, a seam of shadow stretches away between the mountains. 'Is that the Knife?'

She nods. 'I think so. That bit where it twists, near the end, is supposed to resemble a knife's handle.'

'We're going now, then?'

Clementine gives me a quick look, then shakes her head. 'It's too late. I think we should find a spot to camp tonight, and look for a route down there tomorrow.'

I want to agree with her, to succumb to the temptation to sleep again. But I've already cost us enough time today. We have to make up for lost time. If the hunters are scouring these mountains for us . . .

'I reckon we should keep moving,' says Teddy. 'The sooner we get into the Knife, the better.' He turns to face us, but then frowns, as though something behind us has caught his attention. 'Hey, look over there.'

I turn quickly, afraid that we're under attack. But he's pointing to the landscape in general, not any immediate danger nearby. I scan the horizon, trying to figure out what's drawn his attention. There are no more mountains to our south; our current slope just falls down into flat plains. Empty land.

'What is it?' I say.

Teddy frowns. 'Do you reckon that's the wastelands?'

I don't know much about the wastelands, except what I've heard in folklore and ghost stories. They are vast and empty, covering a great swathe of Taladia between the Central Mountains and the southern cities. Down in the far south there are magnificent cities full of richies and the palace of King Morrigan himself. These wastelands, just like the mountains, separate the south from places like Rourton.

'That's why we have to turn east,' Maisy whispers. '*Follow my knife*. If we kept heading south from here we'd hit the wastelands.'

The rest of us nod, a little awestruck. There's a good reason we don't dare cross the wastelands. Years ago, the land was blasted to bits in weapons tests – the soil is toxic and the landscape is dotted with landmines and unexploded bombs. Not just normal bombs, either. They're the first experimental alchemy bombs, from when people were just learning to imbue their weapons with magic. If you trip the wrong wire, or stumble across the wrong patch of rocks . . .

'Does it matter?' says Clementine. 'We're going the other way.'

Teddy glances back towards the Knife, then turns his head to face the wastelands. He frowns again, as though trying to figure out what bothers him about the scene.

'If the wastelands are so empty,' he says, 'then why'd they build a train line between Gunning and . . . *that*?'

He points to a murky shape in the distance. It's too far away to make out any details, but if I strain my eyes I can imagine it's some kind of fortress. A city wall, perhaps, or a stone tower. It's just sitting there, alone, in the middle of the empty wastelands.

And Teddy is right about the train line. I hadn't noticed it in the shadows, but it re-emerges from behind a cluster of crags to our west, pylons glinting in the evening light. It runs straight down out of the mountains, across the wasteland towards the unknown building. The line falls back down to ground level as it crosses the wastes; clearly, this building is its destination.

'What's the king playing at?' says Teddy.

I shake my head. 'I don't know. The building must be some sort of outpost – a base for their hunters, maybe? I suppose the wastelands are a safe place to put a building, if you're worried about defending it.'

'That's true,' says Maisy. 'An enemy army could never sneak across the plains. Even if they weren't killed by the wasteland's dangers, the people in that fortress would see them coming a mile off.'

'There's another train line, further that way,' Clementine says, pointing. 'There must be a fork where the line splits, somewhere up here in the mountains.'

I follow her gaze. In the distance, far to our west, another train line stretches away south to meet the wastelands' horizon. That must be the major line, for richie travellers to return from Gunning to their homes in the south. But first their train – or maybe just a few carriages – can detour to this mysterious building, this fortress in the middle of the wastelands. Perhaps they even keep a second engine up there, waiting in secret to pull those carriages down to the fortress.

'Maybe it's for deliveries,' I say. 'To take supplies to that building. Food and stuff.'

We stare at the building for a while, but no one adds any new ideas. The entire situation makes no sense – and by this point, I'm almost past caring. My head aches, my feet are sore and I just want to find a safe place to collapse. The others must feel the same, because almost simultaneously we turn away from the lookout and head back into the trees.

There are no handy caves to shelter in tonight, but I spot an overgrown ditch nearby. Yesterday's fires didn't spread this far, so the ditch is well protected by branches and undergrowth. When we crawl underneath and drape ourselves in our sleeping sacks, it's almost like we have a ceiling.

There's no hope of a campfire tonight. We're too cramped in this tiny ditch; we'd probably set our sleeping sacks alight, or melt all the snow from our roof. Besides, we've only got one match left and it seems suicidal to waste it. So we share around food that doesn't need cooking: biscuits, fruit and leftover porridge. The porridge has congealed into a sort of glue, so I try rolling it between my palms to restore a little heat.

'Trying to start a street-ball match, Danika?' says Clementine.

I look down at my porridge, which I've unwittingly rolled into a gluggy ball. 'Something like that,' I say, and pop the ball into my mouth. It's not five-star cuisine, but at least it's edible.

'I used to like street-ball,' says Teddy, looking wistful. 'I could win twenty silvers in a good night's betting on a game.'

I snort. 'Is that why you ran off from Rourton? Unpaid gambling debts?'

Teddy shakes his head. 'Nah, not exactly.'

There's a pause as we wait for more details. I suddenly remember Radnor's words to Teddy in the sewer. *'You begged me for a spot to save you from a manhunt, Nort . . .'*

'Well, go on then,' says Clementine. 'Tell us why you joined the crew. I think we're a bit past secrecy at this point.'

Teddy shrugs. 'Well, before we left Rourton, I got into a bit of trouble. So I tracked down Radnor for help – he owed me a favour, you see, and there was word on the streets he was putting a crew together. So I joined up.' He grins. 'And the rest is history, right?'

'Yeah, but what sort of trouble were you in?' I say. 'Must've been pretty serious to scare the great Teddy Nort himself into running out of Rourton. It's not like you'd never been in trouble before.'

'This was a different sort of trouble,' says Teddy. 'It wasn't the guards that were after me. I was hiding out in this richie's cupboard, waiting for night so I could steal his antique brooch collection –'

Clementine rolls her eyes. 'Of course you were.'

'– and I accidentally overheard some confidential stuff in the next room,' says Teddy. 'The richie caught me, and I only just managed to get away. But I reckon what I heard was pretty valuable, because he set half the private detectives in Rourton after me.

'He even offered a secret reward and roped a bunch of scumbags into hunting me down. I've escaped the guards loads of times, no problem. But half my allies were ready to turn me in – that's how good the reward was. I had to get out of town.'

'Why didn't I hear about this?' I say. 'If this richie was offering a reward, I would've thought he'd plaster it all over Rourton.'

Teddy shakes his head. 'Didn't want his bosses to find out the information had been compromised, I reckon. Wanted to hunt me down secretly and get rid of me, without anyone finding out what happened.'

'Must have been some pretty serious information,' I say, impressed. 'What was he up to – assassinating his political rivals or something?'

'Nah, nothing interesting like that,' says Teddy. 'Just some boring trade talk. They kept yabbering on about something called Curiefer – I didn't understand half of it, to be honest . . .'

Maisy sits up. 'Did you just say Curiefer? That's what they're trading?'

Teddy nods.

'Oh no.' Maisy pushes her fingers against her lips. 'I can't believe it.'

'Huh?'

'Curiefer is a liquid metal from the far north. It's very rare and dangerous to extract – people have been trying to mine it for centuries. Someone must have found a decent source, and now they're exporting it south . . .'

'Why? What's it good for?'

Maisy hesitates. 'It's the only known substance that can deactivate magnets.'

'*What?*'

'Curiefer burns easily; it's flammable at the best of times. But if you expose it to a big enough crash . . .' She trails off. 'It explodes on impact, and the radiation scrambles nearby magnets. It wipes them clean, turns them back into normal iron. If King Morrigan has found a source of Curiefer, he could erase any magnetic field.'

She pauses. '*Any* magnetic field.'

There is a moment of silence as her meaning sinks in. Taladia is already at war with other countries in multiple directions. Our king hasn't yet invaded the land beyond the Magnetic Valley, because it's too risky to move his magical weaponry through the gap. But if this mineral gives him the power to erase the magnets' strength . . . .

'The Valley,' I whisper. 'He's going to destroy the Valley.'

'That's why he built a train line over the mountains,' says Teddy, paling. 'That must've been what we saw at the back of the cargo carriage, behind all that mesh. Big vats of this Curiefer stuff coming

315

down from the north. They'd truck it down the main trade road to Gunning, I reckon, but the road over the mountains'd be too unreliable. Snowstorms, rock falls . . .'

Maisy nods. 'Curiefer is volatile – they'd need to move it carefully.'

'Exactly,' Teddy says. 'No wonder they extended the train line! The king pretends the train line's just a treat for richie passengers, so no one guesses what he's up to, but –'

'But the train line has a fork,' I say, 'so they can uncouple the cargo carriage for a detour to that building in the wastelands. But it's not just food supplies they're delivering, it's –'

'Curiefer,' Teddy breathes. 'Blimey, no wonder that richie wanted to hunt me down in Rourton. I stumbled across the secret of the century.'

There is a long pause.

'But if the king's armies break across the Magnetic Valley,' says Clementine, 'it'll mean another war, won't it? There will be more forced recruitments – we don't have enough soldiers to invade the lands beyond the Valley.'

'They'll conscript younger kids,' I say. 'They already take us when we turn eighteen. If they want more soldiers, they'll have to lower the age barrier . . .'

'Nowhere will be safe,' says Maisy quietly.

316

'There will be nowhere left to give people hope. Nowhere for refugee crews to run to.'

No one responds. I try to imagine a world without the Magnetic Valley. That place is a dream for so many young scruffers: a gateway to the lands beyond, a place where the king's bombs cannot fall. And now he is going to destroy it. There will be nowhere left beyond his power. There will be no more hope. And we will have made this terrible journey for nothing.

'But Curiefer only works if there's a big enough boom, right?' Teddy says. 'It's not enough just to set it on fire – there's gotta be a serious impact to make it blow up?'

Maisy nods.

'So how's the king gonna do it? It's not like he can just use alchemy – not in the Valley's magnetic field.'

'How about cannons?' Clementine suggests. 'He could set up the cannons further back from the Valley's entrance, and shoot the Curiefer in from a distance. The impact would come when it hit the ground, and then –'

Maisy shakes her head. 'A cannon would set off the Curiefer as soon as you fired it. You'd need a way to launch it that saves its impact until the end. Something that builds up speed slowly until –'

Teddy slams a fist into his opposite palm. 'Ka-boom!'

We all fall silent.

'That building in the wastelands,' says Teddy. 'I reckon it's some kind of secret military base. Good spot to hide it, really – out in the wastelands, where no one ever goes. It's gotta be where they're stashing the Curiefer. And that fork in the train line's there to deliver it . . .'

'So what?' says Clementine.

Teddy sits up. His eyes are hard now, glinting beneath the snowy roof of our hideout. 'So I reckon that's their weakness. If someone took out that place – blew it up, or burned it down, or something – that'd be a pretty massive blow to the king.'

A prickle runs across my skin. I know what he's angling at now. I know who he means by 'someone'. But it's ridiculous. We're just a bunch of teenagers. We've only survived this long because of luck, and not all of us have made it. A memory flashes hot across my mind: screaming, blood in the water, Radnor's body slipping from my grasp . . .

'Stop it, Teddy,' says Clementine. 'Don't even think about it. We've come so far already to reach the Valley. We just have to turn east through the Knife and –'

'If we don't do something, soon there won't *be* a Valley!'

'But it's not up to us to –'

There is a shout outside. Clementine falls silent. We all stare at each other, suddenly afraid.

'This way!' calls a distant voice. It's distorted by the wind, and muffled through our roof of snowy branches, but there's no mistaking the tone. 'Hurry up. I want to find those brats before the night is over.'

I swallow. The others look nauseated. We all recognise that voice, and what its presence here means. Sharr Morrigan is on the mountainside.

CHAPTER TWENTY-FOUR
THE CHOICE

WE KEEP SILENT FOR SEVERAL MINUTES, STRAINING our ears for any hint of movement outside. It's hard to separate natural noises – whipping wind, or snow clumps falling from overladen branches – from what might be a human footstep. But there is something strange in the wind: a howl that doesn't seem entirely natural.

Teddy suddenly pales.

I bend close and breathe in his ear: 'What is it?'

He looks at me. 'Borrash.'

It takes me a second to recognise the name. Borrash was our last surviving foxary, the one that Lukas sold to a farmer outside of Gunning. How could he be here, in the snow and ice of the mountains? Then I realise. The hunters have brought him here. Sharr Morrigan must have bought him from the farmer – or taken him forcibly, more likely – and she is using the beast to track us down.

Teddy closes his eyes and concentrates. I know he has a connection to the creature, but can they truly sense one another at such a distance? This isn't the time to ask. I keep quiet and try not to distract Teddy from his work. He grinds his teeth together and clenches his eyes so tightly that it looks painful.

I glance at the twins. They look just as lost as I am. We're out of our depth, with no real knowledge of the power Teddy wields through his Beast proclivity. Teddy lets out a low growl. I'm not sure whether the noise is his own, or whether he's somehow channelling the emotions of the foxary itself. I remember how Lukas screeched like a hawk when he borrowed the bird's eyes – perhaps Teddy has made a connection with Borrash. It doesn't sound like a happy reunion.

Teddy's eyes fly open. He looks shaken. 'Sharr's got a whole crew of foxaries.'

'What?'

'She's got four of them, Danika. They're on our scent trail right now – they're going to find us! We've got to move!'

We pack up the sleeping sacks as quickly and quietly as possible. Then we clamber out of the ditch and dash through the foliage into the twilight. My neck itches so intensely now that I have to keep reaching back to scratch it, even in the midst of this terror. My proclivity is clearly on the way, but at this rate I won't live long enough to use it.

'This way,' gasps Clementine.

We head back into the trees, struggling not to trip in ankle-deep snow and foliage. We need a way to disguise our scent, and that means water. A river, a creek, a muddy ditch . . . But everything is frozen solid. We've been melting snow to provide fresh water, never bothering to search for streams. Even if there is a water supply nearby, I have no idea where it is.

The downhill slope is marked by even thicker undergrowth. It knots around our ankles; each of us trips at least once, and my cheeks are soon raw from scratches and cold.

The sounds of pursuit draw closer. We must be leaving a perfect scent trail for the foxaries. The air is crisp; the only competing scents are damp wood and snow. There is no time to search for a pond, I realise. Any second, the foxaries and their riders will burst onto the top of this slope and spot us.

We throw ourselves into a grove of scraggly trees.

Snow and branches hide us from sight, but it's no use – the foxaries will charge down here like rabid dogs when they catch our scent. I wipe a clump of sweaty hair from my eyes, and light glints off my mother's silver bracelet . . . 'The alchemy charm!'

'What?'

I grab the silver rose charm from my bracelet. 'Lukas used this to hide his scent from our foxaries.'

The others' eyes widen. The twins are surely rich enough to have used a charm like this before, and Teddy has probably stolen a few in his time . . . would he have learned to invoke their spells before he sold them?

There is barely enough room on the rose's tiny petals to fit our fingertips. I find a speck of cold silver, just enough space for my pinkie. The last thing I see is a trio of frightened faces with closed eyes. Then I shut my own eyelids and focus. *I'm hidden . . . We are hidden . . . The foxaries cannot sense us . . .*

The air twangs. The rose heats up, painfully hot beneath my fingertip, but I refuse to let go. It feels as though my skin is burning. I can only hope the spell will hold – not just for me, but for all of us. The silence seems to stretch forever. There is no approaching sound, no crunch of paws in the downhill snow.

When I cannot hold my breath any longer I release it in a slow huff. I flutter my eyelids open for half a second to steal a glance at the slope. Nothing. No foxaries in sight. Just silent snow.

The others open their eyes.

'I reckon we should double back,' says Teddy. 'Walk in the places we already left a scent trail. If the foxaries come after us, Sharr might think they're just picking up an older trail that she's already searched . . .'

We hurry back up the slope and through the trees. Occasionally I hear a growl in the distance, but we just hurl ourselves into the undergrowth and engage the charm's alchemy spell until the danger has passed.

It's in one of these hiding places – when I'm crammed between a boulder and Clementine's kneecaps – that my gaze falls directly on Midnight Crest. I stare up at the crumpled fortress and fight a terrible, bizarre urge to laugh. Here we are, fugitives in the snow. And here are the king's hunters, ready to tear us to pieces. A different king, perhaps, but still a Morrigan. Still a tyrant. Has anything changed in Taladia, in the hundreds of years since that fortress burned?

Finally, we find ourselves back up at the lookout point. There has been no sign of the foxaries for a while now. I'm starting to hope they've found our old trail, back down among the burnt regions of the forest. Perhaps they're sniffing around our old cave. We stayed there an entire day, so our scent must be strong.

There is a sudden rattle in the sky.

'Hide!'

We scramble back into the trees as a dozen biplanes roar overhead. They descend, spiralling towards the wastelands beyond the mountains. I venture back onto the rocky edge of our lookout, just in time to see the biplanes disappear below. The dusk is too deep now to make out any details, but I know where the biplanes have landed: inside the walls of that mysterious fortress. Out in the wastelands . . .

Behind me, Maisy gasps.

'What is it?' I say.

'That fortress must be the airbase. I knew the palace had their airbase somewhere near the Central Mountains, but I never thought . . .'

'*That's* where they store their biplanes? The ones that bomb our cities?'

She nods. 'I can't believe it's here. I can't believe they're storing the Curiefer in the same place as their biplanes.' She raises a hand to her lips, stunned. 'Oh no. That's how they're going to do it.'

'Do what?'

Maisy turns on me, her expression desperate. 'They need a huge impact to explode the Curiefer. It's not enough just to burn it; they need it to actually *explode*. So they'll load the Curiefer onto biplanes, and then drop it over the Val–'

'Hang on,' Teddy says. 'You can't fly biplanes over the Valley. The magnets would mess with the engines' alchemy before they even had a chance to drop the Curiefer.'

Maisy hesitates.

'They don't need to drop it,' I say. 'As soon as those planes fly over, the magnets'll bring them down. I'd say a plane crash is a pretty huge impact.'

'But the pilots will die!' Clementine says.

'That wouldn't stop King Morrigan,' I say. 'He could force the pilots to do it. He could hold their families hostage – their spouses, their children. He'd only need to sacrifice a few pilots, a few planes. And then . . .'

I trail off. Images flash like bombs behind my eyes. Magnetic rocks deactivating, in a blaze of biplane wreckage. The rest of the king's air force flying overhead, ready to launch an assault on the land beyond. People screaming, burning, dying. Biplanes clearing the way for troops on the ground, armed with alchemy rifles and cannons . . .

'No wonder they built their airbase in the

wastelands,' says Teddy. 'You'd need a damn good hideout for a place like that. Somewhere to stash their Curiefer *and* their biplanes? I don't reckon they'd want a bunch of refugees to find it.' He pauses. 'Or to do anything about it.'

'What?' Clementine pales. 'You can't still be suggesting . . .'

'I reckon we could do it,' says Teddy. He has a strangely intense look in his eyes. 'It's been done before.'

He points towards Midnight Crest, nestled high among the mountaintops. Its ruins are barely visible in the fading light, but a faint silhouette remains printed on the sky.

'Those people stood up against their king,' Teddy says. 'They burned his prison to the ground.'

A peculiar tingle runs down my spine.

Teddy turns back to Maisy. 'You said that Curiefer stuff is flammable, right? It's hard to make it explode, but it's easy to burn?'

'Yes,' says Maisy quietly. 'That's right.'

Clementine shakes her head. 'Teddy, stop it! We're not warriors – we're just a bunch of kids. Radnor died to keep this crew safe – he wouldn't want us to throw our lives away.'

Teddy scoffs. 'Hate to break it to you, but Radnor's parents were revolutionaries – *real* revolutionaries.

They tried to set up secret meetings, plotting against the monarchy and all that. But someone ratted them out, so the guards in Rourton killed them. Would've killed Radnor too, except I was burgling the place next door and I smuggled him out across the rooftops.'

'What?'

'That's why Radnor let me join this crew,' says Teddy. 'Because he owed me his life. But those guards still shot his parents, and his little sisters . . . If anyone would've wanted us to attack that place, I reckon it'd be Radnor.'

There is silence.

I run a hand through my hair. We now have two routes, and not much time to choose one. To our east lies the Knife: our passage to freedom. We can run away and try to save ourselves. We can leave the king's schemes for someone else to deal with.

To our south lie the wastelands, including the airbase. There lies the palace's fleet of biplanes and – we suspect – a massive stash of Curiefer. If we destroy that stash, we might stop a war. And if we destroy those biplanes, we might stop alchemy bombs from falling on Taladia's own cities . . . including Rourton.

We might be the only ones who know about this base. The only ones in a position to stop this war. How can we turn away?

'*I shan't waste my good life,*' recites Clementine, watching my expression. 'Remember the second verse, Danika? That song is warning us to avoid the wastelands – that's what it means by "waste", I'm sure!'

I shake my head. 'But if we burn that airbase, we could save thousands of lives. Millions, even. How could that be a waste?'

Clementine doesn't answer. She just stares at Maisy, then back at me, as though I'm missing the point. Then I realise what she's really trying to say. She doesn't want to run away to protect *herself*. She's trying to keep her promise to Maisy – to keep her safe. Clementine has sacrificed everything to find her sister a better life. How can we ask her to throw all that away?

Maisy steps forward. 'I think we should try to destroy the airbase.'

Clementine chokes. 'What?'

'I think they're right,' Maisy says. 'We can't just run away. And besides, where would we run? If the king destroys the Magnetic Valley, our hopes are ruined anyway.'

There is silence. We all stare at Maisy. This is not what I expected. Timid, shy Maisy Pembroke is in favour of attacking the airbase?

'The palace biplanes are down there,' Maisy says. 'Those planes killed our mother. Those hunters killed Radnor. And those palace forces, that government . . . those are the people that our father's friends work for. It all comes back to King Morrigan. He's caused everything we've been through. We've got a chance to fight back. I've never had that chance before, Clem. Not really.'

As Maisy speaks, she stares down at the wastelands. She clenches her fists. 'And I'm not afraid any more.'

Against all odds, I believe her. This is not the meek little girl that I met in Rourton's sewer pipes. This is a young woman whose proclivity is Flame.

'All right,' says Clementine. She blinks hard, then nods. 'All right.'

I throw one last glance back at the route to our east. The Knife stretches away through the mountains, luring us to the Valley. But the last streaks of twilight are fading, a dusty crimson, and the colour reminds me of fire. Of my family burning, and Radnor's blood in the water. Of those who will die in King Morrigan's war.

I swallow my fears and turn to face the wastelands.

'I'm in,' I say. 'Let's go.'

CHAPTER TWENTY-FIVE

GLASSES OF HOURS

IT'S PAST DAWN WHEN WE REACH THE WASTELANDS. Empty plains stretch out before us, barren and dead in the morning light. My legs ache from trekking down the side of the mountain; my calf muscles aren't used to moving at such an angle.

I don't want to imagine what lies ahead. The wastelands. I'm heading into the wastelands. The thought sends a queasy jolt into my gut, like I've swallowed a fistful of rotten cabbage. What will we face out there? Unexploded alchemy bombs? An unstable landscape? There could be magical residue in the sand, in the stone . . .

I glance back up towards the mountains. The peaks rise high behind us now: stone and snow against the sky. Despite my earlier resolve, a cowardly part of me wants to turn around. To dart back into the wilderness and follow our song east to the Magnetic Valley.

'We're coming back,' Clementine says. 'After we deal with the airbase, we're coming back to the Knife. This journey isn't over.'

Her words are resolute, but there's an odd sort of quaver in her voice. I think she's trying to convince herself more than anyone.

At the bottom of the slope, we stop to assess our route ahead. The ground itself looks gritty, like wet sand, and frosted over in places. It isn't hard to imagine sinking entirely into the muck. I see no signs of fresh water to drink, so it's lucky we've filled our stolen wineskins with snow. There are gentle undulations – mounds of dirt and rocky plateaus – but compared to the mountain range behind us, the landscape looks flat.

'We won't have much cover,' says Teddy.

'We'll just have to keep to the shadows,' I say. 'You know, lurk around the edges of plateaus and stuff. Avoid the empty patches of rock.'

No one else seems keen to go first, so I force a confident expression onto my face and stride out into the muck. It's reassuring that the ground doesn't explode as soon as I stand on it. Perhaps stories of the wastelands' horrors have been exaggerated. It wouldn't be the first time that a scruffer rumour took on a life of its own.

We cross several kilometres of gritty moorland. Nothing much happens, apart from the itching in my neck. Clementine tells me off for scratching it ('You'll scar yourself before you get your proclivity tattoo!') so I settle for munching candied nuts to keep my fingers busy.

Then Maisy shields her eyes. 'Do you see . . .?'

I follow her gaze. There's a strange sort of shimmer around the next cluster of rocks: a haze of heat and steam that rises from the earth. We venture forward to take a closer look, and a noxious stink curls up into my throat.

'Blimey,' Teddy says, coughing, 'that's worse than my grandpa's old socks.'

The smell reminds me of Rourton's restaurant bins in summer: a piercing combination of rotten fruit and mouldering eggs. I pinch my nose shut and blink away the water in my eyes, straining for a better look at the source of the odour.

It's a shallow pond, its liquid a murky grey. Steam rises in stinking spirals, plinking with sharp little pockets of darkness. A daytime echo of stars: black spots against a sunlit sky. It's our first real sign of magical corruption in the wastelands.

'Come on,' Teddy says. 'Let's get going before our nostrils explode.'

The stench fades quickly once we're past the pond, as though it's incapable of lingering on normal air. But even so, I don't breathe easily until the liquid – and its winking black stars – are far behind us.

About an hour into our trek, I spot an overhang on the edge of a vast plateau. I lead the others across to walk beneath its eaves. It feels much safer here in the shadows. The darkness is oddly comforting on my skin, and after a while my itching starts to subside. Occasionally I spot a shimmer in the distance – a twist of strange smoke, or a glint of abandoned metal beneath the sun. But these sightings are few and far between, and this shadowed pathway feels as dependable as any other route we've taken. Step by step, our footsteps converge into a rhythmic trudge.

'So, how are we gonna destroy this building?' says Teddy eventually.

'If we could get a fire going nearby,' says Maisy, 'I could redirect it towards the biplanes. If those planes are loaded with alchemy bombs . . .' She leaves the sentence hanging.

Teddy lets out a low whistle. 'Gee, we'd want to be a long way off when that lot goes up.'

I turn to Maisy. 'How close would you have to be?'

334

'I don't know. I think it depends on the severity . . . If we could get a big fire going, I might be able to link into its power from further away.'

There's a pause.

'If we're gonna do this,' Teddy says, 'we'd better do it soon. Those hunters are still after us, and we left a pretty obvious trail coming down the mountain. And once they realise we're out here . . .' He gestures grimly at the flat expanse of the waste-lands. 'It's gotta be tonight, I reckon, if we want a hope of getting back to the Knife in one piece.'

We nod in agreement, although Clementine doesn't look happy. 'I still don't see how we're supposed to start this fire.'

I mentally run through the items in our packs. There are clothes, food, sleeping sacks and cooking pots. We have only one match left. There is nothing that could set fire to a plane from afar. Nothing except . . . 'The flare!'

'What?'

'The second flare, from the guard tower in Rourton! Which pack was it in?'

'I don't know,' says Teddy.

We pull to a halt and throw the packs down. I scrabble to open the closest one, hardly daring to hope. I'd almost forgotten about the flare since I removed it from my trouser-leg, back in the forest outside Rourton. What if it was in one of the packs that went over the waterfall?

'Here, I've got it!' says Teddy, yanking the flare from a side pocket. 'Do you reckon –?'

'Worth a try, isn't it?' I say. 'We know these flares can bring down biplanes. If we can shoot one into the building, and Maisy extends the firepower just before it hits –'

'Then we'll get a damn big boom,' Teddy says, grinning.

I examine the flare. It's been partially crushed by its days in the pack, and the tubing is a little flaky. Will it still work after being dunked in water several times? I don't know, but it's the only plan we've got.

'We'll need a high point to launch it from,' I say. 'Somewhere for Maisy to see what's happening, to control the fire. One of the plateaus, maybe?'

'I reckon that'd do it,' says Teddy. 'Hey, it'd be pretty ironic to blow up this place with one of the palace's own flares, wouldn't it?'

I nod. 'Like shooting down that biplane, but on a bigger scale.' I deliberately avoid mentioning Lukas's name. At this point, it seems easier to pretend he never existed.

We wrap the flare in a protective bundle of clothing and place it back into the pack. Then we hoist our packs on again and continue walking.

Just before midday, we stop to rest beneath a pocket of boulders. We allow ourselves a generous swig from our wineskins and a fistful of broken biscuits. But despite my physical exhaustion, I want to keep moving. It's a strange sort of disconnect between body and mind: one yearns to rest, the other to push onward.

I think the others feel the same; there's a new light in their eyes, and a flicker of hope in their voices. I'd put it down to the sugar in the biscuits, but I think it's something more than that. The simple fact that we have a plan – even a rudimentary one – provides a new burst of energy. We have *hope*, we have a *purpose*, and that's better than anything else we've experienced in days.

As morning fades into afternoon, we set off again towards the fortress. We stick to the shadows of a plateau's overhang, and pass the time by sharing tales of life in Rourton. Teddy has fun relating some of his most daring heists – often to the mock horror of Clementine and Maisy, who are personally acquainted with many of the burglar's victims. I join in with tales of mishaps in Rourton's dodgiest bars, and soon we've almost forgotten the danger we're in. And all the while, the fortress grows closer: first a shadow, then a silhouette – and finally a distant building, with contours clear against the sky.

Suddenly, Clementine shrieks. I'm in the middle of a laugh when it happens and it takes me a couple of seconds to register that anything is wrong. By the time I spin around, Clementine's knees are sinking rapidly into the mire.

Teddy swears and grabs her under the arms. Maisy and I each seize a hand and pull, but our efforts make Clementine scream in pain. 'You're tearing my legs off!'

'You're sinking!' says Teddy. He gives her a more violent yank and Clementine screams again. This time, though, terror cuts the sound off short.

'Stop pulling!' says Maisy. 'Clem, you've got to relax. Take it slowly.'

Clementine looks about as relaxed as a lobster in a richie's cooking pot, but she nods. She takes several deep breaths, then lets her limbs slacken.

'Good, that's good. Now just lift your legs out slowly. Don't fight the sand, just slip around it.'

We help support Clementine as she slides herself upwards into our arms. It's slow and hard – my own knees buckle from the strain. Clementine isn't a heavy girl, but the added bulk of her pack is enough to make the weight unbearable. It only took a few seconds for her to sink to her knees, but it seems to take forever to wriggle out again.

'That's it!' Maisy staggers under her own share of

the strain. 'You're almost there. Just stay calm and stay slow.'

There's a final slurp of suction as we pull Clementine free. We tumble back onto the rocks, wheezing and gasping in exhaustion.

'What the hell was that?' manages Teddy.

Maisy shakes her head. 'It's quicksand . . . but there can't be quicksand here. It's not geologically possible – the earth is half-frozen.'

'Yeah, but this is the wastelands,' I remind her. 'This was where the palace tested all their earliest alchemy weapons. Clementine might've just stepped in the wrong place and set off an unexploded spell.'

'Well, I'm not walking on any more sand,' says Teddy. 'I reckon we'll be safer up on the rocks.'

I shake my head. 'We'd be too exposed. We're a lot better hidden down here.'

'So what? We'd be a lot better hidden if we were six feet under the quicksand, too, but I wouldn't call that a happy ending.'

'Do you really think there's more than one quicksand trap around here?'

Teddy nods. 'I reckon that's what the smuggler's song is on about.'

'*How the dark swallows light,*' says Maisy. 'The ground was trying to swallow her.'

'Yeah, exactly. And you know the next line – *When the glasses of hours hold on*. Well, it fits, doesn't it? Hourglasses are about timing things, right? Being quick? And hourglasses are full of sand, so if you put the clues together . . .'

He's right. Quick and sand. Quicksand. I mentally kick myself for being stupid. We shouldn't have taken the song for granted. We knew that those middle lines were about physical locations, but I never bothered to stop and decipher them properly. And as a result, Clementine could have died.

'All right,' I say. 'We'll stay away from the sand.'

We wait about ten more minutes, until our breathing returns to a normal pace and Clementine looks strong enough to walk. She winces with each step, and I feel a surge of guilt for our initial yank against the quicksand. It's lucky we didn't break her ankles.

'Come on,' says Teddy. 'Don't put your feet on anything that's not solid.'

We clamber along the sides of the plateau, grabbing for handholds and places to plant our feet. In any other circumstances this might seem like fun: a troupe of crabs, scrabbling sideways along the rock face. But now, with unstable sand to catch us if we fall, it's terrifying. My pack feels heavier than ever. With every swing of my arms, it seems to drag me backwards towards the sand.

'This isn't working,' Clementine says. 'We've got to get up on top of the plateau.'

I shake my head. 'But we'll be in plain sight – there's no cover up there.'

'Can you make an illusion to cover us, Danika?' says Teddy.

'Not while we're moving. I can only do it if the magnets are still.'

'Well, maybe we should stop,' says Maisy. 'We could hide under an illusion until it gets dark.'

No one else has a better idea, so we agree. Despite our earlier burst of energy, the terror of Clementine's accident has leached our strength. I think we're all secretly keen for an excuse to rest. We scramble up to the top of the plateau and surround ourselves with the magnetic circle. I cast the strongest illusion I can muster. The air shimmers and I know the magnets have caught it.

Finally, I allow myself to collapse. I feel ridiculously exposed up here: no trees, no boulders, no cover at all. We lie upon a bare expanse of rock, in full view of both the mountains behind us and the fortress ahead. If my illusion fails, we are dead. All our lives rest upon my shoulders. It's a frightening thought.

After several hours' rest, we treat ourselves to a meal. The tastiest supplies are running low now;

we polish off the last of the oranges and nuts. There are enough oats to last weeks, but no one fancies eating them raw and we can't afford to waste water to soak them.

When the sun goes down, the wastelands look almost beautiful. The plains turn a murky orange, and the mountains behind us glint gold with snow. Ordinarily I might enjoy this foreign sight – so unlike the smog-choked haze of Rourton – but now I'm just impatient. The sooner it gets dark, the sooner I will feel safe.

'Look,' says Maisy. A flock of birds wheels overhead, swooping across the darkening sky. 'Aren't they beautiful?'

I frown at the birds. As far as I can tell, they're trying to catch insects. From an insect's point of view, this wouldn't be a beautiful sight but a deadly horror. Just another bloodbath upon the wastelands. Then I tell myself off for being so morbid.

'Time to get going?' I say.

Teddy shrugs. 'A few more minutes, I reckon.'

Soon, shadows are chasing the last hints of gold from the sky. We gather up our orange peel ('Better not to leave a trail,' says Maisy), and slip the magnets back into a pack. After one last glance to ensure we've left nothing behind, I lead the others out across the plateau. Not long after this, however,

Teddy points out that it might be safer to leave the packs behind.

'In case we gotta run for it,' he says, dumping his pack in the shadows of the overhang. 'Safer not to be weighed down, I reckon. Always easier to flee a crime scene when you're travelling light.'

I pick out the flare and a couple of waterskins, and pocket a cooking knife for good measure. Then we add our packs to the pile and disguise the site with fistfuls of sand. I take a mental note of nearby landmarks: a double-layered plateau, and a pile of crumpled boulders. If we get away cleanly, we might have a chance to reclaim our packs on the way back to the Knife. And if we don't get away . . .

Well, best not to think about that.

We walk for half an hour, using the moon to guide us. It's dark enough to move with confidence now. No one will see us from up in the fortress, not in these shadows. The only real danger is that I might trip over a bump in the rocks. The fortress itself is mostly dark, except for a couple of windows with lights on.

'There mustn't be many people staying there,' says Maisy.

'I guess the Curiefer mission is pretty secretive,' I say. I don't mention my first reaction, which is sheer relief. If there was an army of people inside the

343

fortress, I don't think I could bring myself to blow it up. Not even if it meant stopping a war.

About a hundred metres from the building, we start to look for higher vantage points. Teddy spots a taller plateau to our left, so we take a detour to set ourselves up on its rocky peak. It's far from an ideal launching point for the flare, but at least it provides a decent view for Maisy to influence the flames.

'Can you see the biplanes?' whispers Maisy.

I scan the shapes up ahead. A stone wall encircles a generous patch of wasteland. A tower rises up on one side of the area, but the wall blocks the other portion of the compound from view.

'No,' I say. 'I think there's a yard or something down low, next to the tower. Should we aim for that, do you think?'

'I reckon they'd store the Curiefer in the tower,' says Teddy. 'That's what I'd do.'

'Maybe,' I say. 'But a flare won't do much damage to a tower.'

We stare at the fortress in silence, trying to weigh up the various options. I get a little antsy as the minutes tick by. I don't want to be stuck out here, exposed on the plateau, for another day of sunlight. The hunters might have figured out our route by now – they could even be combing the wastelands for signs. We have to finish this tonight.

'Come on,' I say. 'Let's just make a decision. The tower or the yard?'

'The yard,' Maisy and Clementine say in unison.

Teddy hesitates a moment, then nods. 'Yeah, all right. I guess one little flare wouldn't do much good against the tower.' He pauses. 'You should fire it, Danika. It's your flare, and you're the one who brought down the plane.'

'That was an accident,' I say. 'It was just luck.'

'Well, maybe you'll get lucky again.'

I step to the edge of the plateau, as close to the fortress as I can get. Clementine hands me the box of matches. I tip out our single remaining match, and hold it up against the moonlight. It doesn't look too healthy, but it just might be enough.

'Ready?' I say.

The others nod. Maisy steps up beside me, ready to strengthen the flame. Teddy balances our flare upon the edge of the plateau, pointing straight at the fortress yard.

'All right,' I say. 'Get ready to run.'

I strike the match. It doesn't catch, but I strike it again and this time there is a sulphuric sizzle. Maisy cups her hands across the flame and it grows – in fact, it grows so quickly that I almost drop the match to save my fingers. But I force myself to hold on and press its nib against the fuse.

Psheeeeooh!

The fuse catches immediately: a whiz of sparking light and metal. I drop the match and grab Maisy's arm – together, we run back across the plateau. The others are already metres ahead, sprinting to get as much distance as possible between their bodies and the fortress. We only have a few seconds, I know, until the spark will reach the gunpowder . . .

Nothing.

After half a minute of running, we stop to look back. The fuse has finished burning; there is no sign of light upon the rocks. But the flare has not exploded, or shot into the sky. My gut sinks, filling with a horrible cold. The flare must have been too damaged by its repeated exposure to water and frost and snow.

'Well,' says Clementine. 'At least we tried.'

There is a horrible laugh from the shadows behind us. Then a figure steps into the moonlight.

'Oh yes,' says Sharr Morrigan. 'You certainly did.'

CHAPTER TWENTY-SIX

WASTE

SHARR SMILES AT ME. SHE DOESN'T EVEN LOOK AT THE others. 'Hello, Danika. It's not every day I meet the girl who blasted my cousin out of the sky.'

'He deserved it.'

'Oh, I don't doubt that. Lukas has always been a disappointment to the family.' Sharr takes a step forward. 'I think his father was secretly relieved when his plane went down. A martyred prince – a hero, even, fighting for his country – murdered by a filthy scruffer. Can you imagine the publicity coup?'

I stare at her. No one speaks.

Sharr takes another step towards us. Her hair gleams like a dark mirror beneath the moon. Are there other hunters nearby? Have they spread out to search for us, or are they lurking just out of sight?

'Better for Lukas to be a martyred hero,' Sharr says, 'than a snivelling brat who won't even fulfil his duties.' She laughs at my reaction. 'Didn't you know, Glynn? My cousin was a secret embarrassment to the monarchy. The king would have named *me* as his heir, if it weren't for that brat getting in the way!

'I thought I had it in the bag, you know. Lukas was dead, and I would be the one to capture his killer. I would be known as the Great Huntress, the Royal Avenger . . . the papers would have lapped it up. The king would name me heir to the throne. I could set Taladia on track to her rightful future, as the greatest empire ever known.'

She steps forward again. Her eyes glint.

'But you slipped through my fingers again and again, and turned me into the laughing stock of the hunting corps. And then my cousin had the temerity to track me down in Gunning. Do you have any idea how distraught I was to discover the brat was still alive?'

Sharr clenches her fists. She looks barely in control of her emotions – a flare just waiting to explode. But she takes a deep breath, blinks hard and forces that smile back onto her face.

I think suddenly of the cooking knife that I took from our packs. My fingers flex towards my pocket, as subtly as I can manage. If I can just grab the knife without Sharr noticing, perhaps –

Then Sharr pulls out a pistol and aims it at my head.

My fingers retract. I know instantly my knife is no use against a gun. To attack Sharr now would be to sign all our death warrants.

Teddy gives an angry snort. 'What, you're using a gun? You've forgotten how to use your proclivity?'

'I don't use Flame against people who share my talent.' Sharr flicks her gaze towards Maisy for the first time. 'I'm not as stupid as your smuggler friend. Why do you think I shot those useless hunters with bullets instead of fire? One of them was a Flame user, just like me.'

I remember the bodies in the forest outside Rourton. Two hunters with bullet holes in their skulls. 'Why did you kill them?'

'They questioned my authority,' says Sharr. 'No one challenges me and survives.' She smiles and cocks the pistol. 'Least of all a filthy scruffer like you.'

A gust of wind trips across the rocks. I want to step backwards, to flee the range of her pistol, but I force myself to stand my ground. Getting shot in the back is not how I want to die. 'Are you going to shoot me?'

Sharr laughs. 'Not unless you force me to. I'd rather get my glory through a live capture and public execution . . . it's much more impressive than a dead body. But if you don't cooperate, I might shoot your friends.' She shifts the gun towards Maisy.

'Stop! I'll come with you, all right? Just don't –'

'Good,' says Sharr.

She whistles: a long, low sound that echoes across the plateau. There's a moment's pause, then a pile of rock rears up from the earth, twisting into the shape of a human in the night. It solidifies with a flicker of unnatural energy and there is suddenly another hunter before us. Obviously his proclivity is Stone.

Another hunter melts down out of the air itself. He paints himself out of the night like a walking shadow. Darkness. The nearness of his power makes the back of my neck itch again.

He slaps a pair of handcuffs around my wrists, then grabs my shoulder to keep me from running. But I have no plan to run. Not while these hunters surround my friends, or while Sharr Morrigan keeps her gun trained on Maisy's face.

'All right,' says Sharr. 'Let's go.'

*

THE HUNTERS ESCORT US TO THE OUTER WALLS OF the fortress. Before the gate is opened, they stuff our mouths with gags and tie blindfolds across our eyes. I wriggle my nose, shifting the fabric to get a glimpse underneath, but Sharr spots my action and slaps me across the cheek.

'Don't even think about it, you little brat!'

There is a noisy creak as the gate opens. The hunter's grip tightens on my shoulder and he yanks me forward across the threshold. The earth changes beneath my feet, from a boggy sand into solid cobblestones. I know now that I was right about the yard. We are clearly still outdoors, because I can feel the night breeze, but we are within the outer walls of the fortress. This yard must be where the biplanes are kept, ready to launch their assaults upon unwitting cities. Cities like Rourton. Ready to blow families like mine into pieces.

A new burst of hatred surges through my veins. I wish I had another chance to light that flare, to blast this place apart. But I'm useless now: just a blindfolded girl staggering through the dark. How did I ever think I could take on the palace and win? I have been so stupid, so arrogant. We should have listened to Clementine and run for the Valley when we had the chance.

We walk on cobblestones for about twenty metres. I feel so vulnerable without my sight; my only clues about the world are the stones beneath my feet and the hunter's pressure on my arm. Back in Rourton, I knew an old scruffer who'd been blinded by an alchemy bomb. He learned to see with his hands, his ears and his nose – he could even identify which street he was on by its smell. I often saw him perform this trick for richies in the hope of earning a few coins.

'The corner of Goddert and Waverly Roads,' he would say, tapping his nose. 'I can smell the baker that way, and there's a sewer on me right.'

Now, I try to copy some of his tricks, but I lack his years of practice to guide me. All I smell is metal and the sweat of my companions. At one point the wind stops abruptly, then starts again. Perhaps I'm walking between parked biplanes.

A door creaks open, and I know we have reached the tower. Hands yank me inside and the cobblestones turn to smoother tile beneath my boots. I'm not sure how many rooms are in this building, or where Sharr plans to take me, but I know the tower is large enough to house dozens of pilots. There seems little hope of memorising my route through the corridors – but still, I try. Left, right, up some stairs, another left . . .

I trip a few times on the stairs. My hands sting with the impact of catching myself, but it's better than smashing my face. Whenever I stumble, a hunter yanks me back upright and Sharr's nasty laughter filters through the dark.

When we have climbed four or five sets of stairs – and I have given up memorising Sharr's circuitous directions – I realise our footsteps are quieter. There are my own feet, of course, as well as Sharr's and those of the hunter who grips my arm, but no one else. I stop and twist aside, shouting muffled names through my gag. 'Teddy, Clementine, Maisy!'

Sharr strikes me again. 'Shut up.'

The hunter pushes me forward. I obey, but my heart is racing. Where have the others been taken? Will they be housed in a separate prison cell? Or will they be executed immediately, given shots to the head like those hunters in the forest?

I yank myself loose and stumble backwards. 'Teddy! Clementine, Mais–'

Sharr smashes me across the forehead with something cold and heavy. I fall, unconscious.

✳

I AWAKE IN DARKNESS. AT FIRST I THINK THE BLIND fold still covers my eyes, but I can't feel any fabr

All I sense is a terrible throbbing and a trickle of blood down the side of my face. Someone is dabbing it. Are they trying to torture me? It certainly feels like it; they're pressing harder now, shoving gobs of fabric into the wound. I let out a moan.

'Danika?'

I freeze. I know that voice . . .

'Danika, hold still. I won't hurt you.'

I open my eyes. Lukas Morrigan crouches beside me, pressing a wad of material against my head. He has a gash across his own cheek, but it looks a few days old; the blood has dried into a crimson crust.

'Where are the others?' I manage.

Lukas looks worried. 'The others? They've been caught too?'

'Yeah. Sharr caught us.'

Piece by piece, my pupils adjust to the dark. There is no sign of my crewmates, just Lukas, and the shadows. The realisation makes my stomach twist. I have to get out of here. I have to find my friends. But I can't do that yet – not when I've barely begun to grasp what's happening. I yank the fabric out of Lukas's hands. Then I take a deep breath to steady myself, and try to make a clearer assessment of my surroundings.

We are locked inside a prison cell, its rough stone lined with metal bars. The bars must be magnetic.

That way, no one could use their proclivity – whether it's Air or Stone or Darkness – to slip between them.

The only light comes from the moon, which shines through a skylight far above our heads. It isn't hard to grasp the skylight's purpose. At noon, the wastelands' sun will strike directly into our prison cell: a trap of heat and misery. How better to keep your prisoners in check, than with the scorch of sunstruck metal?

And the skylight isn't a route of escape, either. The ceiling is at least five metres high; there is no hope of reaching the opening without a ladder. Even if my proclivity were Air, it would be no use; those same magnetic bars form lines across the skylight. I could probably squeeze between them without using any powers, but there's no way to climb that high. We are trapped.

'You shouldn't be here,' says Lukas, sounding distressed. 'I made a deal with Sharr – I handed myself over so she'd let you go.'

I stare at him. And for a moment, I forget the prison cell. I forget everything except the question that hangs in the air between us. '*What*?'

'That's why I left you in Gunning.' His voice cracks, taut with tension. I can't tell if it's shame, or apology, or just concern. 'I'm so sorry I left you. I'm so . . . it's just . . .' He runs a hand through his hair.

'I thought she would catch your crew. Torture you. Kill you. So I left you behind, and I found her. I offered to trade myself into her custody if she would let you escape.'

I stare at him. 'You're her cousin. Why would she want –'

'She wants my place as heir, Danika. No one knows I'm still alive; my own father thinks I died when my biplane went down. I thought if Sharr had the chance to dispose of me and become heir to the throne, she would forget about your crew.' He shakes his head, looking suddenly broken. 'Danika, I'm sorry. I tried. I just . . . I thought she'd leave you alone.'

Silence.

I don't know what to say. Hell, I don't know what to *think*. For days, I thought that Lukas had betrayed us. For days, I thought he left us in Gunning to reclaim his place as royalty. Even now, I don't know whether to believe him. But I think of Sharr's words, back on the plateau: *The king would name me heir to the throne. I could set Taladia on track to her rightful future, as the greatest empire ever known.*

Lukas might be telling the truth. Or it might be just another lie.

'You're a prince,' I say. 'Your father is the king.'

He looks down. 'Yes.'

'You lied to me. You lied to us all.'

'Yes.'

I hesitate, not entirely sure that I want to know the answer. 'Why?'

He glances back up at me, eyes bright in the dark of our cell. 'Would you have let me join your crew if you knew the truth?'

'Of course not!' I squeeze the scrap of bloody fabric in my fist. 'But why would you want to join our crew in the first place? You're the son of the king – you could do anything you want in the world.'

'Could I?' says Lukas quietly.

'Well, coming from someone whose family was blown up on your father's orders, it sure as hell seems like it.'

Lukas looks struck. He stares at me for a long moment, then looks away. I glare at him.

This isn't how it's supposed to go. Just days ago, I dreamed of meeting a Morrigan and inflicting that same pain upon them that they inflicted upon me. I should tear this boy apart. But when I look at Lukas Morrigan, I don't see the son of the king. I see a boy with green eyes and gentle hands, flying a kite beneath the moon.

I don't want to kill him. I want to forget he ever existed.

357

'I never wanted to hurt you, Danika,' he says. 'I just wanted . . .' He gazes up through the skylight. 'I just wanted to escape.'

'Escape from what? A lifetime of caviar and silken clothing? Do you know what it's like to watch your family die, or to hunt for your food in a back alley bin?'

Lukas shakes his head. 'No, I don't. But I do know what it's like to be raised by murderers who only care about war and invading other lands. I know what it's like to have a family who only cares about subduing the masses, whose dinnertime conversations are about which city is due for a bombing.'

He takes a deep breath. 'I know what it's like to have a father who hates me, who thinks I'm a coward. Who probably *celebrated* when my plane went down.'

There is a pause.

Lukas steps into the shadows on the far side of our cell. He turns his back to me and wraps his hand around the bars, gazing into the corridor beyond. 'I just wanted to escape, Danika. I wanted a fresh start in a new land. Is that so different from what the rest of your crew was looking for?'

Almost subconsciously, I touch my mother's bracelet. Lukas's silver rose still brushes the delicate skin on the inside of my wrist. I suddenly remember his expression when he gave it to me, when he said it was a thankyou gift. A thankyou for trusting him. For accepting him. 'Why does your father think you're a coward?'

'Because I'm the best pilot in his air force, but I'm the only one who refuses to drop any bombs.'

An incredulous cough escapes my lips. Of course he drops bombs; he's a biplane pilot! That's what pilots *do*. I open my mouth to argue, to catch him in the lie. But then I remember Sharr's insults, calling Lukas an embarrassment – a brat who wouldn't fulfil his duties. I remember his crashed biplane in the forest, and the cluster of six alchemy bombs still untouched beneath its belly. I suddenly think of Maisy's words on the train, when I was too upset to listen properly. Lukas had a full load of explosives, ready to be dropped on Rourton that night. Yet after the bombing, they remained aboard his biplane.

Lukas isn't lying. He's telling the truth. And if he's telling the truth about the bombs, then maybe . . .

I wet my lips. 'Why'd your father send you on missions, then? Seems a bit pointless, if you never dropped any bombs.'

'I used to think he was holding out hope – just waiting for me to prove myself a worthy heir,' says Lukas. 'But now I think he was hoping something would go wrong. An accident. An excuse to get me out of the way, to promise the throne to Sharr.'

He lets out a slow breath. 'But Sharr's the real threat, Danika. My father is a fool to trust her. She's only kept me alive because I've got information about my father. Things that even she doesn't know.'

He tightens his grip on the bars. 'She'll portray herself as a hero. The huntress who captured my murderer. And she'll convince my father to name her as his heir. But Sharr's too impatient to wait for him to die. She'll dispose of me in secret, use my information to assassinate my father, and take the throne.'

I feel sick. This is not a family. It's so far from how I imagined the royals' lives to be: all glitz and power and full bellies. How can Lukas sound so matter-of-fact about it? How can he just *accept* that his cousin wants to murder him?

I can't help thinking of my own family – my mother's songs, my father's smile, my brother's laugh as we danced around the radio – and suddenly I'm grateful. Grateful that I knew them and loved them as long as I did. That's better than being Lukas, who has never known a real family at all.

'Why did you hang around Rourton that night?' I say. 'When the bombing was over, when the other planes had left – why were you still flying around when I set off that flare?'

There is a long pause.

'Because someone had to see.' Lukas clenches his fists around the bars, then turns to face me again. 'Someone had to bear witness to what my family has done. I'm not a coward who just runs away and hides from the consequences of my actions.'

Silence. Blood is trickling down my lips, so I press the fabric back against my wound. 'They weren't your actions,' I say eventually. 'You didn't drop those bombs, Lukas.'

He doesn't respond.

'You're not responsible for what your father has done, or what Sharr does.'

'That's not what you thought a few minutes ago.'

I pause. The fabric is soaked through, but there's no better bandage handy to stem the flow of blood. I can see now where Lukas took it from; he has ripped off half his own sleeve to tend to my injuries.

'I was wrong,' I say.

Lukas doesn't respond. After a few minutes, he returns to my side and takes the fabric gently from my grasp, ready to dab it back against my wound. He pauses and weighs the sodden fabric, clearly dismayed by the amount of blood. Before I can stop him, he's thrown the cloth away and torn a portion of his other sleeve to press against the gash.

'We've got to find the others,' I say. 'We've got to get out of here, Lukas.' I pause. 'All of us.'

He looks at me, his eyes alight. And there is something in his expression, something so deep and quiet and grateful that it almost takes my breath away. Then the moment passes, and he shifts his gaze back to my wound.

'Why do you think Sharr's put us together?' I say.

'Convenience.' Lukas pauses, his fingers on the fabric. 'She thinks she can use you as leverage to question me.'

'Leverage?'

Lukas looks away. 'Danika, I traded myself into her custody to keep you safe. Sharr isn't stupid. She's going to . . .' He pauses. 'She's going to hurt you, to make me reveal my father's weaknesses.'

There are footsteps in the corridor.

'And she's coming.' Lukas takes a deep breath. 'She's coming now.'

CHAPTER TWENTY-SEVEN

HOW THE STAR-SHINE MUST GO

I SIT UP STRAIGHTER, DETERMINED NOT TO SHOW MY fear. It's hard to keep my head aloft. Somehow, I stop my chin from betraying a tremble. Lukas drops the bloody fabric and steps away from me. Is he trying to convince Sharr that he doesn't care about me, that threatening me will not make him speak?

Sharr appears on the other side of the bars. It's difficult to make out her expression in the shadows, but a flash of teeth reveals that she is smiling. In silence, she stares at us between the bars. There is a lever on the wall behind her, which I assume is used to crank open the bars of our cell, but she makes no move to touch it.

'Where are my friends?' I say. 'What have you done with them?'

'Oh, they're alive,' Sharr says. 'And they'll stay that way a little longer, so long as you both . . . cooperate.'

My breath unclenches from a terrible tightness I had barely been aware of. Alive. They're still alive. It's not too late – if I can just get out of here, if I can find them . . .

'Aren't you coming in here?' I say.

'I'm not stupid, Glynn,' says Sharr. 'Do you think I didn't check your proclivity markings when you were unconscious? I'm not opening this cell while you're awake.'

My skin prickles. I feel dirty, violated. My proclivity tattoo must have finished developing. I don't even know my own power, but this woman has dared to break the taboo; she has examined my markings, despite my age.

'If you're not coming in here,' says Lukas, 'what do you want?'

Sharr picks casually at her fingernail, as though examining a chip in the coloured stain. Then she lowers her hand and smiles at us. 'Oh, I'm just here to chat with my favourite cousin.'

'What about?' says Lukas. 'The arrangements for the Taladia Day celebrations? Because I thought your mother was organising the feast this year, not me.'

'I wouldn't treat this so lightly if I were you,' says Sharr.

She steps into a patch of moonlight, and I cannot quite hold back a gasp. Sharr has changed out of her hunters' uniform into a gleaming satin ball gown. It falls in delicate ruffles across the floor, the fabric a deep crimson that mimics the flames of her proclivity. It is the gown of royalty. It is the gown of a queen.

Sharr smiles. 'Do you know where I'm going tomorrow morning?'

Neither of us answers.

'I'm going south, to the palace. I shall take the Glynn girl with me, and she shall suffer a *very* long death in the city square. After all, she is responsible for killing my darling little cousin.'

Lukas clenches his fists. 'Why are you telling us this?'

'Because you have a choice,' says Sharr. 'If you cooperate, both of your deaths will be quick and private. A nice, clean gunshot wound at dawn. I'll tell the papers that I shot the girl during pursuit in the wilderness.'

I tense up. I had expected Sharr to manipulate Lukas by threatening to hurt me, not by offering to lessen our suffering. But either way, I will die tomorrow. I silently berate myself – *don't look afraid, don't look afraid* – and swallow hard. I have played my cards and I have lost.

I always expected to die on this journey, didn't I? I knew it was a risk when I set out from Rourton. Considering what our crew has been through, I'm lucky to still be breathing now. Isn't it greedy to ask for more, to ask for another day, a year, a lifetime? I've already lived many days longer than Radnor – and I had no more right to claim those days than he did.

'Go away, Sharr,' says Lukas. 'I tried to make a deal with you before and you broke your word. You're going to do the same thing again. Why should I help you steal the throne?'

Sharr doesn't look surprised. She just nods, with a crooked smile still adorning her lips. Despite Lukas's defiance, she knows she has won. 'I will be back at dawn, then, to offer you one last chance.' She turns to me. 'If I were you, Glynn, I'd convince him to take the deal.'

'Leave us alone.' I'm quietly proud of how steady my voice remains. 'You're not a queen, Sharr Morrigan. You're just a thug in a ball gown.'

She raises an eyebrow, gives a casual wave – as though temporarily farewelling a friend between lunch-dates – and vanishes back down the corridor. We listen for her retreating footsteps. When she is gone, I release a shaky breath.

Lukas hurries back to press the fabric against my wound. 'I'm sorry, Danika. I won't let her take you to the palace. I'll think of something . . .'

I pry the fabric gently from his fingers. 'I can do that, Lukas.'

He nods. 'I know.'

There is silence. Lukas slides down the wall to sit beside me, gazing up at the skylight. Our route to freedom, but we have no way to reach it. I can't help thinking of the words to the song: *'Oh mighty yo, how the star-shine must go . . .'* I can see the star-shine now, but it will have to chase the Valley without me.

'I'm sorry, Danika,' Lukas whispers. 'I don't know how to break out of here. I'm trying, but I just can't think of . . . I mean . . . This is all my fault.'

I shake my head. 'No, it's not. All you've done is save our lives. You saved us in the Marbles, and you saved us again last night.' I roll up my sleeve to show him the silver rose. 'I used this charm, just like you said, and it kept the foxaries away.'

There is a pause.

'I'm not a good person, Danika,' Lukas says. 'I wasn't just magically born with a kind heart, you

367

know. Deep down, I'm still a Morrigan. I'm still one of them.'

'Then why do you care about people outside your family? Why did you refuse to drop the alchemy bombs?'

Lukas shakes his head. 'I don't know. I guess it's because of my proclivity.'

I frown. I don't know what sort of answer I expected, but it wasn't this.

'My proclivity developed early,' he says. 'Only a few weeks after my thirteenth birthday. There was a bird outside my bedroom window, getting ready to migrate. I wished I could fly off with its flock . . . and then I did.

'I borrowed its eyes, Danika, and I saw the world outside. That bird flew and flew, and I saw the real Taladia. Shrivelled old men who couldn't afford bread, a bunch of starving children, people who cried and died in the cold of the streets . . .'

'You saw *people*,' I say. 'Real people.'

I imagine a younger Lukas soaring out his window on feathered wings for the first time. The sights, the sounds, the colours. He might have swooped through marketplaces, or soared above the stonework of a city wall. It would be easy to become entranced, especially after a life stuck indoors.

'I'm not naturally a good person,' says Lukas.

'You see, now? There's nothing special about my personality that made me different to Sharr. It was just dumb luck that my proclivity let me see the world, whereas Sharr's –'

'Lets her chuck fireballs at people?'

He nods. 'If I'd got Flame or something else, Danika, I would've been just like her. I would never have known about real people, or realised I've got no right to kill them. I would have dropped those bombs on Rourton, maybe even on *you*, just like every other heartless –'

I raise a finger to his lips. 'I don't care, Lukas.'

'You should.'

'Well, I don't. It doesn't matter why you ended up a good person – it just matters that you did.' I pause. 'And stop apologising, because we're going to get out of here. We've escaped from Sharr before, haven't we? Why shouldn't we do it again?'

Lukas opens his mouth, ready to protest. And without even thinking, I swap my finger for my lips.

He stiffens, but only for a moment. Then we're leaning in towards each other, faces brushing. Lukas's mouth is soft and gentle, with only the faintest hint of stubble above his lip. He reaches around to cup the back of my head.

We break apart, gasping a little. I can hardly process what I've done. We are hours from death;

369

this isn't the time for kissing. But on the other hand, if Sharr has her way, this will be our only chance. I lean forward again and brush my lips across the skin below Lukas's nose. It creases up beneath my lips, and I know that he is smiling.

'Danika,' he whispers. 'We're going to get out of here. I swear to you, no matter what it takes –'

'I know.'

We lean back against the wall, fingers fiercely entwined. I won't let go. Lukas's hand brushes my bracelet, and I feel him touch the rose charm upon the chain.

Suddenly, I remember Lukas's own charm necklace. 'Your padlock charm! Do you still have it, or did Sharr take it?'

'I've still got it,' he says. 'I put a few charms in my pocket, and hid the rest in my boot before I turned myself in. Sharr took my kite and found the charms in my pocket, so she thought that was all I had.' He gives a wry smile. 'She can be a bit too sure of herself, in case you hadn't noticed.'

I sit up eagerly. 'Well, can't you use the padlock to turn that lever? To open the bars?'

Lukas shakes his head. 'The lever's on the other side of the bars. I've already tried, but I can't make the spell work through magnets.'

The disappointment is so strong that it actually hurts. I glance around, searching for another idea, but there is nothing. The skylight is too high above our heads. The walls provide no handholds: just neatly hewn blocks of stone. There is nothing to help – no chair to stand on, no rope to loop around the bars. Our cell is bare.

'Danika,' says Lukas. 'What's your proclivity?'

It takes me a second to remember Sharr's words. After days of itching, my tattoo has developed. 'I don't know. Last time I checked, it hadn't finished maturing.'

I hesitate. Even now, it feels wrong to show my markings to another. But Lukas is not just a stranger off the street, or even a casual friend or acquaintance. I'm not sure what he is, really, but he's something *more*. And besides, my proclivity might be our last hope. If I don't do this, we are going to die. I will never see my friends again. I think of Teddy. Clementine. Maisy. They must be somewhere here, trapped and maybe alone. If there's even a chance I can help them . . .

I take a nervous breath. Then I twist around, offering Lukas the back of my neck.

'You want me to check?' he says.

'Yes. I do.'

He pulls my hair up gently, then he slides away my scarf. A little chill runs through my stomach; I haven't exposed my spine to anyone in years.

'What?' I say nervously. 'What is it?'

Lukas hesitates.

'It's not Flame, is it?'

'No, it's not Flame,' he says. 'You've got a tattoo of the sky. There's a moon, and stars . . .' His voice trails away. 'Danika, I think your proclivity is Night.'

I wrench myself away. 'What? No!'

'There's nothing wrong with Night,' Lukas says quickly. 'It doesn't mean –'

My heart is thudding inside my chest. I almost want to throw up. This can't be happening. People with Darkness or Shadow or Night . . . those people are outcasts. I think of old Walter in Rourton, and his lifetime of playing with shadows in dingy bars.

'Danika, calm down,' says Lukas. 'This makes sense, you know. You're an illusionist; you're natur-ally attuned to –'

'To hiding? To deception, to spying?' I take a deep breath. 'To lurking in the shadows? That's not true, Lukas. Illusionism is just a freak ability – I bet there are illusionists with all sorts of proclivities, like Air or Beast or –'

'Close your eyes.'

'What?'

Lukas touches the back of my neck. His fingers are gentle; they don't flinch away from the markings of darkness. 'Close your eyes, Danika. Please. Like when I gave you the rose charm.'

I wait a moment, then close my eyes.

Lukas pulls his fingers away, and I'm alone. 'Now, what can you feel?'

'Nothing.'

'Try harder.'

There is still nothing, but this time I remain silent. Stale air plays upon my skin, and for a moment I feel blindfolded again. I can't see anything. I can't connect with the world. There is only darkness, only emptiness. But no, wait! There is *something* at the edges of my mind. It laps like water. It tingles against my flesh. It tumbles down through the skylight, mingling with the moonlight.

'Oh,' I whisper.

Because Lukas is right. My proclivity is right there, waiting for me to seize it. And it doesn't feel evil or wrong or twisted. It calls for me to ride away, to slip into the night and share its form. It feels like I can fly.

'Danika,' says Lukas quietly. 'Open your eyes.'

I open them. For a second I'm completely disorientated. Lukas has moved, he has shifted away to the far side of the cell. Is he so disgusted by my proclivity that he . . . But no, it isn't Lukas who has moved. It's me. Metal bars dig into my back, keeping my powers constrained with their magnetic field.

'What happened?' I say.

'You travelled inside your proclivity.'

I glance across the cell floor. The shadows seem to call me back, tempting me to meld into their form. My gaze travels up to the magnet-barred skylight, and the streaks of night that lie visible beyond. And suddenly I know how Lukas feels when he connects with a bird, or Teddy when he communicates with the foxaries. For the first time in my life, I feel whole.

And suddenly, I know how we're going to escape.

CHAPTER TWENTY-EIGHT

FOLLOW MY KNIFE

I FUMBLE WITH THE BUTTONS OF MY STOLEN COAT, trying to undo them as quickly as possible.

'What are you doing?' says Lukas.

'The climbing picks!' I look at him with wide eyes, then remember that Lukas didn't witness my escape down the wall in Rourton. 'Up on the guard turret, when I fired that flare, I stole some climbing picks. I think I can reach that skylight.'

'You've got the picks here?'

I dig through the layers beneath my coat. Sharr confiscated any obvious weapons while I was unconscious, so my cooking knife is gone. But the picks remain deep inside my jacket, cushioned in fabric to protect my ribs. I look up at the skylight. The magnetic bars will prevent me escaping through my proclivity, but not from slipping out as an underfed human girl. Those days of starvation might just save my life.

But there's no hope of Lukas fitting through.

'I can squeeze through those bars,' I say. 'I know I can. And it's night-time, Lukas. Once I'm clear of the magnets, I can use my proclivity if I have to. I'll get back into the corridor and open the cell to let you out.'

He grips my arm. 'You have to be careful, Danika. If there's any danger of being caught, just use your proclivity to escape. Get away, forget about me.'

'That's not going to happen, Lukas,' I say. 'I can do this.'

He takes a deep breath, and releases me. 'Good luck. I . . .'

I want to kiss him again, but I'm scared that if I do then I'll never let go. So I just give a firm nod, yank my boot back on and thrust my climbing picks into the wall. 'See you soon.'

Neither of us speaks as I climb the wall. It feels almost like being back in Rourton, scaling an alleyway or the side of a richie's house when I've been caught sleeping in their doorway. I strike each pick into the mortar between the stones: one, two, one, two . . . It's simple to work up a rhythm between my hands and feet. And with every strike, the shadows seem to float across my skin. They give me courage; if I slip, I can meld my body into the dark. Even so, I'm breathing heavily by the time I reach the roof. The shoulder that I dislocated in Rourton is throbbing again, but it holds steady in its socket.

The skylight bars are welded into the stone. I poke a tentative hand between them, and my sense of the shadows vanishes with a jolt. The magnetic field's power is almost frightening; it tears my proclivity as easily as I might rip a sheet of newspaper. No wonder Sharr Morrigan is confident this cell will hold us.

'Can you fit through?' says Lukas.

I glance down at him. The floor suddenly looks very far away. 'Yeah, I think so.'

I shift my weight to my good arm for a moment, and shove the other hand's climbing pick back into my pocket. With a gasp, I manage to swing across to the skylight. My hands grip the bars, cold beneath my palms. I brace my good arm to take my weight again, before reaching back to snatch my second climbing pick from the mortar.

With both picks pocketed, I dangle from the bars for a moment. My fingers are sweaty but I grip the metal and grit my teeth. I kick my feet up to brace against the bars from below. Then, little by little, I contort my upper body to squeeze through the gap. It's an awkward angle, and my shoulder protests with a stab of pain.

But then my head is through, and my chest. A rush of wind hits my face and I grin, utterly elated. I suck in my stomach and squeeze up higher. My hips become stuck, but a few moments of wriggling and huffing are enough to squish through. I fish my legs up after me and suddenly my entire body is on the roof.

'Lukas, I'm out!'

I peer back down through the bars to the cell below. Lukas grins up at me, practically bouncing on the balls of his feet. I'm not sure whether it's excitement or anxiety – either way, he waves me onward. 'Go, go!'

The roof is flat and bare, but high. I can see the wastelands all around me, stretching to the horizon in all directions but one. To the north lie the Central Mountains, snowcaps lit up eerily in the light of the moon. It's surreal to think that we stood there less than twenty-four hours ago.

I hurry to the edge of the roof, drop to my knees and peer down across the fortress. A large metal silo squats near the base of the tower – is this where the Curiefer is stored? Railway tracks run across the ground. There is a bulk in the shadows on the far side of the silo, where the track bends out of sight. It must be a train carriage, ready to be unloaded.

The courtyard lies below, filled with rows of neatly parked biplanes. The sight fills me with a sudden hatred that clashes with the joy of my escape. Those planes killed my family. They are probably loaded with alchemy bombs, ready to attack another innocent city. Soon they will be filled with enough Curiefer to start a war. If only we had managed to destroy them . . .

But this isn't the time to worry about the war. I must find a way to free Lukas and find the rest of my crew. We had our chance to attack this fortress and we failed. Now we can only hope to escape with our lives.

I double-check that no one is below to see me. Nothing. All I can see in the yard is machinery. Heart pattering, I pull out my climbing picks and slide over the edge of the roof.

It's so tempting to sink into the shadows, to travel weightlessly through the night itself. But my proclivity has only just matured and I don't trust my ability to control it. If I lose myself now, there's no one here to call me back. It's not unheard of for teenagers with Air or Daylight proclivities to disintegrate forever on the breeze. And I can't risk that. Not when Lukas and my friends are still in danger. For now, I must treat my Night proclivity as a last resort.

I clamber down until I reach a window. It's not barred; it's probably a pilots' dormitory rather than a prison cell. The glass pane is slightly ajar, letting a trickle of air inside to refresh the room. I stick my fingers through the gap and slide the window open.

Inside, I bang my shins against an empty bed. This is clearly the room of an important richie. The bedknobs and door handles are laced in gold. A vast picture frame hangs above the bed, containing a portrait of the king, his wife and an infant boy. Lukas. Even in the feeble moonlight I recognise the arch of his cheekbones, the shape of his eyes. His parents are not touching each other. They stand a foot apart, glaring regally into the distance. Lukas's mother holds him like a loaf of bread, not a beloved son. It's the coldest excuse for a family portrait I've seen.

On the far side of the room, I spot another picture. This one is a bird, silhouetted against the moon.

'Lukas,' I whisper. This must have been his bedroom during his service as a biplane pilot.

There's no time to examine the room in any more detail. Every minute I waste is a minute we could be using to flee. I hurry to the bedroom door and open it with a cautious nudge. It creaks and I wince. But the corridor outside is empty, so I risk stepping out onto the tiles.

I round several corners before I find a staircase that leads back up towards the prison cell. My footsteps slap loudly, so I force myself to slow down. For each stride, I peel up my feet and then gently place them on the step above. It takes a painfully long time to move, but at least it's quiet. So long as Sharr keeps her word and stays away until dawn, we should be okay.

Finally, I reach the top of the stairs. 'Lukas?'

When my eyes adjust to the shadows, my gut clenches. I have miscalculated. This is not the top floor of the tower; this is not Lukas's prison cell. It's an unfamiliar stretch of corridor – and at the far end, a hunter stares out the window into the night. I spit out an illusion on instinct, in the very second that it takes him to spin around.

'Who's there?'

My illusion will only last seconds as I have no magnets on hand to prolong it. The guard steps towards me, squinting into the stairwell. I have only one chance: my new proclivity.

I close my eyes and welcome the dark.

Everything falls away. I melt down into the shadows of the corridor. No, I *am* the shadows of the corridor. I slip past the hunter, as insubstantial as his own shadow. The window calls me, summons me out to join the night. That is my home: the darkness, the emptiness, the treacle-coloured sky . . .

No!

I'm not sure whether the shout is real or just inside my head, but it's so sharp and desperate that I jerk to a halt. Then I realise. It's my own voice. I'm about to lose myself.

I force my eyes open. I have reached the far end of the corridor. The hunter stands a good ten metres away, gazing down at the stairs. Before he can turn back this way, I scuttle sideways around another corner. Then I drop to my knees and crawl, holding my breath, keeping as silent as possible. My knees throb from clambering on the stones, but I refuse to sink back into my proclivity. I know, now, that I cannot trust myself to travel that way. Five more seconds and I'd have been lost forever, just another wisp of darkness in the night.

I force myself to breathe softly, even though my lungs nag for deeper gasps. I must be silent, no matter what.

Another staircase lies ahead, narrow and crooked. I rise to my feet and grip the handrail as I climb. Did I come this way when I was blindfolded?

'Danika?'

The voice echoes from up ahead, just beyond the top of the stairs. I hurry towards it. The top step opens into a short corridor, steeped in shadow. At the end lies our prison cell, with Lukas waiting at the barred door. I race forward to meet him.

He reaches through the bars. 'You did it! You did it, Danika.'

I smile. 'Ready to get out of here?'

Then I crank the lever and the bars swing open.

CHAPTER TWENTY-NINE
VOLATILITY

We hurry back down the stairs. It's harder to keep quiet with two of us and we can't afford to run for it – as tempting as it may be. 'Where would Sharr keep the others?'

Lukas shakes his head. 'There are no other prison cells here. She must have locked them in the silo.'

'With the Curiefer?'

'Well, it's the most secure place I can think of.'

At the edge of the corridor, I grab Lukas's arm to make him wait. I peer around the corner, expecting to see the hunter back in place by the window. But the corridor is empty. Has he ventured downstairs, searching for the source of the noise? Or has he gone to find Sharr, to tell her that he suspects an intruder?

'What's wrong?' whispers Lukas.

'There was a hunter here before.'

We exchange glances, then hurry onward. Perhaps the guard has gone to warn Sharr, but we can't stop him by worrying about it. All we can do is move faster. 'Do you know the way down?'

Lukas nods. 'I've lived here since I became a pilot. Just follow me.'

We tiptoe down the stairs and into another corridor, then another. It's lucky that Lukas is here because I'm completely lost. This seems more of a labyrinth than a tower. We scamper around corners, duck through passageways, and even sneak across an ornately painted dining room. I imagine Lukas sitting here for dinner, feasting on gourmet bread and desserts with his fellow pilots.

I wonder whether they feast before they bomb cities or afterwards. Perhaps there is a celebration, a banquet in the aftermath of each mission, while families in the bombed-out cities burn. The thought sends a furious spasm through my body.

'Are you all right?' says Lukas.

I clench my fists. 'Let's just get out of here.'

We reach the ground floor without spotting any signs of human life. I'm starting to worry now; this entire escape has been too easy. Where is everyone?

What could have drawn them all outside into the night?

'We'd better avoid the front door,' says Lukas quietly.

He chooses a window in one of the corridors. It gives a horrible creak when we hoist it open, but the bluster of wind outside is enough to hide the sound. I clamber through and drop onto the cobblestones, with Lukas a second behind me.

The yard is dimly lit by a series of lanterns, spaced along the inside wall. There is still no sign of human life. In fact, the only living creatures are foxaries. They are chained to a post on the far side of the yard, but lie asleep on the cobblestones. Their chests rise and fall gently in the moonlight. 'Where is everyone?'

'I don't know,' says Lukas. 'Unless . . .'

'Unless what?'

I'm answered by the shriek of a whistle. The sound makes me jump – for a terrible second, I think someone has spotted us. But the whistle is the cry of an incoming train, blasting along the tracks to cross from the wasteland into the fortress.

'Must be a load of Curiefer coming in,' says Lukas. 'There are protocols; everyone in the fortress has to help get it into the silo as quickly as possible.'

'Why?'

'Curiefer's too volatile. It's like an oil, designed to burn. The silo's spells keep the vats cool and wet, to stop any chance of a fire. But out in the open air, there's always a risk that something might go wrong.'

I gasp. 'Lukas, this is our chance! If the others are locked inside the silo, and they're about to open the doors to bring in a new load of Curiefer . . .'

He nods. 'Come on, let's go.'

We dart between the biplanes, ducking beneath their wings and around their tails to cross the yard. The silo squats on the far side of the yard, pressing against the back wall of the fortress. As we edge around the yard, human figures finally come into view: hunters and pilots, standing beside the bulk of a train. There is another whistle and the train's wheels stop spinning.

'Unloading protocol, now, now, now!' comes Sharr Morrigan's voice from somewhere in the darkness ahead.

I crouch with Lukas behind a biplane's wheels. The train doors open and people pour into the baggage compartment. A moment later, they emerge with massive crimson vats. Another hunter cranks a lever on the silo door; as soon as it opens, a blast of cold air rushes out. I don't want to imagine what it must be like for my crewmates trapped inside.

'Go!' shouts the hunter.

More people rush forward with trolleys and start to load the vats. The troops' actions are perfectly rehearsed. The scene reminds me of factories in Rourton, with their strictly maintained production lines. As soon as the first vats are loaded, troops push them from the train across the yard and into the silo. Then they re-emerge, running back to the train to reload their trolleys. I spot Sharr Morrigan among the throng, her back to us as she supervises the reloading.

I turn to Lukas. 'This is our chance.'

We dash towards the silo. For a couple of terrifying seconds we're in the middle of the cobblestones with no biplane to shield us from the troops' view. But they're so focused on loading the Curiefer vats, so obsessed with ensuring this flammable material remains safe, that no one spots our movement across the yard.

Inside the silo, the first thing I notice is the *cold*. The air is wet and damp, as though I've stepped into a winter waterfall. Then I spot the sprinklers on the ceiling, which pour mist into the air. The silo is about twenty metres in diameter, and over half the space is stacked high with crimson vats.

I hurry around the side of a huge stack of vats, which hide the back of the silo from view. And there they are: Teddy, Clementine and Maisy, chained to the wall with what must be magnetic wire. The twins' eyes widen when they see us. Even behind his gag, Teddy's face twists visibly into a grin.

But this is no time for soppy reunions. At any second, the troops will return with another round of trolleys to unload. I scurry around to a dark corner behind the largest stack of vats, and squish myself into the gap. Lukas chooses a similar hiding place on the far side of the silo.

There is a clamour as troops wheel their trolleys into the silo. My line of sight is obscured by the vats, so I can only judge people's positions by the sounds of their voices and movement. They seem to be unloading these vats near the front of the silo; no one ventures around the back where we are hiding.

The footsteps patter away, the voices fade, and there is a noisy clang as the door slams shut. 'Will they come back?'

'No,' says Lukas, standing up. 'The train only holds enough vats for two trolley trips. We should be safe for now.'

I set to work on untangling the others' bonds. Someone has knotted magnetic wires around their wrists and ankles, then used padlocks to secure them to the silo wall. I examine the locks; they look like normal brass padlocks, clapped onto the wires as an afterthought.

'Are the locks magnetic?' says Lukas.

I shake my head. 'I don't think so.'

'Good.' Lukas fumbles for the lock-shaped charm on his necklace. 'This should do it, then.'

I step aside as he engages the charm's alchemy spell. There is a snap of power in the air, a loud click, and the padlocks spring open. Within moments we have yanked the gags from our crewmates' mouths, and Teddy is spluttering like a child whose birthday candles refuse to blow out.

'What the hell is *he* doing here?'

'Lukas is on our side, Teddy.' I untangle the wire around his wrists. 'He's not like the rest of the Morrigans.'

As soon as his ankles are free, Teddy jumps to his feet and glares at Lukas. 'You're a filthy traitor. You lied to us, you nicked off in Gunning, you –'

'– surrendered himself to Sharr to save the rest of us,' I cut in with an urgent whisper. 'It makes sense, Teddy. You heard Sharr talking on the plateau – she *hates* Lukas! She wants to steal the throne.'

'But –'

'If Lukas wanted to betray us, all he would have to do is shout. There are dozens of troops out there, just waiting to grab us. Even Sharr's out there.' I take a deep breath. 'Lukas doesn't want us to get caught, Teddy. Just like back at the waterfall, when he fought off those hunters to save us. Or when he gave me the charm that hid us from the foxaries.'

Silence.

'But he's a pilot,' Teddy says. 'A killer.'

To my surprise, it's Maisy who speaks up. Her voice is quiet, but firm. 'He didn't drop any bombs. We found his biplane in the forest, remember? He didn't drop a single one.'

Teddy shakes his head, conflicted. 'You can't trust a royal.'

'A couple of weeks ago, I'd have said you can't trust a richie,' I say. 'Or a pickpocket, for that matter. But we've survived this far as a crew, and we'll survive again tonight . . . but only if we work together.'

There is a pause. And at long last, Teddy nods.

'That's all very well,' Clementine says, 'but how are we supposed to get out of here?'

'I can use this to open the door.' Lukas holds up his padlock charm. 'The silo isn't magnetised; they never expected any enemies to cross the wastelands and get inside the fortress wall.'

'Then what? We'll still be trapped in the yard.'

I try to think of how we might sneak away. We have only one pair of climbing picks, and I doubt the twins could scale a wall anyway. The hunters will catch us before we're even free of the yard. 'The yard!'

'What?'

I turn to the others, suddenly excited. 'The yard is full of biplanes. What if we forget about being sneaky and just steal a plane? We could fly off into the mountains – we'd have the element of surprise, and –'

Lukas shakes his head. 'Danika, it won't work.'

'Why not?'

'Because I'm the only one who can fly a biplane, and there's no room for passengers. They're designed to carry one pilot and that's it.'

We're silent for a moment.

'What about the foxaries?' says Maisy. 'Does anyone know where Sharr is keeping them?'

Lukas and I nod. 'They're tied to a post in the yard,' I say.

'Well, what if we rode off on the foxaries? If we could just get through the gate, we might make it . . . foxaries travel a lot faster than we can on foot.'

Teddy shakes his head. 'They'd shoot us down before we made it five metres, I reckon.'

'Not if they're busy shooting at someone else,' says Lukas.

We all turn to look at him. There is a sudden strength in his voice, a buzz of determination that commands our attention.

'What are you thinking?' I say.

Lukas gives a tight smile. 'I'll steal a plane, fly it up and distract them. While they're shooting at me, the rest of you take the foxaries.'

'What? No! They'll kill you.'

'I'm the best pilot in the force, Danika. I've watched the world through birds' eyes since I was thirteen. I need you to trust me.' Lukas catches my cheek in his hands, and looks straight into my eyes. 'I can do this.'

I swallow hard, trying to fight down my fear. 'I know.'

'But the rest of you will need to run hard,' Lukas says. 'You need to put as much distance between yourselves and this fortress as you can. No matter what, Teddy, keep those foxaries moving. Don't worry about the wastelands, or saving energy, or the hunters . . . just *run*.'

Teddy gives him a strange look. 'Are you gonna –'

'Yes.' Lukas takes a deep breath. 'I'm going to drop an alchemy bomb.'

CHAPTER THIRTY

AND BEYOND

THE SILO DOOR OPENS WITH A QUIET CREAK. I POKE MY head out into the night, but the hordes of troops have clearly re-entered the tower. A pair of guards stands ready at the main gate but there are no other humans outside.

'All right,' I whisper. 'We're clear.'

Lukas prepares to pull away from the group. On a sudden impulse, I grab his sleeve.

'What?' he says.

'I . . . Nothing.' I tighten my grip for a moment, then release him. 'Just don't get shot out of a plane again, all right?'

He smiles. 'I'll see you soon.'

Then he is gone: a shadow flitting between the

biplanes. The rest of us wait for a moment, giving him a chance to select his plane, before we set off towards the foxaries. We duck beneath the metal wings, avoiding the guards' line of sight.

Teddy closes his eyes every few strides, and a low growl escapes his lips. He must be connecting with the foxaries, because the beasts remain silent as we approach. They stare at us, fur bristling a little, but still do not make a sound.

An engine rattles into life behind us. *Lukas.*

The guards shout and rush back into the yard, but it's too late. Lukas steers a pathway between the other biplanes. He is fast, unnaturally fast, propelled by clouds of smoke and silver. For a terrifying moment he seems about to crash into the wall at the end of the runway . . . but then the biplane's alchemy kicks into force. With a scream of raw power, faster and faster, his biplane blasts into the dark.

We run forward to grab the foxaries. Clementine unchains them from their post and we clamber aboard. There is no need to double-up; each of us chooses a separate animal. I can see Teddy's face straining. Most of these beasts are strangers to him, and he is clearly fighting to earn their trust.

People are screaming now, shouting and pouring from the tower like termites. Hunters flicker into place upon the wind, or rise up through the cobblestones, but they are too late. Lukas is soaring above the fortress, beyond the reach of their guns. The guards fling the gates open and charge into the wastelands, firing wildly at the sky.

'Go!' shouts Teddy.

The foxary bucks beneath me. Momentum slams me forward into his neck, and my face fills with that familiar stink of alley-cat musk. I choke, spitting fur and dirt from my lips, and barely lift my eyes in time to see the gate. It's still wide open, so we charge through in a torrent of shouts and screams.

Teddy urges his foxary ahead. 'Faster!'

My own animal bucks again and I almost slip forward across its head. I have a sudden wild recollection of the crew's escape from Rourton, as I watched from the guard turret. My friends are riding out again, in a frenzy of fur and foxary snarls. But this time, I am one of them.

Sharr Morrigan's voice rises above the others, screeching for the hunters to stop us. I find myself laughing, almost hysterical, as I recognise her fury. Sharr is powerless here. She can't use her Flame proclivity so close to the Curiefer, that terribly flammable material.

Our foxaries charge across the plains. Perhaps it's animal instinct that guides them to avoid the sand – or else it's just Teddy, tangled into their minds.

Either way, they leap across the rocky plateaus and keep their claws free from the mire. All I know is that my face is full of fur, and muscles are bunching and releasing beneath my legs, and if I dare loosen my grip I will die. So I dig in deeper, burying myself in the creature's fur, and refuse to let go.

Shots blast towards us, but they can never catch the foxaries. Not out here, on the emptiness of the rocks. I have never felt such speed before; there are no trees, no Marbles, no river . . . nothing to slow the beasts' charge into the night. Hunters scream behind us, yelling and shooting wildly as they charge from the fortress into wasteland. My foxary leaps up onto the edge of another plateau, claws scrambling on rock, and I almost slip backwards. But then we're up, charging forward across the endless stretch of stone . . .

The world explodes.

Pain. Smashes, crashes, blood – one limb aches after another. Everything speeds into chaos, and then it slows. I lie in silence, staring at the stars. It takes me a minute to realise I have been thrown from my foxary. My body lies upon the plateau's hard rocks. Am I dead? I don't think so . . . Surely if I were dead, my limbs would not ache in such a blinding way.

I force myself up into a crouch. My legs shake, threatening to collapse, but I twist my neck to view the fortress behind us. It's gone. There are flames, smoke, screams. In the light of the fire I see the hunters who pursued us, lying stunned or unconscious or dead upon the wastelands. Flowers burst from the ruins: flowers and birds and lights that dance like ribbons across the sky. The alchemy bombs, I realise, dazed. The alchemy bombs from all those biplanes . . .

There is another explosion. The earth shakes. Through blurry eyes I see huge trees burst from the wreckage; their branches twist into vines and then shatter as chunks of stone fly up from the ruins. Fireworks erupt to paint the smoke with coloured light. Broken stones twist and churn on the wind, cracking open into shooting stars – then, with a scream, the site of the fortress comes alive with lightning. Water gushes up into unnatural fountains, higher than buildings, before everything is consumed by flame.

Someone grabs me. 'Get on!'

I obey, clambering upon the back of a foxary. It's one of the twins – Clementine, I think, but I'm too dazed to interpret much beyond the cascade of blonde in my face. Then we are running again, barrelling across the plateau. And above us, a biplane shoots towards the mountains like a flare.

*

ALL NIGHT, WE KEEP RUNNING. THE ONLY PAUSE IS TO collect our packs from the edge of the plateau and knot some rags around our various wounds, before we charge onward to meet the dawn.

We ride up into the Central Mountains: a sweep of rocks and snow. The foxaries slow a little as we move into the forest, but there is no sign of pursuit. That will come, I know. It's only a matter of time. But for now, the surviving hunters are probably fleeing for their own lives, charging into the wilderness before the king hears of this disaster . . .

Before he hears that we have ruined his war.

The day is cold but crisp. We wind ever upwards through the trees, through snow that often reaches the foxaries' thighs. My crewmates are battered; their faces are bruised, and one of Clementine's eyes is swollen shut. Blood trickles down Maisy's cheek, and Teddy's hair is matted with crimson clumps.

I probably look the same. My body throbs, and every upward leap of the foxary threatens to spill me backwards into the snow. But I'm alive. And with that realisation, every detail I notice takes my breath away. The snap of the wind. The rustle of leaves. The throbbing of my head, the taste of blood and mucus in my throat . . .

'Look!' says Maisy.

At first I think she's pointing at Midnight Crest, silhouetted against the sky. I glance at the ruined fortress for a moment, then gaze back down towards the airbase. Its ruins are still smouldering, a distant smear upon the wastelands.

Two burnt buildings. Two kings' ruined schemes. It seems like justice, in a way, and I nod to show my understanding.

Then I realise Maisy's pointing at the crest of the slope, where a figure waits upon the rocks. And there he is. My stomach tightens.

Lukas smiles. 'Took you long enough.'

And I know we are going to make it.

✱

WHEN NIGHT FALLS, WE STUMBLE ACROSS AN OVER-grown ditch. It isn't the same one that we fled from when the hunters pursued us, but it looks similar. Foliage and snow arch across the ditch to form a natural roof. The foxaries slow to a halt, pawing at half-submerged roots in the snow. I stare at the ditch and can't help longing for the safe little burrow inside.

'You know,' says Teddy, 'I reckon we deserve a rest, don't you?'

He settles the foxaries into a nearby thicket,

before we wriggle our bodies into the ditch. We tend each other's wounds with ice from the foliage, then bandage them with strips of a gaudy purple blouse.

'Our mother never liked this one much, anyway,' says Clementine, as I wrap a strip of satin across her eye. 'She'd be happy to see it going to good use.'

We feast on whatever is left in the packs: raw oats mixed with spices, skerricks of dried fruit, and a few stray nuts that Maisy finds in a side pocket. We tell each other stories, explain what we went through while separated. And then we nestle under our sleeping sacks, full and warm.

The twins are the first to fall asleep. It isn't dramatic; they simply drop out of the conversation, lulled into heavy breaths by the warmth of our hideaway. Teddy follows soon after them. His words turn into quiet breaths, and finally to snores.

I turn to Lukas. He turns to me. For a while, we stare at each other. Then Lukas fishes the chain from beneath his shirt, rifles through the charms, and selects the tiny silver star. 'Remember this, Danika? This is my favourite charm.'

'I thought your grandmother gave you that one,' I say. 'You said it doesn't have any alchemy spells attached.'

'No. Just memories.' Lukas presses the star between his fingers. 'My grandmother's proclivity was Night, you know. She was the only half-decent person in my family. Do you know what she told me, when I asked about her proclivity?'

I shake my head, my mouth dry.

'She told me you can't have light without the dark. And you can't have stars without the night.'

I fish my own hand out from the sleeping sack. Our fingers lock. Then we smile, close our eyes, and drift into sleep.

*

WE WAKE UP LATE, ONLY A FEW HOURS BEFORE noon. We panic a little when we count the wasted hours, but there is still no sign of pursuit. Perhaps the explosion caused even more trouble than we thought. I imagine Sharr Morrigan, if she is even alive, must be fleeing for cover in the remotest depths of the wastelands.

There isn't much of a campsite to pack up. Lukas and I roll the sleeping sacks, while Teddy tends to the foxaries. After a breakfast of cold porridge, soaked overnight in snow, we clamber back aboard our beasts.

The day is long and quiet. We allow the foxaries to travel at a walk, and keep a close eye on the sky. There are no biplanes. There is no sound of a train on the mountain's cable system. There is only the rustle of the trees, or an occasional flock of birds across the sky.

By the time we reach the peak above the Knife, it's dusk. The first stars are just appearing. I stare down into the blade-shaped passageway, which slices its way east through the mountains. Beyond lies our route to the Valley.

I whisper the final lyrics of our folk song. *'I shan't waste my good life, I must follow my knife . . .'*

Four voices join me to finish the verse: *'To those deserts of green and beyond.'*

We are not safe yet. We will be hunted and we may face death. But the same may be said of every refugee in Taladia. And at least now, because of our actions, the Magnetic Valley has retained its potency. The king cannot launch his invasion. And countless other refugees might stand a chance.

I glance at the others. Teddy, Clementine, Maisy, Lukas. I don't know whether we will make it to the Valley, but we are still a crew. Lukas squeezes my hand.

And together, we step into the night.

ACKNOWLEDGEMENTS

THIS BOOK WOULD NEVER HAVE BEEN PUBLISHED without the wonderful Anjanette Fennell and Rick Raftos. Thank you for finding my manuscript a home.

I would like to acknowledge the amazing team at Random House Australia. Special thanks to Kimberley Bennett, my brilliant editor, and Zoe Walton, whose tenacity and enthusiasm helped to guide this project from submission to bookshelf.

I am forever grateful to all my teachers, especially Jane Parry-Fielder, David Mann, Margaret Kennedy and Sarah Marrinan.

Finally, thanks to my family:
— my mother, for her love of words and lifelong encouragement;
— my father, for his great advice and for filling my childhood with fantasy books;
— my grandparents, for their love and support; and
— my sister Brooke, for all the stories we've shared.

ABOUT THE AUTHOR

Skye Melki-Wegner is an Arts/Law student from Melbourne. She has worked as a saleswoman, an English tutor and a popcorn-wrangler (at a cinema). In her spare time, she devours a ridiculous amount of caffeine and fantasy literature. *Chasing the Valley* is her first book. She is currently writing the second and third books in the *Chasing the Valley* trilogy.

You can contact Skye at
www.skyemelki-wegner.com

WATCH OUT FOR

BOOKS TWO AND THREE

OF THE

TRILOGY

COMING SOON